I0724332

Nicholas

The Craigdon Family Dynasty

Book Four

CHRIS TAYLOR

© 2020 Chris Taylor

© 2020 by Chris Taylor

(All Rights Reserved)

Without limiting the rights under copyright(s) reserved below, no part of this publication may be reproduced, stored in or introduced into a retrieval system, or transmitted, in any form, or by any means (electronic, mechanical, photocopying, recording, or otherwise) without the prior permission of the copyright owner.

LCT Productions Pty Ltd
18364 Kamilaroi Highway, Narrabri NSW 2390

ISBN. 978-1-925119-80-0 (Paperback)

Nicholas is a work of fiction. Names, characters, places, brands, media and incidents either are the product of the author's imagination or are used fictitiously. Any resemblance to actual persons, living or dead, events, or locales, is entirely coincidental.

Published in the United States of America.

Books by Chris Taylor

THE MUNRO FAMILY SERIES
The Profiler
The Investigator
The Predator
The Betrayal
The Deception
The Negotiator
The Christmas Vigil
The Ransom
The Defendant
The Shooting
The Maker
(Available in Audio)

THE SYDNEY HARBOUR HOSPITAL SERIES
The Perfect Husband
The Body Thief
The Baby Snatchers
The Final Bullet
The Debt Collector
The Lab Test
The Stolen Identity
The Cliff-top Killer
The Likeable Fraudster

THE SYDNEY LEGAL SERIES
An Accidental Murderer
At the Hand of Her Father
A Woman Scorned
Lies and Deception
Ordinary Evil
The Ties That Bind
The Perfect Crime
A Toxic Inheritance
Malicious Love

THE CRAIGDON FAMILY SERIES
Callum
Joel
Isabella
Nicholas
Sophia
Flynn
Noah
Logan
Elizabeth

THE BARRINGTON FAMILY SERIES
Broken Lives
Broken Promises
Broken Bonds
Broken Spirits
Broken Vows
Broken Minds
Broken Dreams
Broken Hearts
Broken Homes

THE FAIRFAX FAMILY SERIES
A Cattleman in Disguise
A Cattleman's Quest
A Cattleman's Daughter
A Cattleman's Secret Baby
To Catch a Cattleman
The Doctor and the Cattleman
To Rescue a Cattleman
A Cattleman's Heart
For the Love of a Cattleman

BACHELORS AND BRIDES SERIES
Matilda
Austin
Farrah

Benjamin
Verity
Denver
Ebony
Tyrone
Willow

Chris Taylor writing as
BELLA CHRISTIAN

THIS IS WHERE IT ENDS SERIES
(in order)
Jessie's Story
Ryan's Story
Holly's Story
Sarah's Story
Veronica's Story

Get a FREE book when you sign up for Chris Taylor's
newsletter at: www.christaylorauthor.com.au

Love Audiobooks? Check out Chris Taylor Books on audio
on Audible.com, Amazon.com and Apple Books.

Join Chris Taylor's Facebook reader group/fan page and be
among the first to receive news of book releases, read and
review books prior to release and other amazing offers. Join
Now at: www.facebook.com/groups/1758023621144744/

Find out more about all of Chris Taylor's books, by visiting her
website at: www.christaylorauthor.com.au

Dedication

This book is dedicated to my children:
Angus, Imogen, Rory, Millie and Madeleine
for your unwavering love, support and understanding…

And as always, to my husband, Linden.
My best friend, my soul mate. I love you to the moon and back.

Acknowledgments

As usual, no book comes into being without a lot of help and support by my friends and family. A world of thanks must go to my wonderful editor, Pat Thomas. Thank you for everything that you do to make my stories even more amazing than I could ever dare to dream. To former Detective Superintendent Michael Kilfoyle, thank you for lending my story credibility. Any mistakes are wholly my own.

To Mary and all of the team at Miblart, thank you for the fantastic book cover. To my sister, Nicole Guihot and to my friends, Ally Thomson and Sue Ricardo, thank you for your excellent editorial comments, proof reading skills and suggestions. I hope you like the final result.

To Amy Atwell, Kirby and the dedicated team at Author E.M.S. who are so much more than book formatters. Amy, once again, thank you for your magic.

To the fantastic writer organizations such as Romance Writers of Australia, Romance Writers of America and Romance Writers of New Zealand for all the help, support and encouragement they offer new and aspiring writers, including me.

To my readers, thank you for your support and love for my stories. Your encouragement and enjoyment make this journey all worthwhile.

And lastly, to my friends and family, especially my husband and children. Thank you for putting up with late dinners and even later conversations as I've emerged day after day from the sometimes scary but always enthralling world I've created on my computer.

Chapter One

Nicholas Craigdon sat behind the impressive large cedar desk that had once belonged to his late father. With his ergonomic office chair twisted slightly to one side, he stared out of the floor-to-ceiling glass windows behind him. The view outside of Sydney's lush botanical gardens, bursting with colorful spring blooms, and glimpses of the deep blue Pacific Ocean were just as impressive as the rest of Henry Craigdon's office, but at that moment, Nicholas was oblivious to the view and to all the other trappings of wealth his father had collected and displayed there proudly over the years.

I'm a fraud. I shouldn't be here... Dad gave this company to Logan...

It was only because of Logan's decency and generosity that Nicholas had a position at Craigdon Enterprises at all. The maliciousness of his father's actions still had the power to hurt...and to anger. Yes. He'd been angry from the moment the lawyer read the terms of his father's will. Seven months, almost to the day, since that catastrophic meeting and Nicholas still felt the keenest sense of betrayal...

How could you, Dad? I gave my life to this company... Every school holiday from the time I was old enough to catch the train into the city all by myself. I studied business at university because one day I hoped to run this company with you by my side. I thought we could be partners... Ha! What a joke!

At least he now knew the reason behind his father's antagonism. A couple of weeks earlier, his sister, Isabella had filled him in. From the moment of Nick's birth, his father had believed Nicholas wasn't his son. It was a shocking revelation and one Nick was still coming to terms with. He was grateful to Isabella for enlightening him and what she'd told him went a long way to explaining his father's attitude, even in death. But it didn't ease the pain.

A knock at the door pulled Nicholas from his depressing thoughts. He swung around in time to see his cousin, Logan shutting the door behind him. Though Logan had assured him many times since appointing Nick Managing Director of Craigdon Enterprises that he had no interest in running the company, Nicholas couldn't help but wonder how long it would take before Logan changed his mind.

"Hey, Nick. How's it going? Who's the hot chick manning your reception desk?"

"That's Harper. The temp agency sent her over," he said, distracted.

"Harper." Logan savored the name. "With all that fiery red hair, I bet she keeps you on your toes. What happened to Margaret?"

Nick sighed at the reference to his late father's secretary. "She resigned. Said it was time. Given she turned seventy last month, I tend to agree. I must say, I wasn't sad to see her go."

Logan grinned. Though the two men were the same age, Logan's casual attitude toward life along with his sun-bleached, surfer-dude hair made him appear younger.

"Come on, Nick. Margaret wasn't that bad." The wink and the grin that followed told Nick his cousin wasn't serious.

Nick rolled his eyes. "Right. Especially if you were happy to have a secretary who hadn't made the leap to computers and still handed you phone messages on slips of paper."

Logan chuckled. "So, what's the delectable Harper's story?"

Nick made a dismissive motion with his hand. "How would I know? She's just a temp. As soon as we fill the position permanently, she'll be gone. Why would I bother to get to know her?"

"Nick, Nick, Nick. I can't believe you and I are related! You have a hot piece of ass right outside your door and you haven't even asked her anything about herself? Do you *want* to stay single your entire life?"

Nick merely shook his head and changed the subject. "So, what brings you to the city?"

Logan's lightheartedness disappeared. He grimaced and ran a hand through his longish, white-blond hair then threw himself down in the comfortable chair opposite Nick's desk.

"It's Dad. He's on my case again. Why can't he leave me the hell alone?"

Nicholas commiserated with his cousin. They had more in common than most people realized. Both twenty-five, both tall, blond and good-looking. Worse still, they'd both had their dreams thwarted by their fathers. Now it seemed both were destined to have their lives controlled by the elder Craigdon brothers.

"I just don't understand it," Logan continued. "I've told Dad over and over. I'm not interested in running Craigdon Super Yachts. All I want to do is design and help build them. I love being where the action is. Working on the factory floor. I don't want anything to do with overseeing the rules and regulations, fighting with suppliers, doing payrolls, mediating staff disputes. The very thought of all that gives me a headache! I wish Dad would accept that and leave me the hell alone."

"At least he's not putting pressure on you to start sailing again," Nick said quietly.

Logan's eyes turned hard. "He knows better than that."

Nick acknowledged the comment with a brief nod. "Of course."

Logan made a sound of frustration. "That's why his insistence that I take over his company is so infuriating! It's like he's offering me a consolation prize. Poor crippled Logan. Never going to be a competitive sailor again. Oh well, offer him a desk job. No doubt he'll be grateful."

Logan screwed up his face in another groan of despair and irritation. "I don't *want* a consolation prize and I sure as hell don't want a desk job! Dad knows the very thought of being locked up in an office all day is enough to drive me crazy. It's like he doesn't give a damn. You have to help me, Nick," he pleaded.

Nick frowned. "What can I do? I have no influence over Uncle Archie."

"No, of course not." Logan paused. "I'm going to tell him any spare time I have will be spent over here, at Craigdon Enterprises. He needs to think that with Uncle Henry gone, the place is in turmoil." He paused again and looked at Nick. "I need you to back me up."

"But—"

Logan held up a hand. "Please, Nick. Hear me out. We both know I'm speaking bullshit. Not only am I hardly ever here, you're running this place so much better than I could—and you love doing it. That's why I put you here. But Dad doesn't know that. I need to let him think Craigdon Enterprises is a mess and I'm needed here every spare minute to try and keep it from going under. As much as Dad and Uncle Henry were often at odds, Dad wouldn't want to see his brother's company collapse."

Nicholas frowned again. If Uncle Archie believed his son's explanation, it would make Nick look incompetent. After all, seven months ago Logan had put him in charge. If the company was on the brink of collapse, it would have to be Nick's fault...

Am I okay with that?

Logan seemed to sense his indecision. "Please, Nick. I'm begging you. It's a lot to ask, but I'm desperate. I need Dad to get off my back. I need him to realize I'm never going to step up and run his company. If he wants to retire, he's going to have to look for someone else."

"Who do you have in mind? Noah? Oh, that's right. He's just been promoted to detective. Maybe Flynn's willing to give up his law practice?"

Logan groaned in exasperation and threw his arms up in the air. "We both know neither of my brothers are interested. They have their own careers. But that's what I'm trying to get through to Dad. *I* have a career, too. Okay, so it's not the one I thought I'd have, but I've come to love the design work I do. Creating a yacht from the floor up. It's exciting. Someone has to do it. I don't understand why he can't see that."

Nick shook his head slowly from side to side. A wry grin tugged at his lips. "We're a right sorry pair, aren't we? I've lived and breathed my father's company since I was a kid and he's handed it over to someone else. You break out in a rash at the thought of taking over your father's company and he keeps trying to force you to do that. It's a shame we couldn't have switched fathers," he joked.

Logan continued to look despondent. "Yeah. It's ridiculous all right."

Nick regarded his cousin solemnly, his earlier humor dissipating. "Are you sure you're okay with me running Craigdon Enterprises? It's part of your inheritance, after all."

The words tasted sour in Nick's mouth. While he'd been left a paltry million dollars out of his father's billion-dollar estate, the bulk of it had gone to his cousin, including the family company. Not that he blamed Logan. Nick knew nothing of his father's reasons but he knew his cousin had not persuaded or influenced Henry to make his decision.

"Of course I am," Logan reassured him. "I told you that right at the beginning. I'm not cut out for office work. Never have been. As for property development, I wouldn't have a clue where to start. It still beats me why Uncle Henry left the company to me."

Nick compressed his lips and nodded grimly. No one could understand why Henry had acted as he did. For years, Logan had spent almost every waking moment out on the water, testing and racing the latest and greatest in sailing boats. He'd been national champion four years in a row and had been headed for a spot on the Australian Olympic team until his accident.

Several serious leg fractures had left him with a permanent limp and had put an end to his aspirations to become a world champion sailor. That was three years ago and Logan was still licking his wounds. Nick was fine with that. He didn't judge. He knew all about crushing disappointment and how difficult it could be to overcome.

Still, it didn't sit right with him, compromising his reputation. As much as he loved Logan, this seemed too much to ask. He said as much to his cousin.

Logan started begging.

"Please, Nick! I know it's a lot to ask, but I really need you to come through for me here. At least until I've managed to convince Dad once and for all I'm not taking over his business. Imagine if our situations were reversed? Imagine how it would feel if your father was forcing your hand in a direction you couldn't even stand to think about?"

Nick drew in a deep breath and briefly closed his eyes. He hated to see Logan in such a difficult position and he certainly sympathized with him, but to pretend to be so incompetent that he needed Logan to hold his hand...? That was too much.

"*Please*, Nick..."

Logan now looked as desperate as he sounded. Nick

couldn't hold out any longer. He let out a sigh of defeat.

"Okay, but on two conditions."

Relief poured across Logan's face. "Anything."

"One, I'll keep up the façade of incompetence only around your father. As far as my family and all of the Craigdon employees are concerned, I'm doing an excellent job and you couldn't be happier with your decision to appoint me managing director."

"Agreed. What's the second condition?"

"That you tell your father once and for all you have no interest in running Craigdon Super Yachts."

"Haven't you been paying attention? I've told him over and over again. He refuses to hear!"

Nick regarded his cousin steadily. Logan was the first to look away. Then he sighed in defeat. "Okay. I'll tell him again. This time I'll make sure he believes it."

"Just make sure you believe it, too."

Logan's frown was immediate and fierce. "What's that supposed to mean?"

Nick refused to look away. "I think you know."

Once again, Logan was the first to break the eye contact. "I've never wanted to run Dad's business. Everyone knows that," he muttered.

Nick merely shrugged. "They're my conditions. Take it or leave it."

"I'll take it. And thank you, Nick. I owe you one."

Nicholas smiled wryly. "Actually, given that you've allowed me free rein to run Craigdon Enterprises as I see fit, I'd nearly call it even."

"And don't forget the generous salary." Logan winked.

"The *very* generous salary," Nick added.

Logan's expression sobered. "I'm more than happy to pay a premium to have you take this off my hands. It should have been yours, anyway."

This time it was Nick who looked away. He agreed with Logan. Craigdon Enterprises should have been his. He hoped to convince Logan to let him buy in when he could afford it. Unfortunately, the million dollars he'd inherited wouldn't be enough. Not by a long shot.

Logan sat back in his chair and stacked his hands behind his head. "So, what else is going on? Anything I need to know?"

"Not really. I fired Dwight Britton. Given that he's facing a string of charges, including attempted murder of Joel's fiancée, Sheridan McClintock, I don't think we'll have much trouble with an unfair dismissal claim."

Logan gave a wry grin. "Yeah. I'm glad Sheridan pulled through. I can't believe Britton shot her! I saw her and Joel together at Callum's engagement party. They looked very chummy."

Nick rolled his eyes. "You're right. Joel and Sheridan are in *lurve*."

"Aren't you happy for them?" Logan asked with a bemused smile.

Nick made a sound of disgust. "Come on, Logan. All that lovey-dovey crap. It's sickening."

Logan merely chuckled. Nick flushed. It was no secret he'd never done well with the ladies. As a teenager, he'd lacked confidence and was shy and awkward. Not a lot had changed. Something he was sure Logan was well aware of and a subject Nick didn't want to get into.

"Do you remember a few months ago I told you and Joel about money missing from the Craigdon accounts?" Nick asked.

Logan frowned in thought. "Yeah, I do. Did you find out anything else about it?"

Nick shook his head. "No. In fact, I'm not sure we can call it missing money. They appear to be payment for some kind of expenses. There doesn't seem to be any rhyme or reason to the withdrawals, but I spoke to our head of finance and though he didn't know the specifics about the payments, he confirmed the transfers had been authorized by Henry."

"How much are we talking?"

"A few million. More than half a million in one day alone."

"Are we sure it was authorized by your father? Remember what happened at McClintock's."

Nick grimaced. It wasn't that long ago Craigdon's biggest rival had been rocked by a scandal involving millions of dollars that were illegally moved to an offshore account.

"You're right," Nick said. "I'll talk to our finance guy again and make sure that money was properly authorized. Assuming it was, I'll set about trying to locate where it went. If it's all above board, I don't care how Dad spent it. It was his to do with what he liked. But out of curiosity I'd like to know what he spent it on.

Logan nodded. "Yeah. I'm curious, too. Keep on it."

"I'm also still trying to reconcile the discrepancies I found with the number of employees Dad had on each building site," Nick added. Do you remember me telling you about that?"

Logan shrugged. "Vaguely. What have you found?"

Nick sighed. "Nothing much. I've visited some of the work sites involved. No one's talking."

Logan frowned. "I still don't understand why he'd employ more laborers than he needed. It doesn't make sense."

"You're right. But don't worry about it. I'm going to keep up the pressure. Sooner or later, someone will spill. They always do. My next step is to talk to some of the more experienced hands. See what they say. If there was something untoward going on, there's bound to be someone feeling disgruntled. He's the one I need to talk to."

"Yep. Sounds like a plan. Anything else I need to know?"

"Actually, there is." Nick paused.

"Fire away."

Nick blew out his breath on a heavy sigh and stared down at his father's desk, unsure how to start. Logan was as aware as any of them of Henry's shortcomings, but still… Was there any reason to bring this up now? The man was dead.

"Nick? What is it?"

He heard the concern in Logan's voice and looked up at his cousin. "I hate to say this, but it looks like Dad was rather unscrupulous with some of his developments."

Logan frowned. "In what way?"

Nick grimaced. "I've found something in Dad's files called the Urban Renewal Program. It was basically the practice of buying large, social housing apartment blocks in the inner city. As each lease expired, he increased the rent until people couldn't afford to pay and then he forced them to leave. It was a strategy he used over and over again to reach his goal. Once Dad had all the tenants out, he came in with the bulldozers, demolished what was there and built brand new, larger apartments, attracting higher rents and a classier paying tenant."

Logan stared at him in surprise. "Wow. Are you sure?"

Nick nodded grimly. "Oh, yeah. I checked and double checked. I didn't want to believe Dad could be involved in something so distasteful. But he was. And it happened more than once."

"Shit. I mean, I'd heard rumors over the years that he could be unscrupulous, but those comments always came from his competitors and I dismissed them as jealous talk. Uncle Henry had his fair share of enemies."

"Yeah. Dad knew that all too well. That was the reason he had those metal detectors installed downstairs. At the time I thought it was a bit over the top, but he insisted it was necessary. I've been thinking about removing them. What do you think?"

Logan shrugged. "Do what you think is best. I don't see a need for them, though I guess we can leave them for a while longer, until we have a better handle on things. There must have been some reason Uncle Henry thought they were necessary."

"I wonder what happened to all the people Dad forced out?" Nicholas mused, unwilling to let the subject go.

"What people?"

"The tenants, the people who were evicted from those apartment blocks. Did they have somewhere else to go, or did they join the long queues at the city's soup kitchens and find shelter in the parks? I mean, where does someone go when they have nowhere to live?"

"I'm sure Uncle Henry made some kind of arrangements for those people. He wouldn't have just put them out on the street."

Nicholas wasn't so certain. He'd known his father better than Logan. Henry hadn't always played fair. It hadn't surprised Nicholas to discover how his father had forced disadvantaged people out of their homes. He was disgusted by the thought.

"I want you to look into what happened to those people," Logan said slowly. "Knowing they might have been treated badly doesn't sit well with me. It might have happened under Uncle Henry's watch, but that doesn't mean we can't try and make reparation, if it's possible. What do you say?"

Nick let out his breath in a rush, feeling relieved. "I think that's a great idea. I wanted to suggest it, but I wasn't sure how you'd react. After all, it's going to cost the company money."

Logan shrugged. "Money isn't everything."

Nick smiled. "You're right. I'm glad we think the same way."

"Absolutely. I have no interest in running this place, but as the new owner, I feel an obligation to make sure things are done right, are above board. I know I can trust you to do that. I want you to know, Nick, you have my full support."

"Thanks, Logan. That means a lot to me. And it makes my life a lot easier knowing we think along similar lines when it comes to making decisions. I'm all for making a profit, but not at the expense of someone else."

Nicholas paused and then continued. "I was speaking to Callum and Grace at the engagement party. They're doing substantial renovations over at the soup kitchen where Grace works. Callum's put his entire inheritance toward the construction of affordable housing for the more disadvantaged in our city. I think your brother, Flynn has also made a substantial financial contribution to their project. It's a noble project and one Callum is passionate about. He assured me it was vitally needed. If you're serious about reparations, I'm wondering what you think about the possibility of us making some changes to that new build we're about to sign off on out at Parramatta?"

"Aren't we building five-star accommodation units on that site?" Logan asked.

"Yes. We are. The demolition of the existing buildings was completed earlier in the year, but the project's been delayed following Dad's death. It's with the Parramatta Council now, but they haven't signed off on it yet. We still have time to make some changes, if we want."

"What did you have in mind?"

"I'm thinking we could downgrade some of the fittings and fixtures to save money and instead of five-star accommodation we could offer apartments as an affordable housing option, with a particular emphasis on those tenants who were displaced when Dad bought and demolished their original homes. Do you think the board would go for it?"

"Not sure, but I'm more than happy to try to convince

them. Draw me up a proposal that I can take to them. With the two of us backing it, I'm sure it will pass the vote."

Nicholas smiled. "That sounds great. Thanks for your support, Logan. It means a great deal to me."

"How long ago did Uncle Henry evict those tenants?"

"I haven't been through all of the files yet, but it looks like it might have gone on over several years."

"How are we going to locate the displaced tenants in order to offer them this new accommodation?"

"I'm not sure. I guess I'll start with Dad's records."

Logan regarded him dubiously. "It sounds like a lot of work with no guarantee of success."

Nick shrugged. He was prepared to put in the hours if it meant making up for what his father had done. At the very least, he'd give it his best shot.

The sound of Logan's phone ringing interrupted their conversation. With an apologetic look, he answered the call.

"Hi, Dad." There was silence while Logan listened. "Yes. Sorry, I forgot. I'm meeting with Nick over at Craigdon Enterprises. Just putting out some fires. No, it's all good. For the most part, Nick's on top of things. Just needed a bit of guidance. Yes. No worries. I'll be there as soon as I can."

Logan ended the call and looked across at Nicholas. He grimaced. "Sorry. That was Dad."

"Yeah, I guessed. Something about the way you called him Dad," Nick said dryly.

Logan flushed. "Yeah. Listen, I'm late for a meeting. I have to get going."

"Of course. I understand. No doubt you have other fires to put out." Nick couldn't resist the dig. Though he'd agreed to the plan, it didn't mean he had to like it.

Logan flushed again and ducked his head. "Yeah. Well, thanks again. I really appreciate what you're doing." He looked around the office. "All of it."

"No worries," Nick said dismissively. "Thanks for stopping by. It's been good to see you."

Logan gave him a quick hug in farewell and slapped him on the back. "You, too. Take care. We'll talk soon." He turned and headed toward the door. "Get me that proposal. Let's take that to the board ASAP," he threw over his shoulder.

Nick gave him a wave and Logan opened the door and left.

Chapter Two

As much as Nick wanted to get a start on the proposal to take to the board, there were more pressing issues to deal with. He turned his attention to his very full inbox. Distracted, he pushed the intercom button and asked his temporary executive assistant, Harper Wyburn, to join him to discuss the day's schedule. There was a sharp knock on the door.

"Come in."

Harper had been with him for the past two weeks, filling in while the position was advertised and though he'd played it cool with Logan, the truth was the whole time Harper had been there Nick had been struggling to concentrate. He wished he'd specified someone more mature, in their fifties, or older. And someone far less attractive. Harper was stunningly beautiful and looked barely out of her teens.

He watched her walk toward him in her smart black suit and impossibly high heels. His appreciative gaze lingered on her full breasts. Her skin was so clear and pale it was almost translucent. Thick auburn hair was tucked low on her neck in a tidy bun. Bright green eyes shone with intelligence.

Nick felt a stirring in his groin and tried to ignore it. An office romance, especially with a temp, was definitely a no go. Besides, he wasn't the kind of guy who engaged in casual flings. Attractive women had always made him nervous. He felt awkward and embarrassed and tongue-tied. Not at all the kind of impression he wanted to make as Managing Director of Craigdon Enterprises.

Harper crossed the room and took the seat recently vacated by his cousin. She crossed one slim, stockinged leg over the other. With pad and pen in hand, she looked at him expectantly. A rush of nerves tightened his chest. He drew in a breath and with an effort, forced himself to speak.

"Good morning, Harper. Thanks for coming in."

She gave him a wry smile that showed a row of even white teeth. "You asked me to, sir."

Nick blushed. "Yes, of course. But I meant, thanks for coming to Craigdon Enterprises. My previous EA was here for many years. I inherited her from my father and though she had some rather antiquated ways of doing things, there's nothing she didn't know about this company. I appreciate you're only here until we find a permanent replacement, but I want to thank you for your willingness to take on such a demanding role, especially given your age."

She frowned. "What does my age have to do with anything?"

Nick squirmed at the sharpness of her tone. "Nothing, but you barely look old enough to have finished high school. You're obviously inexperienced."

Her expression darkened. "Not that it's any of your business, but I was orphaned at seventeen. For the past five years, I've had no one but myself to rely on. I graduated high school and worked nights so I could put myself through secretarial school. Since then, I've worked at some large businesses." She glanced down at her smart tailored suit and heels. "I don't think I've done too badly."

Nick's embarrassment deepened. "I'm sorry. I didn't mean to offend you. If what you say is true about your past, you have nothing but my admiration."

Her gaze narrowed and her cheeks flushed with anger. "What do you mean, *if* what I say is true? Of course it's true! Do you think I'd make up something like that?"

Nick ducked his head. *I've done it again! Why can't I just shut my mouth? It's because she's so sophisticated, so beautiful. I'm the one who feels like an awkward teenager…*

He stammered out another apology. "I-I'm sorry. I didn't mean to accuse you of lying. Of course you wouldn't lie about something like that. And I shouldn't have judged you on your age. I guess I'm used to Margaret who turned seventy a few weeks before she retired. I shouldn't assume age brings wisdom or competence. Of course you're good at your job. The agency wouldn't have sent you otherwise."

Nick heard himself prattling on, but couldn't seem to stop. He risked a glance in her direction. Her cheeks were still flushed and her luscious mouth was set in a tight line. He sighed inwardly. It would take at least a month to advertise, interview and select another EA. In the meantime, he had Harper. A woman who now looked at him like she wanted to throttle him. It was going to be a long four weeks.

Harper fumed in silence. Nicholas Craigdon was as rude and offensive as she guessed he'd be. He was Henry Craigdon's son, after all. What had she expected? He gave off the Mr-Nice-Guy vibe, but it was all a ruse. Underneath that friendly, calm exterior lay a man whose arrogance took her breath away. She hadn't failed to notice the way his gaze had raked over her from top to bottom, lingering far too long on her breasts. While she was used to appreciative glances from men, that didn't mean she enjoyed being ogled so blatantly.

It was just another infuriating display of his arrogance. To rub salt into the wound, he was sinfully good-looking. Of course he was. He was Henry Craigdon's son. Even in his sixties, Henry had had charm and charisma in spades. She'd expected nothing less from his son.

Though Nicholas' hair was a darker blond than his father's and he had blue eyes, not green, she could see the resemblance in the strong jawline, the olive skin, the broad shoulders…the superiority in his gaze. He was every bit as loathsome as his father. *Henry Craigdon.* Her nemesis. The man she held responsible for her mother's death.

With an effort, Harper forced herself to relax and even managed a tight smile. It wouldn't do to put Nicholas offside. He might call her agency and request they send over someone else, someone more amendable. Her carefully laid plan would be stymied before she could put it into motion. That she couldn't risk.

She was finally where she wanted to be, where she *needed* to be. Right there, at Craigdon Enterprises, seated only a few feet away from Henry Craigdon's son. Too bad the asshole had died so unexpectedly. No matter. His son would stand in his stead.

After five long years, she was finally in a position to exact her revenge. No matter how much she hated the Craigdon family and everything they stood for, she had to stay focused and that meant keeping Nicholas Craigdon onside. Though it pained her to do it, through gritted teeth, she offered him an apology.

"I'm sorry. I think I overreacted. Of course you weren't accusing me of lying."

A flare of surprise momentarily widened Nicholas' blue eyes. "Apology accepted," he said with an easy smile.

Harper did her best to return it, but her lips felt like they were being stretched over an abyss. Her cheeks and jaw ached from holding the smile in place. As he busied himself with the papers that were piled high on his desk, Nicholas appeared oblivious to the tension she felt. He looked up at her and grinned.

"Right. Let's get back on track. I have a mountain of correspondence to get through. I've dictated a dozen letters and sent them through to you. I'd be grateful if you can type them up and have them back on my desk within the hour. I also want you to call Steven Rogers. He's the supervisor over at Downer Steel. Tell him to hold off on our order for the Parramatta site until I get back to him. We're making a few changes to those plans."

Harper kept her smile fixed in place and made notes on the pad as Nicholas spoke. It wasn't easy to remain detached from the son of the man she hated. Another surge of anger rose up inside her. Her hand shook from the force of it. She bit down hard on her lip. She needed to prove to him she was as competent as his last EA. She couldn't afford to be replaced.

"Harper? Are you all right?"

She looked up and blinked at the concern on Nicholas' face. *Maybe he isn't as oblivious to my turmoil as I guessed....?* Hurriedly, she offered him a blank smile. "Of course."

His gaze remained trained on her a moment longer before he returned his attention to the paperwork in front of him.

"I have tender documents here relating to three potential purchases. Take a look over them and see if they're in order. Then send them to our legal department and ask them to provide me with a detailed analysis of the conditions. We want to move on these purchases ASAP, but only if the terms are in our favor."

She frowned inwardly, staring blindly at her lap.

Of course the terms have to be in his favor. He's a Craigdon. They always get what they want. Just like this man's father.

As if privy to her thoughts, Nicholas paused for a moment. His gaze held a degree of surprise and uncertainty. "Are you sure there's nothing the matter? You're staring at that notepad as if it's trying to bite you."

Once again, Harper hid her anger behind a bland

expression. She offered him a strained laugh. "Oh, you're so funny."

He continued to regard her with a wary expression, but eventually looked away. She breathed a silent sigh of relief and waited expectantly, her pen still poised over the pad. "Anything else, sir?"

Nicholas shook his head, sending a lock of his longish, blond hair falling over his eyes. Reflexively, she nearly moved to brush it aside, but caught herself in time.

What the hell am I doing?

"No, thanks. That will be all, Harper. You may go."

Annoyance shot through her at his unceremonious dismissal. With a huff, she stood and tugged down her skirt. She glanced at a paperweight that stood on his desk and wondered briefly how much damage it would do if she threw it at his head.

Just then Nicholas glanced up and caught the direction of her gaze. To her surprise, he smiled. Slow, sexy, disarming… With heat stealing across her face, she spun around and left his office, pulling the door firmly closed behind her.

Harper threw herself down in her chair and dragged the keyboard toward her. She opened the software program to deal with Nicholas' dictation. Tugging on her headphones, she clicked on the first document. His deep tones filled her ears, so close and intimate it felt like he was right there beside her. Coupling that with her recent memories of how good he filled out a suit and all of a sudden the air around her felt too warm.

Great. This is going to be even harder than I thought.

She needed to prove she was the best EA ever. One way to do that was to impress him with her speed and accuracy. She needed to do everything better and faster than anyone else so that when the time came, he wouldn't think about replacing her. Not only did she have to be the most competent EA he'd come across, she also had to gain his trust. If her plan to destroy him and his company was to come to fruition, those things were imperative.

With her resolve front and center in her mind, she squared her shoulders and ignoring Nicholas' dulcet tones, she set to work. She was halfway through the second letter when an incoming call lit up the line on the handset beside her. Pausing the dictation, she answered the phone.

"Good morning, Craigdon Enterprises. This is Harper."

"Oh…Harper? Who are you?"

"I'm Nicholas Craigdon's temporary EA."

"Where's Margaret?"

"I believe she retired a couple of weeks ago. May I ask who's calling?"

"It's Sophia Craigdon."

The voice on the other end of the phone was so posh and imperious, Harper's jaw clenched. She hadn't even met this woman, but she already disliked her. *Sophia Craigdon.* No doubt the woman was married to Nicholas. Harper hadn't done any research into whether or not Nicholas Craigdon had a wife because that factor wasn't important to her plan.

"Please put me through to Nicholas," the woman continued in the same haughty tone.

"Of course," Harper replied through gritted teeth. "May I ask what it relates to?"

"No, you may not. Please put me through to him. Now."

The woman spoke with such authority, Harper had no choice but to do as she was told. Quietly seething, she buzzed her boss' office. "I have Sophia Craigdon on line one," she announced in a tight voice.

"Thank you," he replied, seeming oblivious to her snarky mood.

Harper slammed down the receiver and re-started the dictation. Once again, Nicholas was in her ear. This time, all she could see were images of what she imagined the snooty Sophia Craigdon looked like. No doubt she was as good-looking as her arrogant husband. Blond and blue-eyed. Model thin, dressed in designer clothes and with an overbearing attitude to match. Exactly the kind of person Harper loved to hate.

Recalling the way Nicholas had given her an appreciative once-over, her blood started boiling again. The audacity of the man! She wondered what his wife would think. The plain fact was, good looks and charm aside, Nicholas Craigdon was an asshole, just like his father.

Nick depressed the flashing button on his phone and answered the call. "Soph. What's going on?"

"What the hell is wrong with that woman who answered your phone?"

Nick frowned, bemused. "You mean, Harper?"

"Yes! Harper! Talk about an attitude! She gave me the third degree! Asked me what I wanted to talk to you about! Of all the gall!"

Nick grinned at Sophia's outrage. Ever since their late father had treated her so abominably under his will, she'd been mad at the world. Not that he blamed her. He knew what it was like to be treated unfairly.

"Give her a break. She's a temp. She's just doing her job."

"Speaking of jobs," Sophia replied in a more reasonable tone. "I was wondering if you had any vacancies at Craigdon Enterprises? I know! Maybe *I* could be your next EA?"

Nick frowned. Though he loved his younger sister dearly, he couldn't think of anything worse than having her as his EA. Sophia could be as stubborn and pig-headed as their father. She didn't take orders from anyone.

"I've already spoken to Logan," she continued. "He told me to speak to you because you're now in charge."

Nick felt a rush of warmth. Logan had assured him he was the managing director with Logan's full support, but it was nice that he'd told other people that Nick was the one calling the shots, especially after their conversation earlier that morning.

"So what do you think, Nick? Do you have something for me? I'm going mad with boredom!"

Nick swallowed a sigh and tried to think of a way to let Sophia down lightly. "The thing is Soph, you might have finished your degree in teaching, but you don't have enough experience in secretarial to come and work for me as my EA. Being my executive assistant is a very demanding job and requires a specific skillset. Besides, it wouldn't look right to the staff who have stayed loyal to me and Logan since Dad's death. They know you don't have the experience to take on such a position."

"Surely you have something, Nick? I'm desperate!"

"What about a teaching job? That's what you studied at university. Don't tell me you've lost interest in a teaching career already?"

"Of course not. But it's the middle of September. We only have one more school term before the end of the year. No one's hiring right now."

He heard the despondency in her voice and wished he could help her, but taking her on as his EA wasn't the solution. He and his youngest sister had always fired each other up. If she took on a position as his subordinate, answering directly to him, they wouldn't be talking by the end of the day. Keeping her at arm's length was best for both of them.

"I'm sorry, Sophia. The best I can do is a junior administration position. You'll be paid minimum wage."

"Nick! You're the managing director of a billion-dollar company. You must be able to find me something better than that!"

Her sulky tone filled him with irritation. "I'm sorry, Soph. I don't have time for this. I have plenty of real problems on my desk to deal with. That's my best offer. Take it or leave it."

"I'll think about it," she finally responded. "By the way, Mom asked me to tell you she wants us all over for a family dinner tomorrow night. Seven o'clock. Don't be late."

Chapter Three

Harper continued to plow through the lengthy dictation. All the while, she fumed over Nicholas' total lack of decency. She was glad he was every bit as reprehensible as his late father. That would make it easier to carry out her plan for revenge.

When she'd first caught sight of Nicholas Craigdon, her body had reacted instinctively to his good looks and charm. Physically, he was model-perfect, with a dazzling smile to match. His welcome had appeared genuine. It was just as well she knew firsthand how deceptive a good-looking Craigdon could be. She'd do well to remember that. She'd worked hard to get where she was and she wasn't about to jeopardize everything she'd planned over a way-too-sexy man.

As a temp, she'd worked at a number of companies including, most recently, for McClintock Properties. It was there she got the idea to seek a position with Craigdon. The rivalry between the two businesses was legendary, going back at least two generations, although things had recently calmed between the two companies. Apparently, a Craigdon and a McClintock were now dating.

Not to be put off, Harper broached an ambitious employee in the contracts office at McClintock's about providing some inside information once she'd established herself inside

Craigdon Enterprises. The offer was readily accepted and even encouraged. Christopher Barrington was a snake but if he helped her exact revenge, her association with him was worth it.

She'd thought the most difficult part would be getting access to useful information, but Nicholas had just handed her three tenders. She could hardly believe her luck. But first, before she got to those she had to finish the dictation.

Typing as quickly as she could, she finished the last two letters and added them to the pile. Collecting them, she pushed away from her desk and headed back to Nick's office. She knocked briefly on the door before stepping inside. He looked up in surprise as she entered.

"Yes?" he asked.

"I have those letters ready for you." She put the pile down on his desk.

His eyes widened. "You've finished already?"

"Yes."

"All of them?"

"Yes."

He shook his head and smiled. "Wow. I know I asked for them to be returned within the hour, but I expected it would take much longer."

She shrugged, inwardly pleased. "No."

He laughed. "I guess I was used to Margaret. She wasn't exactly speedy on a computer."

She gave him a quick smile. "Then I guess you're lucky I am."

The look he gave her was filled with admiration. "Absolutely. How long can you stay?"

Her stomach clenched in anticipation. *Yes! This is exactly what I hoped for!* The longer she was there, the more time she had to destroy his company. She deliberately kept her tone casual. "As long as you want me to."

Nick's grin widened. "That's great. We've just started advertising for the position, but you're welcome to stay here until it's filled. I might even convince you to apply." He winked.

Her belly somersaulted. It wasn't fair that he was so damned attractive. And nice. No, he wasn't nice. He'd ogled her the first time he'd seen her that morning—he had no right to do so. He was a cad. Just like his father. She had to remember that.

"Is there anything else you'd like me to do?" she asked.

"How are you doing with those tenders?"

"They're next on my list."

He nodded. "Good. Are you familiar with that type of document?"

"Yes. I've worked for other property developers. In fact, my last position was in the contracts office. I'll check these ones thoroughly."

He gave her another grin that might have curled her toes if she'd allowed herself to be interested.

"That's great. But don't worry too much about the legal jargon. Like I said earlier, every tender goes to our lawyers for final approval once I've finished with them."

She gave him a tight smile. "Right. Well, if you have nothing further, I'll get back to my desk."

⌒

Nick frowned at Harper's departing back. Logan was right. She was incredibly attractive. Something about her dark-red hair and porcelain skin. Her delectable figure. Petite and curvy. And those eyes. So green. Like emeralds. It was too bad she was his EA, even temporarily.

And then he shook his head. It was almost laughable that Nicholas Craigdon would come right out and flirt with someone like Harper Wyburn. In fact, he didn't flirt with any woman. His father had cured him of that.

Refusing to let his mind dredge up those painful memories, he turned his attention to the proposal he'd started to put together on the affordable housing project. Though the company had been hemorrhaging money in the months before his father died, the stream had stopped upon his father's death. With other more important issues to deal with, Nick still hadn't identified the recipient of the funds, or whether there was more than one, but he was determined to get to the bottom of it at some stage. There was plenty of time. It wasn't like the company was broke.

Despite the millions of dollars that were unaccounted for, Craigdon Enterprises was in good shape. Over the months since his father's untimely death, Nicholas had discovered the late Henry Craigdon had a knack for putting his money into investments that paid off many times over.

Of course, some of those investments had resulted in the removal of vulnerable people from their homes, but Nicholas was determined to make reparation for that. If they managed to secure the majority of the tenders they expected to bid on over the next few weeks, the company would be in an even better position. There would be no reason for the board to reject Nick's affordable-housing proposal. At least, that's the way he hoped the cards would fall. But the way his luck had been running lately, he wouldn't count on anything until it was a done deal.

Harper pored over the tender documents, looking for any detail that might be valuable to Craigdon's competition. She'd already snapped off a picture of the front page with her phone which contained all the essential information, such as the property address, the vendor's details and most importantly, the tender price. It was information she was sure Christopher Barrington would be pleased to get his hands on.

She hadn't given any thought, beyond the obvious, as to why the McClintock employee had responded so positively to her suggestion she feed him confidential information on Craigdon Enterprises. She assumed the longstanding rivalry between the two companies was reason enough. It was well known among the industry that there had been no love lost between Henry Craigdon and Michael McClintock. Even though both men were now dead, Harper had been confident she'd find someone at McClintock's eager for dirt on their competitor. She'd been right.

It was an added bonus that Christopher had offered to pay her for her information. She could certainly do with the extra cash he'd promised, but as far as she was concerned, bringing Henry's company down was payment enough. It was a shame he hadn't lived long enough for her to get her revenge on him personally. No matter. Craigdon Enterprises and the man who now ran it would have to suffice.

Checking to make sure the way was clear, Harper took a few more photos of the proposed terms and conditions on the following pages and saved them to a folder on her phone. Slowly, she worked her way through all three tenders, taking photos of relevant information as she went. Satisfied she'd recorded everything of value, she attached the files to an email to Christopher Barrington and tapped SEND.

There. It was done. She sat back against her chair and took a moment to relish the satisfaction that filled her veins. It was only the first major step in putting her plan for revenge into action, but boy, it felt so good.

That's for you, Mom. The first of many. I swear I won't stop until this company's bankrupt. Wish me luck...

Moments later, Christopher sent back a response.

Good job. The money's in your account. I've included a bonus to keep you interested. Nice doing business with you. Keep up the good work.

It was right on seven o'clock when Nicholas walked up the wide stone steps to his family home the next evening. Punctuality had been drummed into him by his father from an early age. It was a habit that was hard to break. His mother, Elizabeth Craigdon, met him in the entryway.

"Nick! You're right on time."

"Hi, Mom," he said and kissed her on the cheek. She looked lovely in a cream-colored, linen suit. "Is everyone else here?"

"Well, Jett and Isabella are both at work, but everyone else is here. We're just waiting on Sophia."

Nick rolled his eyes. "Of course we are. I don't know how the rest of us learned how to be on time, but somehow that courtesy escaped our baby sister. What's her excuse this time?"

"Now, now," his mother gently admonished him. "There's no need to be like that. This past seven months have been so difficult for her. Cut her a bit of slack."

"So difficult for *her*? What about me?"

Elizabeth patted him on the arm. "Of course, Nick. Your father treated you abominably. You have every right to feel put out."

"More than put out, Mom. I'm furious."

She frowned. "Still?"

"Yes, Mom."

"But Logan as much as handed you the company. You're managing director. Isn't that enough?"

Nick sighed. He was there to enjoy a family dinner. He didn't want to bring up past hurts. "No, Mom. It isn't enough. But let's not get into it tonight. All I want to do is forget all about Dad and the will and Craigdon Enterprises and relax with my family for a few hours. Is that all right?"

His mother's expression softened. "Of course it is, darling." She reached up and smoothed back a lock of hair that had fallen over his face. "You look tired, Nick. Are you getting enough sleep?"

"I'm fine, Mom. I have a lot going on, that's all."

"With the company?"

"Yes. And other things. Margaret finally retired. I've had a temp working in the office for the past couple of weeks. It always takes a bit of adjusting to a new staff member."

Elizabeth blinked in surprise. "You didn't tell me Margaret retired."

He gave his mother a droll look. "She turned seventy not long ago, Mom. It was well and truly time."

"Yes, of course. I wish I'd known. I would have arranged for a farewell gift. She was with your father for many years."

"Yes. Anyway, now she's gone and I need to replace her. I've put in calls with the job agencies and we've started running some ads in the newspapers. In the meantime, I have Harper Wyburn."

"Is she the temp?"

"Yes."

"What's she like?"

Nick was immediately besieged with images of the beautiful EA. He hurriedly pushed them aside. "She's fine. She knows her way around a computer, which is a bonus. More than Margaret ever did."

"Does Harper have any experience as an EA?"

"Yes. The agency wouldn't have sent her if she wasn't qualified. And so far, she's done good work."

"Where has she worked before?"

"I don't know. She's a temp, Mom. I didn't look into her credentials."

His mother shrugged. "Fair enough."

"So, what's for dinner?" Nick asked, steering the conversation away from the woman who'd already occupied far too many of his thoughts.

His mother smiled. "Amy's outdone herself. Beef Wellington with roasted baby potatoes, steamed green beans and honey carrots. All your favorites."

Nick grinned. "Sounds great. I'm starving."

"Good. Because there's crème brûlée with fresh whipped cream for dessert."

"Did someone say crème brûlée?"

Both Nick and his mother turned as Sophia topped the last step and walked across the foyer toward them. She looked glamorous as usual in a long, sky-blue halter dress made out of some kind of floaty material that swirled around her legs. Huge gold circles adorned her ears, along with a chunky necklace that was a few shades darker than her dress.

"Soph. It's good to see you." Nick pecked her on the cheek.

"Have you found me a job yet?" she asked, only half-joking.

"I already offered you one," Nick replied. "You told me you'd think about it, remember?"

Sophia rolled her eyes. "I'm not doing some menial job in the mailroom, Nick! I want to be where the action is."

He shrugged, not at all moved by her plea. "Take it or leave it. Beggars can't be choosers."

"Come on, you two. Let's not bicker," Elizabeth gently chided. She looked at her daughter. "If you need money, you can always come to me."

Sophia pouted. "That's the thing, Mom. I shouldn't *have* to come to you. Daddy should have left me what he gave everyone else."

"A measly million dollars?" Nick asked. "That's all he left me."

"At least it was a million," Sophia replied. "If you recall, my inheritance had quite a few less zeroes than that."

Nick compressed his lips into a thin line. The sting of hurt and disappointment at the discovery of how unfairly their father had treated some of his children was as sharp as ever.

"Oh, I recall all right," he muttered. "Just like I remember how Dad left Isabella twenty million. Even Jett, Joel and Callum got ten million each. It's so unfair."

Elizabeth looked distressed. "Please, Nick. Sophia. Let's not get into this right now. I want us all to enjoy our time together this evening. We don't spend near enough time together as a family."

"I thought you said Jett and Isabella weren't joining us," Nick said.

"That's right. But everyone else is here. Why don't we go through to the dining room?"

With that, Elizabeth led the way across the travertine-tiled floor and into the formal dining room where the long table had been set for ten. Nick offered easy greetings to his brothers, Callum and Joel and their respective fiancées, Grace Gunning and Sheridan McClintock. Callum and Grace were due to get married right before Christmas.

Seated beside Grace were her two children, Seth and Alyssa. They were cute kids and over the months since Callum and Grace had become a couple, had easily become part of the Craigdon family. At the head of the table sat Uncle Archie.

"How are things, Uncle?" Nick asked, taking the vacant seat beside him.

"Can't complain, Nicholas. How about you? I hear you're facing some uphill battles over at Craigdon Enterprises."

Nick opened his mouth to respond to the contrary and then remembered his promise to Logan.

"Yeah, I guess," he mumbled. "Dad sure left some big shoes to fill."

"Well, I'm sure if anyone can fill them, it's you," his uncle replied with confidence, "no matter what my son says."

Nick looked at the man in surprise. "Thank you, Uncle. That's very kind of you to say."

Archie's physical likeness to Nick's father was evident. Though Henry had been a couple of years older and had green eyes and white-blond hair flecked with gray and Archie had dark-blond hair and brown eyes, the resemblance between the two men was undeniable. Anyone would have guessed they were related. It was only their personalities that were starkly different.

For one, Nick couldn't imagine his father ever giving him a compliment. Henry had been a hard taskmaster who demanded excellence from all those around him. His children were no exception. He barked orders more often than anything else and refused to tolerate fools. Uncle Archie couldn't have been more different.

Perhaps it was something to do with the fact Archie was younger, but there wasn't the same level of intensity in Archie's demeanor, the same drive to prove himself right, no matter what. Archie laughed more than he argued and always seemed to have a way of defusing a tense situation. No doubt he'd picked up that skill early in life, while learning to deal with the irascible moods of his charismatic, older brother.

Archie's easygoing attitude toward life might have been construed by some observers as laziness, but Nick knew better. His uncle had built up a world-renowned super yacht design and construction business from scratch. His designs, and now those of Logan's, were sought after by some of the most influential, wealthy people in the world. The attention to detail and Archie's insistence they use only the finest materials in the upscale fitout was legendary. The painstaking hours of labor used in the construction were obvious. No, despite his laid-back attitude, there was nothing lazy about Archie Craigdon.

Dinner was served and the beef Wellington was as good as

Nick remembered. One of the things he missed most about living at Craigdon Manor was the food. Though his mother had been more than happy for him to remain at home, at twenty-five Nicholas thought it was well and truly time to move out and strike out on his own.

He'd bought a modest apartment on the western outskirts of the inner city with a portion of his inheritance and money he'd been given by his mom. Though sparsely furnished and without a decent stove, it was somewhere he could be alone with this thoughts. But on nights like this, after enjoying a restaurant-quality meal, he wondered if he'd made the wrong choice. Amy had been with the family for more than two decades and was a wonder in the kitchen. She also knew the likes and dislikes of every Craigdon member.

"Please offer my sincere thanks to Amy for this superb dinner, Mom," Nick said, filling his plate for a second time.

Elizabeth smiled. "She'll be pleased to know you enjoyed it, Nicholas. She's always had a soft spot for you."

Sophia gave an exaggerated eye roll. "Only because he'd spend hours keeping her company in the kitchen. We all know it's because he wanted to be the first one to sample her cookies."

Nick grinned. "Too right. And it worked. Amy always let me have some when they were fresh from the oven. Almost too hot to eat. I used to get in at least two or three before the rest of you wandered in."

"It's a wonder you're not the size of a house," Sophia grumbled good-naturedly.

Nick patted his taut stomach. "Good genes, I guess. Oh, and the time I spend in the gym lifting weights and doing crunches."

Callum groaned and slapped his hand against his forehead. Nick laughed. It was well-known Callum tried hard to stay as far away from the gym as possible. It was fortunate for him he kept himself fit in other ways, at the construction site of his new building project, for one.

"How are the apartments coming along?" Nick asked.

Callum put down his fork. "Not too bad. We ran into some problems with the plumbing early on, but it looks like it's sorted out now."

"How many apartments are you building?" Nick asked.

"Sixteen. Four on each floor."

"It's a good number," Nick mused.

Callum nodded. "Yes, sixteen is better than nothing, but that's a long way from making a dent in the affordable housing shortage in this city. There's only so much private companies can do. We really need the government to come more on board."

"As a matter of fact, I've been looking into it myself. I'd like to add affordable housing to Craigdon Enterprise's projects."

Joel started in surprise. "I thought CE was synonymous with luxurious apartments. Are you sure this is the right thing to do?"

Nick nodded. "You're right. Dad built up a reputation for five-star buildings and I don't want to interfere with that. I'm not taking CE in a new direction, but I want to diversify, just a little."

Sophia stared at him, frowning. "Why? I love the luxury and sophistication a Craigdon Enterprise's building offers. Dad worked his whole life for that reputation. I hope you're not going to turn your back on all he achieved."

Nick blinked in surprise. The last person he expected to come to their father's defense was Sophia. He grimaced. He hadn't made a conscious decision to tell his family about what he'd discovered, but now he felt the need to explain.

"The thing is, I discovered something untoward in Dad's business dealings."

Elizabeth frowned. "Untoward? What do you mean?"

Chapter Four

Nick looked around at his family. While none of them suffered under the delusion their father had been perfect, Nick wasn't sure how they'd react to what he was about to say.

"It seems Dad was in the habit of purchasing low-cost housing and then increasing the rents until the tenants were forced to move out. Then he'd go in and demolish the building and start again, replacing it with five-star, luxury accommodations."

Callum and Grace looked appalled. "Are you kidding?" Callum cried.

Nick shook his head. "I'm afraid not."

"How many times did this happen?" Joel asked, his expression grim.

"At least four. Maybe more. I haven't been through all of Dad's files, yet."

Elizabeth paled. "Four times? What happened to all those poor people?"

Nick's lips thinned. "I don't know. They sure as hell weren't offered apartments in Dad's shiny new buildings. I guess they were forced into other, less expensive accommodation."

"Which is in very short supply," Callum added somberly.

Nick nodded. "That's why I want to do something about

it. I feel I owe those people. Dad treated them abominably. I'm hoping we can do something to rectify that. It might not be the exact people Dad misplaced, but at least someone in similar living conditions will reap the benefit."

Seated across from him, Elizabeth reached out and patted his hand. "That sounds like a wonderful idea, Nick. I'm appalled to learn that's how your father treated these people, but I'm so proud of you for wanting to do something about it."

"Yeah, Nick. Good job," Callum added.

There was a mumbling of assent around the table. Nick fought off a wave of embarrassment.

"I'm not doing it for the accolades. I'm doing it because it's the right thing to do."

"Of course," Joel agreed smoothly.

Sophia looked unconvinced. "Are you sure you want to do this? What Daddy did was horrible, but it had nothing to do with you."

"You're right, Soph. I could just as easily have remained silent about my discovery. This was all on Dad. But I can't ignore what he did to those vulnerable people. I need to make amends. I promise I won't sully the reputation of CE, but I need to do this."

"Does Logan know about it?" Archie asked.

Nick turned to his uncle. "Yes. I discussed it with him earlier. He's all for it. He told me to put together a proposal he can take to the board."

Archie regarded him solemnly. "It sounds like a big project. Are you sure you're up to the task?"

Nick tamped down a spurt of irritation. It wasn't his uncle's fault that Logan had told him Nick was struggling with the demands of the job. With his gaze steady on Archie's, he replied. "Didn't you just tell me how you were confident in my abilities to fill Dad's shoes?"

Archie flushed and then nodded briefly. "You're right. No doubt Logan's exaggerating the difficulties you've been having over there. What you're doing is admirable, Nick. I wish you the best of luck."

Nick felt a rush of warmth. He couldn't remember ever receiving such praise from his father. No doubt because Henry had spent Nick's entire life believing Nick wasn't his. Nick swallowed a sigh.

Elizabeth clinked a spoon against her glass to get everyone's attention. They all stopped what they were doing and looked in her direction.

"I just want to thank you all for making the effort to come tonight. I know it isn't always easy for us to get together, what with work schedules, sick children and whatnot. But I always appreciate it when you come. I also want to remind you all of the upcoming baptism. Jett and Danielle have arranged for Annalise to be christened the first Sunday in October. It will be held at St Monica's Catholic Church in Richmond and afterwards, we'll have lunch here. I hope you can all make it."

There was a general murmur of agreement among those gathered around the table. "Are fiancées invited?" Joel asked and then winked at Sheridan.

"Of course. Everyone's welcome," Elizabeth replied. "Just let me know who's coming so I can inform the caterers."

Nick's thoughts zeroed in on Harper and he immediately shut that down.

What the hell am I thinking about her for? I've never brought a woman to a family function. My siblings would rib me mercilessly. They'd ask questions I have no answers for. And even if I found the courage to ask her, she'd probably say no. We hardly know each other…

With a silent groan, Nick forced the thought from his mind. After dessert, the family moved into the music room for coffee and liqueurs. Elizabeth entertained them with some lively tunes on the piano. Several tunes were familiar to Nick, having heard them many times during his childhood, but others were new.

Once, his mother had dreamed of being a concert pianist, but life had other plans. She'd never gone into the details of why she hadn't pursued that. He'd always assumed it had something to do with his father. For all his faults, Henry Craigdon had been an incredibly charismatic, persuasive man.

He smiled at his mother from his position on the couch. "You haven't lost your talent, Mom. How often do you play?"

She shrugged. "Not as often as I used to. Lately I seem to be busier than ever. We have Joel and Sheridan's engagement party at the end of next month and then the usual Christmas mania. And of course, I've been helping Grace with the wedding preparations."

She shot a fond glance in Grace's direction. Nick smiled at the genuine affection on his brother's fiancée's face. Callum had turned his back on their father's dream that Callum would become a priest and had found love with the widowed Grace. Nick had never seen his brother so happy.

I wonder if I'll ever know happiness like that…

Once again, images of Harper Wyburn flooded his mind. He didn't know what it was about her that drew him. He normally steered well clear of beautiful women. Could his attraction have something to do with the anger and sadness he sensed behind her fiery green eyes? He got the impression life hadn't always been kind to her. He knew exactly how that felt.

Perhaps we're kindred spirits? I wonder if she'll let her guard down long enough for me to find out…

It surprised him to discover he very much hoped the answer would be yes.

❧

Harper sat back against the headboard of her single bed and tapped on her phone to open up Safari. Typing the address of her bank into the search bar, she waited for the site to load. Christopher had come through on his promise. The sum of five thousand dollars had recently been deposited into her bank account. It was more than she'd expected. It was obvious Christopher was not only wealthy, but he had a significant beef with Craigdon Enterprises. Why else would he be willing to pay so much for her information?

For most of the time Harper had worked at McClintock Properties, she'd been stationed in the contracts department. Christopher had barely noticed her, but she'd paid plenty of attention to him. Though he was more than twice her age, he was still undeniably good looking. But it wasn't his attractiveness that intrigued her. It was his attitude.

He was often rude and demanding for no good reason. It was obvious he was only tolerated by his staff. Some of them displayed outward dislike for him, but all of them did his bidding. It was as if he had some invisible power over them.

As far as Harper could see, Christopher brought the negativity on himself. He seemed to go out of his way to embarrass people or make their life uncomfortable. He continually berated the secretarial pool, which did nothing to endear him. It was like he had a grudge against the world. Harper had kept her head down and got on with her job. The longer she stayed there, the more time she had to put her plan together. Then Henry Craigdon dropped dead unexpectedly from a heart attack and she was forced to revise everything. Christopher had immediately come to mind.

She could no longer bring Henry down, but she could bankrupt his company. Selling trade secrets to the enemy seemed like the perfect way to do it. And now she'd set the plan in motion. The first piece of information had been sold and her bank account was looking much healthier than it had a few days ago. The best part of it was, it had been so easy.

She'd set herself up with the agency to ensure that if

Craigdon Enterprises ever requested the services of secretarial staff, she'd be the first one selected. And then it had happened. A request came through for a temporary executive assistant to the Managing Director of Craigdon Enterprises.

It was like the stars had aligned. This was the opportunity she'd been waiting for. Not only did she know someone who might be interested in the commercial secrets of the Craigdon empire, she now had direct access to the managing director's office. It seemed too good to be true.

Leaning back against the pillows, she smiled at the thought of how everything had fallen into place. Unable to help herself, she took another look at her bank account. Five thousand dollars for a few minutes of snooping and a handful of photographs. If she managed to send Christopher something of worth at least once a week, it wouldn't be long before she could afford something better than her shabby studio apartment. She might even find somewhere big enough for a double bed. Wouldn't that be a step up?

She looked around at the place she called home. Sandwiched between a dry cleaners and an empty shop, the small window that looked out onto the street let in only a modicum of daylight. Though she kept the place as clean as she could, there was no hiding the cracked and aged linoleum, the peeling paint, the tattered rug she'd found in a nearby alley and washed in the kitchen sink...

Still, she'd lived in far worse. At least as long as she continued to pay the rent, this was hers. As shabby as it was, she was grateful. She could still remember what it was like to take refuge in a homeless shelter. Though it was better than sleeping rough, it was far from ideal. She was glad she'd had her mom for protection, at least during those early years.

With an effort, she pushed aside the sad memories and focused on her anger. Anger was good. It was anger that kept her going. She'd made a promise to her dying mother that

Henry Craigdon would pay for what he'd done. Now he was gone, thwarting her plans. But his son was alive and well. Nicholas Craigdon might not be directly responsible for what had happened, but he'd taken over the reins. No doubt he was as unscrupulous and greedy as his father. She'd make damn sure, one way or the other, the Craigdons would live to regret the day they set eyes on Harper Wyburn.

Harper's next opportunity came sooner than she expected. Five days after she'd texted Christopher she was called into Nicholas' office. He smiled as she walked in. She self-consciously tugged at her short skirt and tried not to notice how nice he looked.

He wore a navy-blue suit that set off the color of his eyes. His dark-blond hair was curling at the edges, like he was in need of a haircut. Again, when a lock of hair fell over his eyes her fingers itched to push it back.

Oh, no. This isn't good. Don't get caught up in his looks. He's the enemy. Stay focused.

The problem was, over the few weeks she'd been there, Nicholas Craigdon had been nothing but nice. He treated her with courtesy and respect and aside from the first time he'd openly checked her out, he'd been the perfect gentleman in her company. He always couched his orders in the form of a request and he never shouted or yelled. He went out for his own coffee and sandwiches and always offered to get something for her. Though she always declined, sometimes he'd turn up with a surprise treat anyway.

Once it was a fresh blueberry muffin. Another time it was an éclair. Only yesterday he'd brought her a latté. His thoughtfulness was both disarming and surprising. At those times he seemed to be the antithesis of his father who Harper couldn't imagine ever doing something so nice for anyone, let alone his staff.

"Do you need something?" she asked now, keeping a safe distance from his desk.

She'd learned the hard way if she got too close she'd be overwhelmed by the smell of his expensive cologne. The last time it had stayed with her for the whole day, driving her mad. Her enemy wasn't supposed to smell so woodsy, so fresh, so good. Neither was he supposed to look like he'd just stepped off a fashion shoot. Even this late in the day, his tie was impeccable, his shirt a pristine white, with no creases in sight. It wasn't right for a man to look that good.

In contrast, she felt disheveled in her cheap tailored suit. She'd bought it from the bargain bin and that day had teamed it with a pale green blouse she'd found in a thrift shop. The entire outfit had set her back fifteen dollars. The only thing she'd been extravagant with was her shoes. The shiny black stilettos elevated her height an additional three inches. Even then, she only came up to Nicholas' shoulder. Still, the sandals made her feel good and though it had been hard to part with the seventy-five dollars, she was glad she had.

"Harper, I've just received the paperwork on a new development out at Badgery's Creek. I've already had my team work up a bid. I want you to take a look at it and make sure everything's in order."

"Badgery's Creek? Isn't that where the new airport's going to be built?"

"Yes. Every developer worth his salt is itching to get out there. The good news is, there's still prime land up for grabs. McClintock Properties have been wining and dining some of those vendors for the past few months. It's time we got in on the action."

Harper's ears pricked up at the mention of McClintock's. Maybe she was about to get her hands on the next piece of information she could sell…

She took the sheaf of papers from Nick's hand. Their

fingers touched. Warm tingles ran up and down her arm. She steadfastly ignored them.

"No problem, sir. I'll check them over."

He smiled and her heart tripped over. She flushed, annoyed by her reaction.

"Harper, you've been here three weeks. Please, call me Nicholas."

She inclined her head in response in an effort to hide the fact her pulse had taken off at a gallop. She didn't want to call him Nicholas. It was too familiar. It was making him into a real person, not just the son of her sworn enemy.

Oblivious to her inner turmoil, he spoke again. "How are you doing with the job applications? Have we had much response?"

"A few have come in," she said offhandedly, thinking about the piles and piles of résumés that sat in the bottom drawer of her desk.

"Good. Well, if you wouldn't mind, I'd like you to go through them and do the first cull. Narrow it down to the top twenty and we'll go from there. Is that all right?"

She gave him a tight smile. "Of course. I'll get right on it," she lied.

Harper had been purposefully ignoring the responses she'd received to the advertisement for Nicholas's permanent EA, hoping he might forget about them. While she didn't want the job herself, she needed more time to bring her plan to fruition. At some point, he was sure to raise the issue again, but the longer she could put him off from making a decision, the better.

"Will that be all, sir?"

He gave her another disarming grin. "Is it so hard to say my name?"

She blushed. "I-I… I'd prefer not to."

He sat up in his chair and frowned. "Why?"

She clenched her jaw together and cast around frantically for an excuse.

How can I tell him I need to keep a barrier between us, something to hold him at a distance, so I can continue to carry out my plan?

"I… It's a sign of respect," she managed through gritted teeth. "You're my boss. It's not right for me to be so familiar."

He looked at her like she'd sprouted two heads and she could well understand his confusion. It was the twenty-first century. People were expected to call each other by their given names, boss or no boss.

Then Nicholas shrugged as if it was of no consequence and she breathed out a silent sigh of relief. Unwilling to risk any further questions, Harper turned on her heel and escaped.

Chapter Five

*N*icholas stared after Harper in bemusement. When she pulled the door to his office closed behind her, he restlessly pushed away from his desk. The girl had been there three weeks and she still made him unaccountably nervous. He should have gotten used to her by now. Better still, learned to ignore her.

But the truth was he thought about her more than was acceptable. Even when the door was closed between them he found himself wondering what she was doing. From time to time he'd hear her voice on the phone or the tap of her fingers on the keyboard. More than once, he'd called her into his office for no reason at all. He'd make up some excuse for why he needed her, but all he really wanted was to be near her.

His infatuation with the temp was maddening. As soon as he found a permanent replacement she'd be gone and though he'd hinted more than once that he'd like it if she threw her name into the ring, each time she'd brushed him off. It was as if she only wanted to be there for the short term; that the thought of being his permanent EA was completely undesirable.

Nick felt a familiar stab of self-pity. Though he tried hard to maintain a healthy self-esteem, over the years it had been a struggle. During his teenage years, his father had taken every opportunity to ridicule him.

Though blessed with the Craigdon genes, Nick had been shy and awkward as a teenager and Henry had gone out of his way to draw Nick's inadequacies to everyone's attention. And then his father's cruelty had culminated in the most despicable act of all. Nick could remember it like yesterday.

He'd been all of sixteen. He'd finally found the courage to ask the prettiest girl in his class out to the movies. He and Katrina came home afterwards and were making out in the cabana by the pool when Henry came across them. Nick hadn't even known his father was home.

Though Nick was still a virgin, he'd managed to get past second base. Katrina was as keen to get the deed done as he was. She'd already pulled off her top and bra when Henry found them. Nick was still fully clothed. He'd never forget the look of derision on his father's face as Henry took in the situation.

"What the hell are you still doing with your clothes on, boy? Can't you see she's panting for it?"

Nick could still feel the fire of his humiliation. But Henry wasn't finished. He moved further into the cabana and reached out and ran a finger across Katrina's cheek. His eyes were fixed firmly on her naked breasts.

"You're one hot little piece of pussy, aren't you? If you want a real man, come and find me. I'll be ready and waiting." Through his suit pants, his father cupped his erection and gave Katrina a suggestive wink.

Nick had felt sick. Too embarrassed to even look at his date, he'd barely managed a muttered goodbye as she gathered her clothes in outrage and left. Later, Henry had taken him aside and told him to forget about her.

"She's only after the Craigdon money. Do you think a girl like that would be interested in the likes of you if you were poor? That's the only reason she agreed to come home with you. Mark my words."

Nick had never breathed a word of what happened to anyone, but he never forgave his father for the hurt and humiliation inflicted upon him that day. Naturally, Katrina wanted nothing to do with him after that and as the years went by and Nick remained single, wondering if maybe his father had been right.

All through university, Nick mostly kept to himself. Never did he bring another girl home. He was now twenty-five years old and still a virgin. What a joke.

His father was right. Girls like Katrina and Harper weren't interested in guys like him. He was kidding himself that now he was managing director of his father's billion-dollar company things would be different. He was still the same awkward, nervous kid of his youth and beautiful women like Harper Wyburn would always be out of his reach. It was time he set aside any fanciful notions to the contrary and accepted it.

I just wish the knowledge didn't hurt quite so much…

Harper couldn't believe what she was reading. The new tender documents contained so much valuable information her head was in a spin. Now that she knew how keen Christopher was to get his hands on this kind of information, she was determined to raise her price. Five thousand dollars just wasn't enough for the kind of gold she held in her hands.

Not only did the documents detail what Craigdon Enterprises was prepared to pay for the much-coveted, Badgery's Creek land, it also contained precise terms and conditions that were acceptable to the company for the deal to go ahead. All McClintock's would need to do was to set their bid slightly lower and make their demands a little less stringent and the deal should be theirs for the taking.

Checking that she was alone in the reception area, Harper pulled out her phone and began photographing the documents. As she took pictures of the pages she thought about how much such information would be worth. Ten thousand? Twenty? The very thought made her giddy. She couldn't begin to imagine having that kind of cash. This time, she'd negotiate the payout before she gave Christopher access to the documents. With that in mind, she sent him a text.

I have something you want. It's even better than what I gave you the last time. I want 20k.

She bit her lip in indecision. Her finger hovered over the screen.

Am I asking too much? I hated Henry Craigdon for being so greedy. Am I the same? Am I no better than him? She shuddered at the thought.

No, she refused to put herself in the same category as Henry Craigdon. Deleting the reference to twenty thousand, she replaced it with ten. Before she could change her mind, she sent the text. She didn't have to wait long for Christopher to respond.

You have to be kidding! Five thousand. No more.

There was no way the detailed information she had on the tender was worth the same as the information she'd supplied him previously. She sensed that if she stuck to her guns, Christopher would come up with the cash. In order to pique his curiosity, she attached the photo of the first page of the tender documents to another text.

Ten thousand, or this page is all you get.

The response was a little slower in coming, but when it did, it made her smile.

OK.

Harper had to bite her lip not to cry out in triumph and disbelief.

Christopher Barrington has just agreed to pay me ten thousand dollars! On top of the five thousand she'd already received! It was almost unbelievable. But she wouldn't let him know how ecstatic she was, or how desperately she needed that money. No, she had to play it cool or next time he'd negotiate much harder. And she was almost certain there would be a next time.

Quickly, she sent off another text.

I'm glad we're in agreement. I want half upfront.

Christopher: *You drive a hard bargain.*

Harper: *Do you want the information, or not? It makes no difference to me.*

She held her breath, waiting for his answer. She hoped she hadn't pushed him too far.

Five thousand dollars has just been transferred to your account. You'll get the other half when I get the information.

"Oh my God! Oh my God! Oh my God!" she squealed, unable to believe she'd pulled it off.

"Is everything all right out here?"

Harper froze. Nicholas stood in the doorway to his office. He had no way of knowing about the text conversation on her phone, but it was obvious he'd heard her. She cast around for an excuse.

"Um, sure. I just… I just had some good news."

To her consternation, he walked closer, a half-smile on his face. "Oh? Care to share?"

She hurriedly dropped her phone into her handbag that was stowed beneath her desk and turned to face him. "Um, no. Not really. It's nothing really."

"You seemed pretty excited."

She thought quickly. "It's my sister. She's having a baby!" she lied.

His smile appeared genuine. "That's great news! Is this her first?"

Hating her continued deception, Harper replied. "Yes! I'm going to be an aunty! How amazing is that?"

Nicholas laughed. "It's the best feeling ever. I have two nieces and a nephew. All three of them are under five. They belong to my brother, Jett and his wife, Danielle. I don't get to see them as much as I'd like, but when they stop by it's always a riot."

"I can imagine," Harper said, feeling bad about the story she'd spun and silently hoping he'd let it drop.

"Do you have any kids?"

His question took her by surprise. She blinked. "Um, no. I don't have any children."

"Do you want some one day?"

Her eyes widened and then she frowned. His questions weren't exactly appropriate for the workplace. Still, she surprised herself when she answered him.

"Yes. I'd love to have children one day."

His smile was dazzling. She had to look away, unable to bear it another minute. This whole conversation was wrong and she was the one to blame.

What the hell were you thinking, telling him your sister's pregnant? You don't even have a sister!

Looking at Nicholas' open, smiling face, she felt a twinge of guilt. For all his father's nasty characteristics, so far she hadn't seen anything like that in his son.

Is it fair for me to punish the son for his father's sins?

The thought gave her pause, but then an image of her dying mother filled her mind. Tammie Wyburn had only been thirty-five years old when she lost her life. She'd suffered right to the very end. Harper had sat beside her, holding her hand, praying for the nightmare to be over.

Her heart hardened. Someone must pay for what she and her mother had endured. It wasn't possible to hold Henry Craigdon to account, so it would have to be his son. End of story. She needed to put aside any softening she might feel toward Nicholas and keep her eye on the end goal. She'd vowed to destroy Henry Craigdon. She intended to do that in whatever way she could and nobody would stand in her way.

Harper was knee-deep in dictation when she took another call from Sophia Craigdon. The woman really was a pain. She called her husband at least twice a day, sometimes more.

How does she expect the man to get any work done?

No doubt Sophia was one of those pampered wives who had nothing better to do than to attend the beauty salon, lunch with friends, or annoy her husband. And then Harper made an impatient sound in the back of her throat.

What do I care what kind of woman his wife is? It's none of my business. He can be married to the nastiest bitch on earth for all I care.

But that wasn't true. Over recent weeks, she'd gotten to know her boss better and though she wasn't prepared to let go of her plan for revenge, she was willing to concede Nicholas Craigdon was a nice man. Polite, respectful, funny. A little awkward and shy. Nothing like his arrogant, domineering father. Harper cared too much about the woman Nicholas was married to. She didn't want Sophia to be clingy or whiney or a bitch. Nicholas deserved someone sweet and kind and caring. Someone who looked past his shyness and saw the decent man underneath. Perhaps Sophia was all of that and more. It wasn't fair for Harper to judge a woman she'd never met.

"Harper? Are you still there?" The voice was sharp with impatience.

Harper gritted her teeth and forced her attention back to the phone. "Yes, Sophia. I'm still here. What can I do for you?"

"Funny, Nick told me at least a week ago he'd advertised for a new EA. I thought the position would have been filled by now."

"No, not yet," Harper managed.

Guilt flooded through her at the thought of the résumés that continued to pile up in the bottom drawer of her desk. She'd deliberately ignored Nick's request to cull them and was dreading the moment when he asked her for an update. So far, he'd been too busy dealing with other issues to raise it with her, but she was living on borrowed time.

"Well, anyway. Please put me through to Nick."

"I'm afraid he's not in," Harper replied sweetly, pleased that this time at least she could tell the truth.

"Not in? Where is he?"

"At an outside meeting."

"How long will he be?" Sophia's tone had turned petulant.

Harper clenched her jaw and tried her best to remain pleasant. "I don't know. He went out to one of the construction sites. He could be another couple of hours, at least."

"Another couple of hours!"

"At least," Harper added in a cheery tone.

"But I need to talk to him! It's important!"

It always is…

"I've already tried his mobile," Sophia continued. "It went straight through to voice mail."

"I'm afraid I can't help you, but I can take a message and let him know you called," Harper offered with false sweetness.

There was a dramatic sigh on the other end of the line. "If that's the best you can do, I guess it'll have to do."

After taking down Sophia's details, Harper ended the call. Slamming the receiver back onto the phone rest, she pulled her keyboard toward her and typed an email to Nick.

Call Sophia. She says it's important.

On a burst of irritation, she clicked SEND. As much as she didn't want to judge his wife harshly sight-unseen, the woman wasn't making it easy. She interrupted Harper's work so often it was becoming annoying. Surely the woman had more important things to do with her time than to incessantly call her husband?

Maybe it's time to admit I feel the tiniest bit jealous of the woman who managed to capture Nicholas Craigdon's heart…?

The admission wasn't as shocking as it should have been, but it was every bit as unwelcome as the first time she'd had thoughts about softening her attitude toward her boss. She should welcome the news he had a wife. It meant he was safely out of bounds. Any feelings of fleeting attraction could be swiftly put to bed. That was the sensible thing to do. She needed to focus her energies on her plan. No matter how nice Nicholas might be, he was the son of Henry Craigdon and for that he would pay.

Chapter Six

Over the next week, Harper kept her resolve firmly in place. Every time Nicholas joined her in casual banter, asked her about her weekend, made friendly overtures, she rebuffed him. If he was confused about her cool attitude, he didn't say anything but she noticed that as time went on, he called her into his office less and less and their friendly repartee faded away to almost nothing. She wished she could say she didn't miss their conversations.

On a brighter note, her information gathering for Christopher was gathering steam. It seemed she'd gained Nicholas' trust and as his EA, she had access to highly confidential information. She didn't want to draw attention to herself by passing on everything that came across her desk, but at least every second tender document ended up in Christopher's hands. And he was generous with his thanks.

They'd eventually agreed on a lump sum payment of fifteen thousand dollars for every tender document she provided. Her bank account was bursting at the seams. She'd never imagined she could make so much money. For her, it had been all about bringing Craigdon Enterprises to its knees, but she had to admit, the financial gain was an extremely attractive added bonus. It was too bad her mother was no longer around to help her spend it.

The intercom on her desk buzzed. She picked up the receiver. "Yes, sir?"

"I need you to book me a car. I'm driving up to Brisbane in the morning for a business meeting."

She blinked in surprise. The drive would take at least ten hours and that wasn't counting rest stops.

"You're driving?" she asked.

"Yes."

"Wouldn't you rather fly?"

"No. I don't fly."

She frowned, even more confused. "You don't fly? Are you for real?"

"Yes. I'm for real." There was a pause. "I'm terrified of flying."

Once again, Harper was taken by surprise. "It's like…a ninety-minute flight. You're barely in the air before you're coming down again."

"It's not a matter of the time it takes. I don't fly." His voice was tight.

She knew she should leave it alone, but she was intrigued. She didn't know anyone who'd choose a ten-hour road trip over a ninety-minute flight. It was crazy.

"Have you ever been in a plane?"

"Yes. Once. I was thirteen." He sighed. "My father had a four-seater Cessna Skyhawk. We got caught in a storm. Dad had to bring the plane down in an emergency landing. We were lucky to survive. I've hated it ever since."

He spoke in clipped tones. It was clear the memory of his near-miss still had the power to shake him. A rush of compassion surged through her. She could almost picture a young Nicholas being caught up in the terror of a mid-air emergency. No wonder it still affected him.

"I understand," she said softly. "I'm sorry I asked."

"It's fine," he said brusquely. "You weren't to know. But if you don't mind, I'd like you to arrange a car."

"Of course, sir. Do you have a preference?"

"Something with plenty of grunt. I'm thinking a Porsche."

She could hear the good humor returning to his voice and smiled. "Color?"

He laughed. "Red, of course. They go faster. Everyone knows that. Oh, and I want a decent stereo."

"Leave it with me."

Harper hung up the receiver and pulled her keyboard toward her. After what he'd just shared with her, she was determined to find him the perfect ride. After spending a few minutes searching online, she clicked on a reputable company based in the city. It didn't take her long to find what she was looking for: A cherry red, 911 Turbo Cabriolet. If the weather was good, he'd be able to open the roof and feel the breeze in his hair.

She could almost see him with his longish blond hair blowing in the wind, singing along at the top of his voice to his favorite tunes. She had a sudden yearning to go with him and wondered fleetingly if he'd ask her to accompany him. After all, he said he was attending a business meeting and she *was* his EA. She pulled herself up short.

Don't be an idiot. If he's taking anyone it will be his wife. Fancy thinking for even an instant he might ask you…ridiculous! It might not even be a business meeting. He wouldn't be the first man to lie about something like that. It could be something completely different, something he didn't want her to know about…

Curiosity got the better of her. She picked up the phone and buzzed Nicholas' office. He picked up right away.

"How did you do?" he asked without preamble.

She took a moment to make the connection. "Uh, yes. The car. How does a 911 Turbo Cabriolet Porsche sound?"

"It sounds exactly like the kind of car I want to take on a road trip. Is it red?"

"As red as can be."

"Good." He paused and then added, "Is there anything else?"

Harper flushed. What he did with his time was none of her business. Still… "Yes, um… I was wondering if you needed me to book you any accommodation."

"Thanks. Yes, I'll be away a couple of nights. Book a room at the Hilton. It's on Elizabeth Street in the city."

"For how many people?" she asked as casually as she could.

"Just me."

She let out her breath in a *whoosh* of relief and then silently castigated herself. It shouldn't matter to her if he were getting away for a romantic interlude with his wife or not. He meant nothing to her.

"No problem," she managed. "Consider it done."

"Thank you, Harper. I appreciate your help."

She blushed, at a loss for words.

"Oh, by the way, how are those résumés coming along? Do we have a shortlist yet?"

And then her cheeks heated for an entirely different reason. Guilt flooded through her. "Um, not quite. I'm still making my way through them."

"Well, we need to do something about them sooner or later. Unless of course you've decided to hang around?"

She heard the hope in his voice and panic tightened her insides. There was no way she was hanging around for the long term. Her plan was to get in and out before anyone suspected what she was up to. By the time the boss of Craigdon Enterprises realized his empire was crumbling, she'd be long gone.

"Um, no," she replied.

"Too bad. I've kind of gotten used to you being around."

His disappointment was almost tangible.

She swallowed past the lump of guilt and did her best to reassure him. "Don't get me wrong, I enjoy being here. It's just that, I like the freedom of being a temp. I can come and go whenever I please, meet new people, new situations. A week here, a month there. It keeps the job interesting," she said in a rush, hoping he'd buy her lies.

"Of course," he agreed. "I just thought I'd ask. Again."

She gave a strained laugh, feeling even more uncomfortable. Nicholas Craigdon was a decent man. He didn't deserve this. But neither had her mother deserved to die such a dreadful death. Slowly drowning as fluid filled her lungs. The hacking cough, the sunken cheeks, the breathlessness... Harper wouldn't forget the sight of her mother's dull, pain-filled eyes for as long as she lived.

Once again, the reminder of why she was there fighting this fight flooded Harper with steely determination. Nicholas was a Craigdon. No matter how she might feel about him personally, everything came back to that. She'd come this far in her quest to destroy his family company. She wouldn't go soft now.

Harper walked into Marty's Youth Club situated in an old warehouse in Blacktown's industrial area. The journey took the better part of an hour, but there was a direct train from central station in the city to Blacktown, which made the trip easier. The club was within walking distance of the station, which was a good thing, especially when it was raining, like it was now.

"Harper! It's good to see you!" Marty Hannaford greeted her with his usual cheery smile.

She set her dripping umbrella aside and gave the old man a hug. "*Brr.* It's really coming down out there."

"You should have called me from the station. I would have come and picked you up."

She laughed. "It's only a bit of water. I'll dry."

She left her handbag in one of the staff lockers and then moved to the storeroom and began to gather her supplies. She wasn't sure how many of her girls would turn up in such nasty weather, but she hoped at least a few of them would brave the elements. They only had two more classes before the etiquette and deportment course came to an end.

She felt a twinge of sadness at the thought. Over the eight weeks the course ran, she and her students always grew close. This group was no exception. All ten of the girls had come from disadvantaged backgrounds and were eager for attention. They were also keen to learn the skills Harper had on offer.

The focus of her course was to get teenagers and young adults ready for the workforce, starting with preparation of their résumés, interview skills and the last few weeks concentrated on making the most of their appearance. It never ceased to surprise her just how little young people knew about personal grooming.

Still, she could remember being that young girl, wanting to use makeup and do her hair in more sophisticated styles, but not knowing how to go about it. Losing her mom right when these things became important hadn't helped. So she'd learned the hard way, on her own and with the assistance of online tutorials and public computer access. Now she made it her mission to do what she could to ensure other young women didn't need to do it the same way.

It was the main reason she volunteered at the youth club. She'd come across an advertisement in the paper quite by accident and had been intrigued by what it offered. Marty Hannaford was an ex-boxer with a national featherweight title to his name. He was passionate about doing something for the young people in his suburb.

He'd started the club in Blacktown with the idea of getting young people off the streets. Too many of them were out and about getting into mischief when they should have been home in bed. Their nightly wanderings frequently resulted in them engaging in criminal activity, which often saw them go to jail. It was a downward spiral from there. Marty wanted to try and change the direction of the lives of these young, vulnerable people with a viable alternative, and before it was too late.

It was a noble cause and one Harper was immediately attracted to. She approached Marty with her idea of providing deportment and grooming lessons for the young girls. Marty had jumped at the idea and the course had gradually expanded to include other things, with a particular focus on gaining employment.

Marty concentrated on the boxing. He saw many benefits to the sport, including fitness, self-discipline and respect. He wanted to instill some of those benefits in the kids who lived in his neighborhood and from the growing number who continued to turn up each night, it was obvious he was well on the way to achieving his goal.

As she pulled out containers of hair brushes, makeup cases and curling irons, she watched Marty begin to line up boxing gloves in a neat row on the bench outside the makeshift boxing ring. Unaware of her scrutiny, she saw him frown and shake his head. Curious, she wandered closer.

"Is everything all right, Marty?"

He looked up in surprise and gave her a smile, but this time she saw the strain around his eyes.

"Of course. Why wouldn't it be?"

She shrugged. "I don't know. You just seem kind of down."

And then his shoulders slumped and his eyes welled up with tears. Alarm ratcheted through her.

"Marty! What's wrong?"

His lips compressed and she could tell he was trying hard

to maintain his control. She touched her hand to his arm in a gesture of concern and that simple movement seemed to push him over the top. His eyes filled with tears.

"I don't know how we're going to keep the club open," he cried.

She frowned. "What do you mean?"

"Barrons have pulled their sponsorship," he said referring to the local hardware store that provided much of the financial assistance to allow the club to function. "Times are tough. They have to cut back. They've decided their sponsorship of the youth club is one of the things that needs to go. It's a heavy blow. If we don't get another sponsor on board soon we won't have enough to cover the rent and the utilities, let alone anything else."

She stared at him in shock. She couldn't imagine all of Marty's hard work dissolving into nothing. And what about the kids? Where would they go? What would happen to them? In the years the club had been running, there had been many inspirational stories from ex-students who'd gone on to lead happy, successful lives. Harper loved those evenings when past graduates returned to tell their stories and the current cohort of students listened wide-eyed and inspired. Now that might all come to an end.

"Don't worry about it, Marty. We'll think of something. There must be other sponsors out there willing to take on the club. It'll be all right." She murmured the words of reassurance in an effort to cheer him up. She wished she believed them.

To her relief, he gave her a weak smile. "You're right, Harper. Thanks for lifting me out of the doldrums. We'll be all right."

On her way back to where she'd set up tables and chairs along one side of the room, she waved to Alan, the judo teacher who also donated his time and expertise to the club, along with all the volunteers who worked there.

As the clock drew closer to opening time, more and more kids trickled in. The boys headed straight for the boxing ring or the judo mats. The girls made a beeline for her.

"Hi, Miss Harper!" Cherie greeted her with a shy smile.

"Hi, Cherie," Harper replied, giving the young Aboriginal teen a grin. "How did you get on with those braids?"

"Not so good," the girl replied. "But I tried. I even tried to show my sister, but we both ended up in a mess."

"No worries. I'm sure you're not the only one in the class to find it a bit tricky. I'll make sure we go over it all again."

More girls filed in. Harper greeted them all by name. These girls, from all backgrounds and ranging in age from fifteen to twenty, were like her family. Every time she started a new course, she cautioned herself not to get too close to her students, and every time she failed.

What will happen to them if the youth club closes its doors?

She enjoyed being a part of their lives and having them a part of hers. She'd shared the fact she'd come from an underprivileged background, the challenges she had finding work, her day-to-day struggles. In turn, they opened up to her and told her about their families, their friends, their own struggles.

Some of the stories were even more heartbreaking than her own. At least she'd had her mother until she was seventeen. One of the girls had lost her mother when she was a toddler to an overdose. Another one never knew her biological parents and had been given away at birth. Though she spoke well of her adoptive parents, it was clear she felt there was something missing in her life.

"What are we learning tonight, Miss Harper?" a sweet fifteen-year-old by the name of Sasha asked.

"Tonight, we're learning about good posture. You might not realize how much the way you walk says about you."

An eighteen-year-old Asian girl with short black hair and

a ready smile, by the name of Mia, giggled. "You're kidding me, right? Who cares about the way I walk?"

Harper grinned. "You'd be surprised, Mia. Just wait and see. I'll show you what I mean."

As the girls took their seats, Harper set out the materials they'd need. "You'll see I'm giving out the hair accessories again. I also want to go over the braiding techniques we learned last week. Neat and tidy hair is a must for a successful job applicant. I'm sure Cherie's not the only one who had trouble, right?"

There was a murmur of agreement and a few wry chuckles. As Harper took her usual place in front of the class and her gaze scanned the girls who'd braved the elements to come there that night, she was filled with a deep sense of contentment. Being here, helping these girls, was the most satisfying thing she'd done in her life. Even her ever-present quest for revenge against the Craigdons, which had consumed her for so many years, paled into insignificance when she took time out once a week from her everyday life and gave of herself to these young women.

At another time, she might be inclined to spend some time thinking about that, but right now she had a class to teach. Hopefully it wouldn't be her last. Clapping her hands together to get their attention, she began.

Nick walked into the office Monday morning and barely acknowledged Harper where she sat behind her desk. He'd had a lot of time during his road trip to Brisbane to think about her and he'd come to the conclusion he needed to take a step back. He'd been trying way too hard to be her friend. It was obvious she didn't think of him in any way other than as her boss—and only a temporary boss at that. She had no interest in staying on at the company. She'd made that quite clear. He had no choice but to accept she also had no interest in him.

Things were made more difficult by his feelings. For weeks, she'd been all he could think about. They got on well. Shared a similar sense of humor. She was smart, outgoing and confident. And beautiful. All the things he wanted in a woman. Only, she didn't seem to feel the same way about him. He'd returned from Brisbane determined to keep her at arm's length, to treat her no differently than he would any other EA.

Think of her as Margaret. That should put an end to those fantasies you've been entertaining for so long...

The pep talk had worked and he'd been able to pass by Harper's desk on the way to his office with only the briefest murmured greeting. She'd looked up and smiled at him. He'd felt the brilliance of it all the way to his toes, but it didn't bring a halt to his progress. When he made it safely to his office and closed the door behind him, he breathed a sigh of relief.

See! You can do this! She's just your secretary. And a temporary one at that. As soon as you find a permanent replacement, she'll be gone. Don't forget that.

Dropping his briefcase on his desk, he pulled out his notepad and a sheaf of papers from the appointment he'd had with some private investors in Brisbane. They'd contacted him and asked for the meeting. He'd discussed it with Logan and though they were both of the opinion Craigdon Enterprises probably didn't need outside investors, Nick went along anyway. It didn't hurt to build relationships with people who could give you access to money. You never knew when you might need it.

For the next couple of hours he looked over correspondence, signed letters and returned phone calls. He'd kept up with most of his emails while in Brisbane. What he hadn't had time for was his proposal for the affordable housing development project. Though he'd researched the possibility of altering the current plans to include the proposed changes, he still needed to put it into a format that would convince the board of directors it was a viable option. The company wouldn't make the kind of money they usually did on their high-priced apartments, but Nick hoped to appeal to the board's sense of common decency and the need to give back to their community, a community that had helped make them all rich.

The phone in his pocket rang and he pulled it out and checked the screen.

Logan.

He answered the call. "Hey, mate. How are things?"

"Can't complain. How was your trip to Brisbane?"

"Yeah, good. I met with the Harris Consortium. It was as we suspected. They want a piece of the Craigdon pie. I told them we were flattered, but we were all good for money right now."

"I hope you didn't offend them."

"Of course not. I kept it all very friendly. Told them if things ever change, we'll get in touch. No sense closing doors in someone's face for no reason."

"Good. That day might be closer than we realize."

Nick frowned. "What do you mean?"

Logan sighed. "We've lost another bid to McClintock's."

"How do you know?"

"I got a call from the vendor."

"Why would he call you?"

"Hey, keep your shirt on. Apparently he tried to call you, but was told you were out of the office until today. So he called me."

"Shit," Nick cursed. "Which one?"

"That piece of land you had your eye on out at Badgery's Creek. I thought they'd have enough on their hands, given they're knee-deep in negotiations with Simon Blackhall's consortium. Seems I was wrong."

"How far out were we?" Nick asked.

"I don't know. No one would tell me. Just that McClintock's offer came in well below ours."

Nick shook his head in disbelief. "You're fucking kidding! That's the fifth time that's happened in the last few weeks. What the hell's going on? We've always been in the ballpark before. Now all of a sudden we're too difficult to deal with and too expensive. It doesn't make sense."

"You're right. Something's off, but I'm not sure what. You need to keep your ear to the ground. We can't afford too many more disappointments. I have a board meeting in a couple of weeks. They're not going to be happy. We need to get to the bottom of it so I can at least assure them we're on top of it, or else you might be heading back to Brisbane, cap in hand, sooner than you think."

After promising Logan he'd find out what the hell was going on, Nick ended the call. He tossed the phone on his desk. With a curse of frustration, he threw himself into his chair and scrubbed his hands through his hair.

What the hell is going on?

Five out of nine tenders submitted on various projects in and around the city had gone to McClintock's. How could Nick's team be so off with their costings? It didn't make sense. It was the same team of experts his father had used. Many of them had been with the company for years. They'd been tendering successfully on projects for months since Henry's death. Now, all of a sudden, things were going awry. And in a very big way.

Something was definitely wrong. Of one thing he was certain: There was no way he could take his affordable housing to the board while the company was suffering like it was. He'd have to put it on the back burner until things settled down. And that pissed him off even more.

Chapter Seven

From her position outside Nick's office, Harper heard the muttered profanity coming from inside. Her hand had been poised to knock when the sound of him cursing gave her pause. She'd been intent on delivering a pile of letters for him to sign. Now she hesitated. It was obvious something was wrong. In all the time she'd been there, she'd never heard him raise his voice or show any other display of temper and yet she could tell even behind the closed door that he was far from happy.

With the weekend falling right after his last day in Brisbane, it had been three days since she'd seen him and even though he'd checked in with her a couple of times while he'd been away, it wasn't the same as seeing him face to face. She hated to admit that she'd missed him. Then she heard another curse and what sounded like something hard hitting the desk. Coming to a decision, she knocked sharply on the door and called out.

"Is everything all right?"

There was a moment of silence before Nick bade her to enter. She opened the door and found him scrubbing his hands over his face.

"Are you okay?" she asked again, filled with concern.

His answering bark of laughter held no humor. "Okay?

No, Harper. I'm not okay. We've just lost another contract to our biggest rival. That's five altogether. In the past few weeks. Those contracts were worth a combined three hundred million dollars. It's not enough to break us, but it'll put a serious dent in our profits. We might even have to lay off some staff. The worst part is, I don't have a clue why it's happening."

Harper stared at him, feeling sick. This was the reality of her plan. Three hundred million dollars… That was staggering and so was this confusion, this devastation that was plastered over Nicholas' face. It was all her fault. She was the one responsible for the way he looked right now. She fought against a wave of guilt.

For the past five years, she'd stoked the fires of her revenge. No one was going to get in her way. And now her plan had finally been put into action and if Nicholas' words were anything to go by, it was working well. This was what she'd dreamed of. To bring Craigdon Enterprises to its knees. She shoved her guilt away. Now wasn't the time for a fit of conscience.

Henry Craigdon had felt no compunction about tossing her and her mother out on their ears, along with hundreds of other unfortunate tenants who could no longer afford his ridiculously high rents. They'd had no choice but to leave the only home she'd known. From the age of fourteen, she and her mother had been forced to live in shelters and on the streets, accepting kindness from strangers, always hungry, always afraid to sleep at night.

Her mother had found work in a café washing dishes. The pay was paltry, but it was enough to allow Harper to stay at school. Her uniform was often dirty and she didn't get to shower every day, but at least she was able to continue her education and it was the best her mother could do.

But three years of living rough took their toll. Her mother died of pneumonia when Harper was seventeen. Harper had been devastated. She'd lost the only person she had in the world.

The anger she felt was enormous and she didn't have to look far to find someone to blame. She could trace every piece of misfortune back to the time when she and her mother had been evicted from their home. There was only one person responsible.

It took a few months, but eventually she was given an audience with Henry Craigdon. She'd lied her way in, telling the elderly EA who guarded the reception area outside Henry's office with the vigilance of a corrections officer, she was a long-lost relative. To her surprise, though the woman regarded her suspiciously, she bought her story and had taken her to Henry's office. The same office now occupied by his son.

It was the first time she'd set eyes on the infamous Henry Craigdon. He was every bit as intimidating as she'd heard, especially to a seventeen-year-old. Tall and broad-shouldered and weighing at least two hundred pounds, he was a formidable sight. On top of that, was his overbearing attitude. He'd regarded her with a sneering arrogance that held just a tiny amount of curiosity. After all, he had to know she wasn't a relative.

As soon as Margaret closed the door behind her, he'd given her a sleazy once-over. Her skin crawled, but she forced herself to stand there. She'd come this far. She wasn't going to bail out now.

"My name is Harper Wyburn," she declared, proud that her voice didn't show even a hint of the fear that almost paralyzed her.

"Harper Wyburn," he replied, as if savoring the sound of her name. Once again, his gaze drifted over her, lingering on her breasts. She fought against the urge to cross her arms over her chest.

"What can I do for you, darlin'? Don't bother giving me that bullshit you're a long lost relative. Let's just cut to the chase. What do you want?"

She lifted her chin and stared him down, trying to hold on to her courage. "My mother was Tammie Wyburn."

Henry gave her a blank look. "You say that like I should know her."

Anger ignited in Harper's stomach, firing up her determination to hold this man accountable for all that had happened to her family.

"My mother was one of the hundreds of tenants you kicked out on the street."

"You're talking bullshit," Henry said dismissively. "I didn't kick anyone out on the street. Every one of those tenants either left of their own accord or failed to pay their rent. I gave them more than three months to catch up on their arrears before I took the action that was afforded me under the law."

Harper's cheeks burned with anger. "Don't you dare preach to me about the law! You increased the rents until they had no choice! You did it deliberately so you had an excuse to evict them. Yes, you might have had the law on your side, but what you did was reprehensible! You destroyed lives! Because of you, my mother died! And you didn't care! You still don't care! I can tell it doesn't affect you in the slightest. You're totally, completely morally bankrupt. How can you stand to look at yourself? You make me sick," she spat.

To her fury, Henry only laughed. "Well, well, well. Little Harper Wyburn has fire to match the color of her hair. I like that. I like that a lot."

He moved closer. Before she knew what he was doing, he reached out and picked up a lock of her hair and rubbed it between his fingers. Shocked and angry, she wrenched out of his way with a gasp. Once again, her actions were followed by an amused chuckle.

"You seem very upset about what happened, darlin', but what you don't understand is business. I'm in the business of making money. If some people are disadvantaged by that, it's a small price to pay. No one makes it to my heights without treading on a few people along the way. You and your mother were part of that. Nothing more, nothing less. If you expect me to apologize, you're going to be disappointed. I did what I had to do. It was just good business."

Fury like she'd never known rendered her speechless. She opened her mouth to roast him, but to her horror nothing came out. Instead, her eyes filled with hot tears and a lump formed in her throat.

Oh, God, I'm going to cry. Please, God! No! Please don't let me cry!

Henry moved back beside her and patted her on the arm. "Oh, come now. There's no need for that. I understand you're upset and I'm sorry about your mom. You're way too young to be alone in the world. How old are you, anyway?"

"I'm seventeen."

"Seventeen? So young and yet so beautiful." His hand stroked up and down her arm in a deliberate caress.

She froze.

"I'm sure you came here looking for compensation and I wish I could comply, but the thing is, I might not be willing to hand over cash, but there are other ways you and I could come to an agreement." His hand moved higher and then drifted across her breast. "You're a beautiful woman, Harper Wyburn. But I'm sure you know that. What say you agree to spend some time with me? We could start with dinner and then go from there. I can be a very generous man to my friends." He cocked his head and looked at her. "Are you and I friends, Harper Wyburn?"

She stumbled away from him. Every fibre of her being burned with fury and disgust. "Stay away from me, you filthy old man! And let's get this straight: You and I will *never* be friends. Mark my words. I'm going to destroy you! You're going to regret you ever heard the name Harper Wyburn."

She'd left his office feeling dirty. She caught a bus to the shelter and scrubbed herself under the shower until her skin was raw. Still, she felt unclean. As the years passed, her desire for revenge simmered to a slow boil. She had no means to do anything right then, but one day that would change.

She'd finished school and had managed to put herself through a secretarial course at night while working part-time at a local grocers. With only herself to look after she'd found a cheap studio in which to live. Once her grief had lessened, Harper began to plan her revenge. And now that day had come.

"Harper? Harper? Are you okay?"

Nicholas regarded Harper with a frown. She was staring off into the distance as if lost in thought. Not only that, she was trembling like a leaf and looked like she'd seen a ghost. One moment she'd been asking if he was all right and when he started railing about the loss of some important tenders, she looked like she might faint.

What the hell's going on? She's only been with us a month. Okay, so it's a lot of money to lose out on, but I wouldn't expect her to care so much...

"Harper?" he asked again, this time a little more sharply.

She blinked and her eyes came back into focus. Finally he seemed to have gotten through to her.

"Y-yes?" she stammered, looking guilty.

"I asked if you were all right. You went somewhere for a while. Is everything okay?"

Her answering smile looked strained. "Yes, of course. I'm sorry. Something you said… It brought back a memory."

"From the look of you, it was an unpleasant one," he ventured.

She flushed and looked down at her feet. "I'm sorry," she said again. "I don't know what got into me."

He brushed away her apology. "It's fine."

She raised her gaze to his. He was relieved to see the normal clarity back in her eyes.

"No, it's not," she said. "You're the one with a right to be upset. I can't believe you've missed out on so many contracts."

He scowled at the reminder and then sighed. This wasn't Harper's fault. It wasn't fair for him to take out his disappointment and frustration on her. He told her as much.

"I'm your EA. You're allowed to do that. It's in the job description." She smiled hesitantly and the action brought life back into her pale face.

He smiled wryly back. "You're too kind."

"There's a lot of money at stake. You have a right to be upset."

"Yeah. The worst part is I'm going to have to put my plan for affordable housing on the backburner."

Harper's eyes widened. Her quick intake of breath indicated the level of her surprise. "A-affordable housing?"

Nick grimaced. "Yeah. But it doesn't matter now. Our failure to secure those contracts means the board won't look favorably on my proposal. At least, not right now."

Harper moved to take the seat opposite him. She crossed one leg over the other, immediately drawing Nick's gaze. Her short skirt rode high on her slim thigh, exposing an ample amount of tanned skin. She caught him looking at her. Blushing hotly, he tore his gaze away.

"Tell me more about this proposal of yours."

She appeared genuinely interested. For a few moments, he vacillated between wanting to share every detail with her and telling her there was no point. She seemed to sense his indecision.

"Please, Nicholas," she urged. "I'd really like to hear about it."

Nick blinked in surprise. It was the first time she'd used his given name. He liked the way it sounded on her lips. He liked it a lot. Decision made, he filled her in on his plans to try and fix a wrong done by his father and his proposal to include in the latest rebuild some affordable housing for not only the current lot of displaced tenants but also to create more low-cost housing apartments for others.

When he'd finished, he sat back in his chair. She stared at him, her eyes wide with disbelief. The silence between them lengthened. He stirred uncomfortably, embarrassed now that he'd spilled so much of himself to her. And then she finally spoke.

"Oh, my God! What a wonderful idea! You must do everything you can to convince your board to back you. There's a great need for affordable housing. So many people are living on the streets, or in meagre shelters that are filled to overflowing. Without proper housing, these people are at risk of dying from exposure and neglect. Their deaths could be avoided if only there was somewhere for them to live."

When she finally stopped speaking, her breath came fast and tears shimmered in her eyes. Nick was shocked at how passionately she spoke about the plight of the disadvantaged. It seemed she had an even more active social conscience than his.

Or was there something else behind her impassioned speech?

"You seem to know a lot about it," he probed.

Harper's lips twisted into a grimace. She looked away as a blush stole up her cheeks. "I… I had a relative die from exposure after losing her accommodation because she couldn't afford the rent," she muttered.

Nick felt a wave of sympathy. It seemed his EA had firsthand experience of exactly what he wanted to help fix. That kind of knowledge could be a bonus if he had any hope to convince the board to back his project.

"Would you like to look at my proposal? Maybe you can think of some ideas to make it more palatable for the board?"

She started in surprise and sat back against her chair. Just then, his phone rang. Checking the screen, he grimaced.

Christopher. What the hell does he want?

"I'm sorry," he said. "I'm going to have to take this. We can talk later."

Harper pushed back her chair and stood. "Of course. I'll leave you to it." With that, she turned and left the room, closing the door behind her.

Nick sighed and answered the call. "Christopher. How are you?"

Chapter Eight

Christopher Barrington responded in kind to Nick's half-hearted greeting. At the same time, he pushed his chair away from his desk and spread his thighs wide, giving the girl on her knees between his legs a little more room. Now that he had his own office, he was afforded the luxury of privacy and he made sure to take advantage of it.

He'd met the young secretary in the staff cafeteria a couple of weeks earlier and had got chatting to her in the line. She was pretty in a bland kind of way and had a vapid smile. Not usually his type, but he could tell after only a few minutes of conversation she might be interested in his proposition. It wasn't the first time he'd succeeded in flattering young women into giving him a head job in return for a vague promise of a promotion in the future.

Of course, he was careful never to put a timeline on the end goal. It wouldn't do for them to be badgering him forevermore about the promised promotion. A promotion that most of the time wasn't forthcoming.

By then he'd gotten from them what he wanted and there wasn't much they could do. After all, who wanted to admit they'd been taken in by the oldest trick in the world? It was mean and spiteful, but no one forced the silly twits to get on their knees. Besides, ever since his father completely and maliciously failed to even make mention of Christopher in his will, he'd been feeling mean and spiteful toward everyone.

"What have you been up to?" Nick asked, bringing Christopher's attention back to their phone conversation.

"The same old, same old," he replied in a surly tone.

"We haven't spoken much since the funeral. I just wanted to tell you I'm sorry about the way Dad treated you, both before and after his death."

The genuine sympathy in Nick's voice only irritated Christopher. It was rich for one of the legitimate Craigdon offspring to feel sorry for him. Nick had at least been acknowledged by their father.

"Yeah. Well, that's the way the old prick was. Malicious and nasty right to the end."

There was a pause. Nick cleared his throat. When he spoke again, Christopher heard the impatience in Nick's voice.

"I'm sure you're disappointed at being overlooked. God knows, he didn't treat me very fairly, either. He knew how much I wanted to be CEO of Craigdon Enterprises and yet he handed the whole company over to Logan."

Christopher smiled to himself. Having Nick pissed off at their father might work in his favor. They could join forces in the lawsuit he'd filed and double their efforts in suing the estate. It was the reason for his call.

"I was wondering if you had time to meet me for coffee. I want to run something by you," Christopher said.

"What, now?"

Christopher could hear the reluctance in Nick's voice. "Yes."

"Can't we discuss it over the phone?"

"I'd rather do it in person. I'm sure you can get away for a bit."

There was another pause and then Nick responded. "Sure. How about we meet at The Venue. It's within walking distance for both of us. I take it you're at work?"

"Yes. I've been here since half-past eight."

"Same here. A break would probably do us both good. See you there in ten."

Christopher ended the call and dropped his phone back into his pocket. The girl between his legs renewed her efforts and within minutes he exploded in her mouth. He zipped up his pants and summarily dismissed her. She shot him a disgruntled look, which he ignored. Shrugging into his jacket, he left for his appointment.

He completed the walk to The Venue in less than ten minutes. Nick was already seated at an outdoor table when he arrived. He put in his order over the counter for a long black before joining Nick. As he took a seat opposite his half-brother, he noticed Nick's gaze on him. The pointed look was followed by a frown.

"What the hell's wrong with you?" Nick asked.

Christopher scowled. No doubt Nick was referring to the bags under Christopher's eyes. He'd also lost a few pounds. It had been close on eight months since his father died and he hadn't had a decent night's sleep since. Brushing away Nick's question, Christopher replied with one of his own.

"Have you given any thought to challenging the will?"

Nick shrugged. "What, like you?"

"Why not? Both of us were fucked over. You can't argue against that."

Nick shrugged. "You're right. But suing the estate… It seems kind of…undignified. I might be pissed off at what Dad did, but it was his company to do with what he wanted. He gave it to Logan. I'm just lucky Logan didn't want to involve himself in the day-to-day operations. He's given me free rein."

Their coffees arrived and both men murmured their thanks and waited for the waitress to depart before resuming their conversation.

"You're lucky Logan's been so generous. No one's offered me a scrap of their inheritances." Christopher heard the bitterness in his voice and it only fueled his anger. He shot Nick a sardonic look. "Just don't get too comfortable in the managing director's office. If my lawsuit's successful, Craigdon Enterprises will be mine. And rest assured, I'm not going to walk away from my responsibilities like Logan has."

Nick stared at him in shock. Eventually he spoke. "Well, I guess I ought to thank you for giving me fair warning. At least I know where you stand."

"Too right. I'm not making any bones about it. Craigdon Enterprises should have been mine and I'm going to fight like hell to get it. You can come on board and get a bigger piece of what was owed to you or you can sit by like a pussy and do nothing. Your choice."

Anger lit up Nick's face. Christopher remained unmoved by his half-brother's show of temper. Christopher had never been one to play the nice guy. He sure as hell wouldn't start now.

Nick took a sip of his coffee and with a muttered curse, set it aside. Not even bothering to excuse himself, he pushed away from the table and made a speedy exit. Christopher leaned back against his chair and watched him leave. His chuckle was totally devoid of humor.

Nick returned to the office deep in thought. Though he'd dismissed out of hand Christopher's suggestion he join the court action against Henry's estate, he couldn't deny the idea held appeal. Whenever he thought about how miserable and mean his father had been when he'd divided up his estate, his blood boiled. One of his sisters had been left twenty million dollars. Three of his brothers had received ten million each. Nick had been left a paltry million. The greatest insult was handing over the ownership of the company Nick loved to his cousin.

Nick could understand Christopher's antagonism and his desire to hit back. He'd been left out of the will altogether. It was a deliberate and unforgivable insult. Sophia had also been treated shabbily. The whole thing was a mess all round.

With a sigh, Nick leaned back in his chair and stacked his hands behind his head. Logan had insisted Nick occupy his late father's office. Apart from the spectacular views, it was furnished with tasteful, expensive furniture, including a wall safe hidden behind an original Brett Whitely painting. Though Nick hadn't yet found the time or inclination to go through the papers his father had kept there, he wondered if now might be as good a time as any.

Maybe I'll find something to explain his nasty and mystifying actions? Then again, maybe it's best I not know…

One of the reasons he hadn't been able to bring himself to go through the contents of the safe was because he didn't know what he'd find. He wasn't sure he could stand any more surprises. Still, his meeting with Christopher had left him feeling discontent and restless.

Perhaps it's time?

Before he could change his mind, he pushed away from his desk and strode across the room. Removing the painting and setting it to one side, he studied the directions and dialed in the combination. The door to the safe opened and he stared at the bundles of papers stacked inside.

Now that the moment was upon him, he was filled with indecision. Adrenaline surged through his body. His heart beat fast. Fear of what he might uncover kept him momentarily immobile, but with a resolute shake of his head, he reached inside and pulled out the first of several packets.

Taking it back to his desk, he switched his phone to "Do Not Disturb" before sliding his finger beneath the seal. The legal documents had been prepared by his father's lawyers. As he scanned the typed pages, he realized it was the paperwork relating to the setting up of the charitable institution known as the Stella Taunton House for Widows and Orphans.

Weird.

It appeared his father had set up the charity himself and had then bequeathed it the sum of fifteen million dollars. The sole trustee of the charity was Stella Taunton. Nick had never heard of the woman. He wondered who she was and what her connection was to his father. The fact Henry had left the charity fifteen million dollars was evidence enough of an important relationship. He set the papers aside for further reflection.

Emboldened, he returned to the safe and retrieved another packet. This one contained a bundle of letters between Henry and a man by the name of Daniel Gunning. From the contents of the letters, Nick ascertained that Gunning was a junior urban planner employed by the City of Sydney Council involved in assisting the progress of some of his father's developments through council.

Some of the letters were handwritten. Nick scanned the contents. It seemed his father had struck an arrangement with the urban planner to issue occupation certificates without the usual engineer's checks. They were breaking the law by circumventing the checks that were meant to ensure the building was safe for occupation and it seemed the motivation for doing so was money. The earlier Henry got his hands on the occupation certificate, the sooner he could finalize the sale of the building. Nick was ashamed to admit his father had been involved in such a scheme and from the projects mentioned in some of the letters, the arrangement had been in place for some time.

The tone in the next bundle of letters was a lot less friendly. It seemed Gunning had upped his terms.

I want ten thousand dollars or it's not happening… Don't you tell me what to do! This is my ass on the line!

Wire the money by midnight tonight or you can kiss your Penrith project goodbye. I can make sure it's stalled for months…

There were no dates on any of the letters, so it was impossible to tell when they'd come into existence, but what snagged Nick's attention was the name "Gunning."

He frowned. The name was familiar. In fact, he was sure Callum's fiancée's last name was Gunning. Was this Daniel Gunning her father? Her brother? Her husband? There was no way to know if they were related. He needed to talk to Callum about that.

Setting the letters aside, he returned to the safe for a third time and retrieved yet another packet. This time he pulled out a stack of loose sheets of paper held together with a paperclip. The pages were covered with names and dates. Each entry had notations of money against it. Taking them back to his desk, he read through them, but couldn't work out what they meant.

There were page after page of entries, but there were no clues as to what the notations referenced and there was no discernible pattern to the entries. The only thing he was sure of was that the information was important. His father wouldn't have felt the need to keep the documents in his safe if that wasn't the case.

With a sigh, Nick set them aside. It had been a long day and he was beat. He glanced at his watch and saw it was a few minutes before five. Time to call an end to the day and go home and crack a beer. He'd deal with the contents of his father's safe and what it all meant some other time.

Harper shut down her computer and bent to retrieve her handbag from where she'd stowed it under her desk. It was the end of another day at Craigdon Enterprises and at the moment she was feeling torn. On the one hand, she enjoyed watching her growing bank balance and the satisfaction she got from knowing she was instrumental in the failure of this company to secure lucrative contracts. On the other hand, she was afflicted more and more with guilt that what she was doing was hurting her boss and possibly affecting much-needed affordable housing.

Nicholas.

She couldn't believe she'd broken her own rule and referred to him by his given name. She'd prayed he wouldn't notice, but it was obvious from the flare of surprise and pleasure on his face that he had, and it was too late to take it back. It was just that he'd taken her by surprise with his announcement about affordable housing and his name had just slipped out.

She was still shocked to discover he intended to make reparation for his father's terrible deeds. She never expected the son of Henry Craigdon to have an ounce of compassion, let alone be prepared to right a wrong, especially one that had nothing to do with him and would come at a heavy price. She'd worked at Craigdon Enterprises long enough to know the company specialized in high-quality, top-of-the-line apartments where the starting price for even the smallest of them had six zeroes. Making a commitment to building affordable housing would no doubt see them losing substantial money, not making it.

Of course, it could be all talk. She didn't know Nicholas well enough to know if he was genuine in his desire to help the disadvantaged and to set right what his father had done, especially when there was so much money at stake. But he'd certainly been passionate when he'd explained the details of his plan to her and had even invited her input. He'd also appeared genuinely upset at the prospect he might not get his proposal past the board.

Nicholas Craigdon kept surprising her. The fact he wasn't the ruthless businessman she'd envisaged was unsettling. The more she got to know him, the more her preconceived notions of what the son of Henry Craigdon would be like were sent awry. It was definitely cause for further contemplation.

As if on cue, the door to Nicholas' office opened and he came striding out, briefcase in hand. His hair was ruffled and his tie had been loosened and was slightly askew. He looked tired and there was a slightly defeated air about him that touched Harper. She didn't want to feel anything for this man, the son of her sworn enemy, but it seemed the choice had been taken out of her hands.

"You're off for the weekend." She blushed as she stated the obvious.

"Yes. I've had enough. It's been a tough day. Hell, it's been a tough eight months."

She pretended ignorance. "Is that how long your father's been gone?"

"Yes, almost. Though taking over the reins is what I wanted, it's certainly come with its challenges."

"You're talking about the lost tenders?"

"Yes. And other things," he said, his expression turning bleak.

She felt another stirring of compassion and bit her lip. He started to walk past her on his way to the lifts. She opened her mouth before thinking.

"Wait."

He came to a halt and turned back to face her, a questioning look in his eyes. "Is there something you want?"

"No. Yes." She blushed furiously and hurried to explain. "What I mean is, would you like to go somewhere for a drink? You look like you could use one."

Surprise flashed briefly across his face. "You're right about that. In fact, I was just thinking about heading home and cracking open a beer."

"I was thinking more of the wine bar down on the corner, but whatever suits you."

He grinned and inclined his head. "The wine bar sounds good."

Chapter Nine

The George St Cellar boasted high white ceilings divided by dark wooden beams from which huge wooden wagon wheel chandeliers hung, filling the space with soft yellow light. The bistro-style tables were spaced far enough apart to provide a modicum of privacy, but by the time Nicholas arrived with Harper in tow, the place was buzzing. That wasn't surprising, given it was late on a Monday afternoon in the city. Young twenty-something professionals lined the bar and most of the tables, inside and out.

"Stay here. I'll try and find us somewhere to sit," he told Harper.

She acknowledged his words with a nod and he pushed his way through the crowd. Finally, he spotted a couple leaving at the far end of the bar and he hurried back to Harper.

"Come with me." Reflexively, he reached for her hand and pulled her along behind him through the press of bodies.

Slowly, he became aware of her hand in his. Warm and soft and slender, it fitted perfectly inside his. Their fingers were threaded together and he liked the way that felt way too much. Like they were together. A couple. Not just two work colleagues enjoying a Friday night drink. And as they always did when he was in the company of a beautiful woman, especially one he was interested in, nerves danced in his stomach.

Still, he was glad she'd issued the invitation. It had come as a complete surprise, and despite his pep talk on the way home from Brisbane, he was excited at the thought of getting to know her better. Now they were away from the confines of the office, he hoped she might let her hair down, or at least reveal a little more of herself.

He was relieved to see the two recently vacated seats at the bar were still unoccupied. As they took their seats, Nick caught the attention of the barman.

"What can I get for you?" the man asked.

Nick looked at Harper.

"I'll have white wine, please."

Nick asked for a beer. A short time later, the barman arrived with their drinks. Harper reached for her handbag, but Nick halted her movement.

"My shout," he said.

She smiled. "Thank you."

Another rush of nerves flooded his veins, but he merely inclined his head and then gulped his beer. To his embarrassment, the cold liquid went down the wrong way and triggered a fit of coughing.

"I'm so sorry," he gasped when he could finally speak again.

She merely smiled. "Don't be sorry. You're fine. It happens to me all the time."

"Really?" he asked on a rush of hope.

She shook her head and laughed. "No, but I don't want you to feel bad about it." She reached out and touched his arm. "You need to relax and unwind. You've been working so hard. You must be worn out from your drive to Brisbane and back."

The warmth from her fingers on his arm reminded him how good it felt to have her hand in his. All too soon, she removed her hand and picked up her glass. She took a sip and gave a contented sigh.

"Ah. That tastes so good," she said, giving him another smile.

"It's nice to have the chance to kick back."

"Absolutely," she agreed.

He took another mouthful of his beer, grateful that this time he managed it without incident.

"I just want to say thank you for your help this past month. Jumping in without any prior knowledge of the company and taking over from Margaret couldn't have been easy. It's been a smooth transition, at least as far as I'm concerned. I want you to know your efforts have been appreciated."

Her smile widened and warmth filled her green eyes. "Thank you, Nicholas. That's a nice thing to say."

"It's true," he said.

"I've been a temp all my working life. You're the first boss to compliment me on my work and thank me for turning up. Most bosses hardly notice the temp."

He gave her a shy grin. "You must know by now I'm not like most bosses. In fact, it's only been since my father's death I've been a boss at all. Prior to that, I had much less important roles in the company."

"Tell me about your father." She'd tilted her head to one side and her eyes were filled with sharp curiosity.

Nick took another sip of beer and then set his glass on the bar. His shoulders slumped on a sigh.

"My father was an enigma. He was larger than life, the father of six children, the head of a billion-dollar company. He was arrogant and tough and sometimes he could be unbelievably cruel, but I also believe he loved his family. I lived my life in his shadow, wanting so much to be like him, but hating the thought I might *become* like him."

"I'm not sure I understand," Harper said.

Nick sighed again. "There was much I admired about my father. He was a hard worker, smart at business. He knew how to handle people and how to negotiate a good deal. But there was a lot I didn't like." He glanced at her and then continued. "For starters, he was a serial womanizer. I don't know how soon into his marriage it started, but it was a well-known fact among the family that he didn't know the meaning of fidelity."

"How did your mother handle that?" Harper asked softly.

"I'm not sure. On the surface, she seemed to ignore it, it was almost like she thought if she didn't acknowledge it she could pretend it wasn't happening. But it must have hurt her. As a child, I didn't give it a whole lot of consideration. It was just something I was aware of and felt uncomfortable about. But now I can only imagine how awful it must have been for my mother to have a husband like that. No wonder she turned to someone else for love."

Harper's eyes widened in surprise. "She had an affair?"

"Yes. But I only recently found out about it. Apparently it happened a long time ago." He paused and wondered if he should tell her about his other recent discovery. Harper seemed to sense his indecision because once again, she reached over and touched him on the arm.

"Talk to me, Nicholas."

Her gentle urging was all it took for him to blurt out what his sister, Isabella, had told him more than a month earlier.

"I recently found out my father always believed I wasn't his biological son. That explains so much." He shook his head. "My father always treated me like a pariah. No matter what I did, it wasn't right. He belittled me at every opportunity. Still, I took it. I loved him and I wanted to be loved by him. That was one of the reasons I wanted to be part of his company." He paused and then added. "Now I know why he was so awful to me."

Nick's voice hitched on a lump of emotion that had formed in the back of his throat. The understanding and compassion in Harper's eyes only exacerbated the rawness of his feelings.

He took a couple of gulps of beer, swallowing them quickly.

"That's terrible," Harper said quietly. "What kind of man does that? Whether he thought you were his or not, *you* believed you were his son. If he wanted someone to blame, he should have blamed your mother. It sounds like she was the one who had some explaining to do."

Nick compressed his lips. "Maybe he did? I wasn't the only one he treated badly. The irony is, it wasn't true. I *was* his biological son. It both saddens and angers me that he died not knowing that."

Silence fell between them as they busied themselves with their drinks. Nick ordered another beer. Harper nursed her wine.

"So, what does Harper Wyburn like to do in her spare time?" he asked in an effort to lighten the mood.

She hesitated a moment and then answered. "I'm pretty boring, actually. I usually potter around the house, doing laundry and other mundane jobs. If the weather's nice, I might go to the beach. Mostly I like to read and do jigsaw puzzles."

She looked faintly embarrassed by the admission. Nick grinned in delight. "I love jigsaw puzzles! I've got one half-finished on my dining room table. It's a thousand pieces and it's doing my head in. Too many shades of blue. I should have known better than to pick an ocean scene. I don't know what I was thinking!"

She laughed and the sound of it filled him with warmth. Here he was enjoying the company of a beautiful woman and it felt so…easy. His nerves had receded and his usual awkwardness had disappeared. He hardly dared to believe it. He'd grown up surrounded by confident alpha males, but somehow that innate confidence had escaped him. He guessed it had something to do with the fact he could never measure up in his father's eyes. It had a way of grinding a person down, destroying their self-esteem until they were only a shell of the person they could have been.

He liked to think he'd overcome some of that and the support from the rest of his family had helped. His two sisters, Isabella and Sophia, were staunch and loyal defenders, even though Sophia could be a bit of a pain. He put that down to her age. At twenty-one, she'd barely dipped her toes into the adult world. Up until now, she'd been cosseted in the world of a student, first at school and then university.

But now she was out on her own and navigating the world and all its pitfalls. She kept bugging him about a job, but he knew she had her heart set on being a teacher. If he gave in to her demands and offered her a position in the family company, it would be too easy for her to ignore her passion and find solace in something safe.

Life wasn't about finding a safe haven. It was about putting yourself out there, taking risks. He wanted to push her to find a teaching job and put her passions and training to good use. She'd make an excellent teacher. She just needed to believe in herself.

"I can't believe a guy like you is also interested in jigsaws."

Harper's comment drew his attention back to her. He grinned. "What do you mean, a guy like me?"

She blushed adorably. "Well, you know. You're confident and charming, in control without being domineering. You're smart and personable and sinfully good-looking. Poring over jigsaws is kind of…dorky. You don't seem at all dorky to me."

Her words filled him with warmth. He leaned closer. "You think I'm good looking?"

Her blush deepened. All of a sudden she seemed terribly interested in the contents of her glass, but eventually she looked up and met his gaze.

"Of course I think you're good looking. You must know that. You're not blind."

He shrugged. He'd never given it much thought. There were always more important things on his mind. Like trying to please his father. He told her as much. Once again, her eyes filled with compassion.

"It must have been tough growing up with a father like that."

He blew out his breath on a sigh. "Yep. It definitely wasn't easy."

Harper saw the change in Nick's mood and wished there was something she could do about it. Any mention of his father had an immediate negative effect. She could understand his reaction. From what he'd told her, he was as much a victim of his father's maliciousness as she had been.

She didn't want to feel sympathy for Nick. Nor did she want to accept they might have more in common than she could have guessed. Those thoughts and feelings were in direct competition with her quest to destroy Craigdon Enterprises. Though Nick had never been directly in her sights, she'd known since discovering his father was dead that there was a good chance he'd become a casualty.

That knowledge now made her uncomfortable, but now wasn't the time or the place to think about it. She wasn't prepared to let go her promise to avenge her mother, but neither did she want to see Nick hurt. As if aware of her tumultuous thoughts, he took another sip from his beer and regarded her somberly. Wanting to lift his mood, she cast around for a different topic.

"You know what else I do in my spare time?"

He gave her a slight smile. "Tell me."

She drew in a breath, hardly daring to believe what she was about to share. She usually shied away from making personal revelations to anyone and yet here she was about to tell Nick something no one in her day-to-day life even knew. She drew in a deep breath.

"I volunteer at a youth club one day a week."

His eyes crinkled in a surprised smile. "Wow. That's great. What do you do there?"

She told him about the program she'd set up to help young women grow in confidence, with the eventual aim of securing a job. She also talked about the boxing and the judo and the other programs run by volunteers at the club.

Nick's eyes shone with admiration. "You never cease to surprise me. What you and the others are doing sounds amazing. How long has it been running?"

"Marty Hannaford set up the club about ten years ago. Up until now, it's been going great guns."

Nick frowned. "What's happened to change that?"

Harper sighed. She hadn't meant to share so much of the youth club with him. It had been meant as a way to lift him from his sad mood more than anything. But she found she enjoyed talking to him about the club and how proud she was of what it had achieved.

"The last time I was there, Marty told me we'd lost our major sponsor. It's a big blow. Without sponsorship, we won't be able to keep the lights on. The kids don't pay to attend. None of the volunteers get paid. But we need money to pay the rent and utilities and to provide things such as boxing gloves, protective gear, judo mats, makeup, hair brushes and accessories. It all adds up."

Silence fell between them. Harper finished her wine. Looking thoughtful, Nick ordered her another and added another beer to the request. This time it was she who felt depressed. The possibility of the youth club closing saddened her. She fished around for a more positive subject.

"Tell me more about your plans for affordable housing. "We got interrupted by your phone call last time."

Nick smiled. "You're right. I remember I suggested you share some of your ideas. You mentioned a female relative of yours had fallen on hard times. Did she live in public housing?"

Harper bit her lip against a rush of emotion. Images of her mother, sick and dying filled her mind. She pushed them aside and forced herself to respond.

"Yes. She did. When she could no longer afford the rent, she was forced to live in shelters and on the streets. It was tough. She eventually caught pneumonia and died."

Nick looked appalled. "It's terrible to think something like that could happen in Australia. It makes me even more determined to do something about it, especially when my father was responsible for uprooting his fair share of vulnerable people."

"I'm glad you share a different outlook than him. That it's not all about the profits," she said.

Nick grimaced. "The more I discover about my father, the less I admire him. He was a man of many different faces, not all of them pleasant."

I couldn't agree more…

She compressed her lips into a thin line. "So I gather."

Nick reached for his fresh beer and took a drink. "So, what are your thoughts about my housing project? Do you have any suggestions?"

She looked at him and smiled a little uncertainly. "Do you really want to know?"

"Of course. You've had some experience by the sound of it. Were you close to your relative who died?"

"Yes. I was very close. That's how I know how hard it was on her."

"What would you like to see included in the development?"

Harper drew in a deep breath. "A place to call their own is important. A separate bedroom, a well-equipped kitchen, a laundry. It's so hard to find somewhere to launder clothes in the city."

"I didn't know that," Nick replied. "What else?"

"It's important to have other services nearby, things like a pharmacy and grocer, a medical center. They could all be incorporated in the design. You could have retail space at street level and apartments above. What do you think?"

He laughed. "You're amazing! I think it all sounds great. You've given this some thought."

She ducked her head in embarrassment. She didn't want his praise. "Not really. But I know what's important to people in these situations. It's more than just having a roof over their heads."

"Of course," Nick agreed quietly. "And I'm grateful for your input. We make a good team."

His gaze locked on hers and all of a sudden, the air between them grew charged. Her chest went tight as oxygen became in short supply. Then Nick leaned toward her. His eyes drifted closed. She pulled back with a jerk.

"Oh, God. Nicholas, I'm sorry."

She heard the panic in her voice, but there was nothing she could do about it. There were so many reasons why kissing Nicholas Craigdon was a very bad idea, not the least that he was married.

His eyes flew open. At the same time, he pulled back as if he'd been burned. His cheeks turned crimson with embarrassment. She could almost read his thoughts.

Oh, God, he thinks I don't like him like that. He thinks I'm appalled he might even think I'd like him like that. It's written all over his face. I can't hurt him like that. I can't let him think his advances wouldn't be welcome if he wasn't married...

"Nicholas. Stop. Please, whatever you're thinking, it isn't right."

His expression remained hard. She could tell he was still

consumed by the embarrassment of her rejection. She couldn't let him keep thinking that. She reached out and put her hand on his arm.

"Please, Nicholas. Don't take offense. But I draw the line at married men."

He frowned in confusion. "Married? What are you talking about?"

"Your wife. Sophia."

"Sophia? She's not my wife! She's my sister!"

Harper gasped in surprise. "Your sister? I thought… All the phone calls…" Now it was her turn to feel embarrassed.

Nick sighed. "I get it. She calls me constantly. She's a pain. But she's going through a rough time right now and she's my little sister." He shrugs. "What can I do?"

Can this guy get any nicer? He cares for his little sister, even when she must have been driving him nuts…

"Oh, God. I'm so sorry," she said. "I should never have made such an assumption."

"There's nothing to apologize for. I was the one out of line. I should never have tried to kiss you."

She wanted desperately to set him straight, to tell him exactly how much she wanted him to kiss her. But such a move wouldn't be wise. It was better they keep some distance. She merely shrugged in response.

He frowned, and then spoke again, as if needing to make her see. "I tried to kiss you and you didn't want me to. I don't know what I was thinking. I should have realized a girl like you would never be interested in a guy like me. The alcohol must have gone to my head."

She blinked in surprise. He had no idea how wrong he was. She thought of all the times his father had ridiculed him, not even believing he was his son. He'd been hurt so many times by people who were meant to love him. She couldn't contribute to his pain.

"You're wrong, Nicholas."

He gave her a half-hearted grin, but she could see the strain in his eyes. "Which part?"

"All of it," she said with emphasis. She wondered if she was brave enough to continue. The look of sadness that warred with hope in his expression decided it for her.

She moved closer and eyed him steadily, so he knew she meant what she said. "Despite the fact I thought you were married, I wanted you to kiss me. I… I've been struggling against my attraction to you from almost the moment we met. I don't want to like you. But I do. I like you a lot and there's nothing I can do about it."

Hope blossomed in his eyes. "Why do you sound so dismal about it? Is it such a bad thing?"

"Yes. No." She sighed. "It's complicated."

Nicholas rolled his eyes. "Of course it is."

She wasn't fooled by his attempt at levity. Hurt continued to shadow his expression. All of a sudden, she felt the urge to make him understand, even if it meant exposing herself in the process.

"No, Nicholas! You don't understand! I'm not just saying that to be polite. It's the truth. I have a lot going on in my life and falling in love with you isn't in the plan."

He held her gaze. "Do you plan everything?"

She shrugged and looked away. "Yes. For the last five years I've had no choice. My plan's what's kept me going."

"That sounds rather ominous."

She almost choked on the lump that had lodged itself in her throat. "It hasn't been easy, that's for sure."

His expression turned earnest. "Plans can be altered. They're not written in blood. Is there anything I can do or say to make you change your mind?"

She looked at him, feeling torn. Here was a good and decent man. A man who cared about people. A man who enjoyed doing jigsaw puzzles. What she wouldn't give to have met him under different circumstances, a different lifetime, without the specter of his father and what he'd done filling the space between them.

For a few long seconds, she almost did it. She almost came clean with the truth. But something inside her shied away. For years she'd been focused on her plan. She owed it to her mother to see this through. Slowly, she shook her head. "No. It's best this way for both of us."

Nick stared at her. Her words held such finality, he was flooded with disappointment. For a moment there, he thought she'd been giving serious consideration to his suggestion. But then she'd told him no. Her plans were her plans. There was no changing them.

Something told him it hadn't been easy for her to arrive at that decision. That meant she wasn't entirely convinced. He'd always been a fighter. No matter how many times his father knocked him down, he kept getting up and coming back for more. He knew with certainty there was something about Harper that was worth fighting for.

She hadn't said she couldn't fall in love with him—just that it wasn't in her plan. All of a sudden he was filled with determination to make her see having him in her life wasn't so bad. That some plans were worth changing after all.

Then there were her revelations about the youth club. It was obvious how much the place meant to her and he was sure her work there made a real difference to the kids who attended. It seemed a shame to see the place close, especially if it were only a matter of a shortage of funds.

Money was something he'd always had access to. Even though his father had been less than generous with Nick's inheritance, he'd never wanted for anything. His mother had set up a trust fund for each of her children and given them access from the day they'd turned eighteen. Nick had spent a decent portion of it on his apartment, but there was still plenty to draw on.

The more he thought about the youth club, the more he knew what he wanted to do. In order to get Harper to fall in love with him, they needed to spend more time together, getting to know each other outside of work. He needed to make her realize falling in love with him was possible. Not only possible, but the best thing she could do. He didn't know how he was going to achieve that, but he was determined to give it all he had.

The youth club could be a starting place. Another possibility was introducing her to his family. Jett and Danielle were having their daughter baptized that very weekend. Harper would be able to see where he came from, how good and decent his family was.

She'd told him she was an orphan. The only family she'd mentioned was a sister. He had no way of knowing how close they were, or if they even spoke. Perhaps if she saw how loving and supportive his was, she might come to like him more. Enough that the idea of falling in love with him wouldn't seem so impossible. It was worth a shot.

Before he could change his mind, he opened up his mouth and blurted, "My brother and his wife are christening their daughter this weekend. On Sunday. Would you like to come?"

Chapter Ten

Harper blinked at Nick in surprise at the sudden change of subject. She couldn't believe she'd admitted she had feelings for him.

What was I thinking? I'm doing everything I can to destroy his company! How can I even hint that I like him way more than I should? It's madness!

Now he wanted her to meet his family. Attend a family baptism, no less. She shuddered at the thought of coming face to face with Craigdons *en masse*, but then she paused. She'd always been curious about Henry's family. Over the years, she'd wondered about what kind of woman could be married to a man like that. She'd also wondered about his children.

She'd done some basic research of Henry's family on the Internet and knew well before Nick had told her that Henry had six kids. Five of them to his wife and one to an earlier relationship. She hadn't bothered to look into his family any further. At that time, they weren't important. It was only Henry in her sights.

But then Henry had keeled over with a heart attack and her plans went awry. It had taken her a few months to regroup and come to the decision to pursue her plan for revenge anyway. Back then, it hadn't mattered that the people who'd suffer from her actions weren't directly responsible for what had happened. The only important thing was avenging the death of her mother.

But now she'd met Nicholas and he was nothing like his arrogant pig of a father. He was sweet and kind and sensitive. He was thoughtful and caring and he concerned himself with the plight of others. And he was single. Under different circumstances, he was a man she could come to care for, maybe even fall in love. The thought was confounding.

She'd never been in love. Not even in high school. Her family circumstances after the eviction and later, after her mother's death, weren't conducive to a happy-go-lucky, without-a-care-in-the-world attitude she was sure was necessary in order to give herself over to the giddy, nonsensical feeling of love. Instead, she'd been focused on completing her education and getting her revenge on Henry Craigdon. That was the sole reason she'd gone to secretarial school.

Right from the time her plan for revenge had taken form, she was certain she'd have to take Henry on in his world. It wasn't possible for her to become a competitor, but she could definitely cause him trouble on the inside. Her plan was to get employed at Craigdon Enterprises and once there, work out a way to make Henry pay.

She leapt at any job that came along even remotely related to property development. She'd worked at several similar businesses around the city and had been thrilled when she got a job at McClintock Properties. She'd done her research on the who's who of the developers and knew McClintock and Craigdon often went head to head. She was another step closer to seeing her plan come to fruition.

Then Henry had died and the rest was history. Now his son wanted her to meet his family.

What do I do? Do I take the opportunity to learn more about my enemies? Am I willing to take the risk I might like them? That I might realize they're good and decent people, like Nick? That if I do like them, it might interfere with my ability to see my plan through to the end?

The thoughts went back and forth through her head. She bit her lip in indecision. Nicholas made a noise of impatience and looked at her with resignation.

"It's all right, Harper. I understand. It's too much, isn't it? I'm always screwing things up. The thing is, you make me so nervous I can barely think straight. I'd love you to meet my family, but I don't want to scare you off. I—"

"It's okay, Nicholas. I'll come."

His eyes went wide with surprise and delight. "You'll come?"

She gave him a grudging smile. "Yes. I'll come."

Harper was pleased for the extra money in her account when she went shopping for something to wear to the baptism. Though she'd accumulated a tidy sum thanks to Christopher and the secrets she'd sold him, she hadn't yet spent any of the spoils. She couldn't explain even to herself the reason why, and right now she wasn't prepared to give the issue closer examination.

In the past, she'd never had the reason nor the money to splurge on an expensive outfit, but a baptism at Craigdon Manor seemed the perfect excuse to go on a shopping trip. And after doing some research, she knew just where she wanted to do it. With a spring in her step, she caught a bus into the city to the heritage-listed, late nineteenth century Queen Victoria Building and headed straight toward Leona Edmiston's store.

According to the online article, Leona Edmiston was one of Australia's leading fashion designers and was known as the "Queen of Frocks." The article went on to say that Edmiston designed for the sophisticated, urban woman and one could be guaranteed her frocks would be timeless, elegant and effortlessly glamorous. It all sounded good to Harper. Elegant and effortlessly glamorous were exactly what she was aiming for.

One such woman met her just inside the store. The saleswoman was dressed in a superbly tailored, white silk suit that contrasted perfectly against her fake tan, clear blue eyes and bright smile.

"Good morning. May I help you?"

Harper gave the woman a smile. She looked like she might have been in her late thirties, but with her flawless makeup and impeccable hair style, it was difficult to tell for sure.

"Thank you. I'm looking for something to wear to a baptism."

The woman nodded and gave Harper a quick, assessing gaze. Dressed in bargain basement jeans and a T-shirt, Harper expected the woman to frown. To her credit, she merely turned away and walked over to one of the stands.

"Are you looking for a pantsuit or a dress?" the woman asked, flicking through clothes on a rack.

Harper wandered closer. "I think I'll go with a dress."

The woman merely nodded and continued to sort through the rack. At last she pulled out a dress that was so beautiful, Harper was momentarily lost for words.

"I like this one," the woman continued. "It's made of a soft textured crepe that will cling to your curves and though you're petite, I think this mini dress will look sensational. Why don't you go and try it on?"

Harper nodded and took the dress. The material was as soft and silky as it looked. The dark-green and white floral pattern was something Harper would never have chosen in the past. She preferred somber colors like black and navy-blue, serviceable colors that wouldn't show the dirt or go out of date. But as she stepped out of her jeans and T-shirt and shimmied into the dress, she couldn't believe how good it looked and felt.

Its shirt-style sleeve and button-down front bodice gave it a semi-casual look, but the cut and cost of the fabric ensured the outfit looked anything but cheap. The curved seam detail meant the skirt flared out around her legs, making her feel sexy and feminine. There was a separate belt with a wooden-look buckle that cinched in Harper's waist. Coupled with some nude-colored heels and a matching clutch purse and she could already envision the final result. She looked and felt terrific. The best part was, she didn't even ask about the price.

"How are you going in there? Do you need any help?"

Harper pushed aside the curtain in the change room and stepped out in the dress. The saleswoman's eyes went wide with pleasure.

"I knew it would look good!" she exclaimed.

Harper stood before her a little self-consciously. She'd never paraded around to show off her clothes before. Usually it was a matter of finding something cheap and serviceable. Often she bought things without even trying them on. This was a whole new experience and one she found she enjoyed.

"Do you like it?" the woman asked.

Harper smiled widely, excitement and happiness flooding through her veins. "Oh, yes! I love it!"

The woman nodded, pleased. "I'm so glad. You're going to be the envy of every young woman at the gathering."

With that the woman turned away and Harper returned to the change room. She'd been filled with apprehension at the thought of meeting Nick's family, but all of a sudden, her fears were swept away. Wearing such a magnificent dress would give her the confidence she needed not to feel self-conscious and out of place. Who knows? She might even enjoy herself. The thought made her smile.

All of Harper's newfound confidence disappeared the moment she and Nicholas pulled up outside his family's impressive home. Not wanting him to know about her modest living arrangements, when he'd offered to stop by and collect her, she'd given him an address more than two blocks away from where she lived. He'd made no comment on what he thought was her neighborhood and he had no reason to. It was an average neighborhood in the inner west. Popular with young professionals and students, it was only a few miles from the city. Exactly the reason why she'd chosen to deceive him into thinking that's where she lived.

He'd greeted her warmly and shot her a look of admiration as she'd climbed into his luxurious sports car. She'd settled herself against the soft leather seat, determined to enjoy herself. They'd filled the silence with casual conversation all the way to the church. Even then, catching glimpses of his family in the pews in front of him, her confidence had remained in place.

Then they turned into the double wrought iron gates that led to the Craigdon mansion and Harper's nerves had returned. Taking in the acres of manicured lawns, beautiful gardens and established trees, it hit her like a sledgehammer between the eyes how incredibly wealthy the Craigdon family was.

Oh, she'd known in a general sense that Craigdon Enterprises was worth billions, but to have that opulent wealth displayed so overtly in front of her made it all too real. The thought of the crowded shelters and other forms of dismal accommodation she and her mother had been forced to live in following their eviction filled her heart with bitterness. Being in Nicholas' company over the past few hours had lulled her into a sense of false contentment. Here was a stark reminder of the reason she was really there.

The circular driveway that ended outside the house was already crowded with expensive cars. Harper stepped out onto the paved walkway and was immediately beset by nerves. She hadn't been given the opportunity to meet any of the family at the church and was now terribly apprehensive about meeting them *en masse*.

"Will your whole family be here today?" she asked, her voice displaying her nerves.

Nicholas gave her a reassuring look. "Yes."

"All five of your siblings?"

"Yes. And their significant others. Jett is the only one married, but Joel and Callum and Isabella have all found the love of their lives. Callum's wedding is only about six weeks away. Then of course, my cousins will be here. You've already met Logan. He has two brothers, Flynn and Noah. Then there's my mother, of course. And my uncle. And by the look of the crowd at the church, at least fifty or sixty of Jett and Danielle's closest friends."

Harper's pulse rate kept climbing by the minute. Her chest went tight. She felt like she might faint.

What was I thinking when I agreed to come? This is a nightmare! How will I keep up the subterfuge in front of so many Craigdons?

Nicholas shot her a look of concern. "Are you all right?"

She sucked in a breath and worked desperately to get her pulse back under control. At the same time, she managed a tight smile. "Yes. I'm fine. I guess I'm just a little nervous. I've never done this before."

Nick gave her a teasing smile. "What? Attend a party?"

She grimaced. "It's not just a party. It's…" She waved in the direction of the mansion, the magnificent grounds, the rows of luxury cars. "All of this. I mean, who lives like this?"

They'd started walking toward the wide stone steps that led to the front door. Nick caught her by the arm and pulled her to a halt.

"Hey," he said softly. "It's my family. They're just like any other family. Okay, so they own a nice house and a big yard and they have friends with nice cars. But they have their faults and failings like everyone else. They're not monsters. They're normal people. You'll be fine."

She stared at him, unconvinced. Nick was oblivious to her ulterior motive for being there, but what if other members of his family were more astute? What if someone asked her what she was doing there? After all, she was his EA. It seemed ludicrous he'd invite someone like her, a mere employee and a temporary one at that, to a family celebration. She was a fraud.

"You're overthinking this, Harper," Nick cajoled. "Come on."

With that, he began walking again and this time he took her hand, giving her no choice but to follow. With dread swirling around in her stomach, she sent up a silent prayer heavenwards to help her get through the next few hours.

The first person they ran into was Sophia. She was every bit as tall and poised and beautiful as Harper imagined, if not a fair bit younger. Harper had assumed the woman was around Nick's age, but she looked closer to nineteen or twenty. She also looked nothing like her brother. Her hair was a medium brown color, lightened with blond highlights. Her brown eyes looked at Harper with frank curiosity.

"Soph. You look lovely as always," Nick said and pecked his sister on the cheek. He drew Harper in close. "This is Harper Wyburn."

Sophia's eyes widened. "Harper? Not your EA?"

Nick didn't look the slightest bit uncomfortable. "Yes, my EA."

Sophia's assessing gaze went from her brother to Harper and back again. "I see."

"No, brat. You don't see at all. Now, stop being rude and say hello to Harper."

Sophia's smile was overly bright. "Hello, Harper. Welcome to Craigdon Manor."

Harper forced a response through her dry lips. "Hello, Sophia. It's nice to finally meet you in person. You're so much lovelier than I expected."

Sophia flushed and looked away. Nick laughed. "You deserved that, Soph. You've been a pest, calling me non-stop. No wonder Harper thought you were my wife."

Sophia looked appalled. "Your *wife*? *Ewww*."

Now it was Harper's turn to feel embarrassed. "I'm sorry. I just assumed…"

Sophia gave her a wry grin. "I can be pretty demanding, can't I? Is that what wives are like?"

"I don't know," Harper replied. "I've never been married."

A gleam of speculation entered Sophia's eyes. Once again, she looked from her brother to Harper. Her gaze lingered on their still-joined hands. Harper tried to pull her fingers from Nick's, but he tightened his hold.

"Well, it was nice to meet you, Harper. Enjoy the party. I know I will." With that she blew her brother a kiss and moved away.

Nick turned to Harper. "So, that was Sophia. One down, four to go—not including my mother. Come on. Let's go and get a drink."

With her hand still in his, Nicholas led her through throngs of people gathered in small groups in the entryway, the living room and all the way outside to a large covered deck, complete with cabana and swimming pool. That was where the bulk of the guests were gathered and the tinkling of glass and the buzz of conversation filled the air.

Nick dragged her over to a makeshift bar. Music from a string quartet set up not far away was pleasant and calmed her nerves a bit.

"What's your poison?" he asked.

"I'll have a glass of white wine, thank you."

Nick gave her order to the barman and then asked for a

beer. With drinks in hand, they made their way over to where a tall, regal-looking woman with a head of thick, white, perfectly coiffed hair held court near the swimming pool. Harper immediately knew who she was. As the woman turned toward them, Harper was almost frozen with nerves.

"Mom. It's great to see you. You're looking well." Nick gave his mother a kiss and a hug before turning to Harper.

"Harper, this is my mom. Elizabeth Craigdon."

"It's… It's nice to meet you, Mrs Craigdon."

The woman smiled. "Please, call me Elizabeth. It's lovely to have you here."

"Thank you for letting me share this special day," Harper replied.

Elizabeth smiled again and then turned to her son. "Nicholas, would you mind getting me a glass of orange juice? I'm feeling rather thirsty. The day's warming up."

Nick shot a glance in Harper's direction, but dutifully complied without comment. As he disappeared back the way they'd come, Harper was filled with panic. She took a gulp of wine.

Oh, God. Please don't leave me here with Nick's mother. What am I going to say? For the past five years I've been consumed with getting revenge on her husband. How am I going to conceal that kind of hatred

Chapter Eleven

The warm smile and keen intelligence in Elizabeth Craigdon's eyes was disarming and helped to calm Harper's turbulent thoughts. She didn't know what she'd expected of the wife of the late Henry Craigdon, but this friendly, pleasant woman wasn't it.

"So, Harper," Elizabeth said, moving them a short distance away to where the crowd had thinned. "Tell me about yourself."

Harper's heart skipped a beat. Nerves rushed through her veins. It had been a long time since she'd shared herself with anyone. Even Nick didn't know much about the woman beneath the professional façade. She couldn't risk Elizabeth discovering the truth. It would devastate her son.

The thought gave Harper pause. Since when did she care about the way Nicholas Craigdon felt? She'd been upset to learn how badly he'd been treated by his father, but that didn't wipe away all the pain and anger she'd lived with every day of the past five years.

Elizabeth regarded her expectantly, waiting for Harper's response. She thought fast. "I was born in Sydney. After I finished school, I put myself through a business administration and secretarial course. I've been working as a temp ever since. That's how I met Nick."

Elizabeth smiled encouragingly. "You've done well for one so young. Your family must be proud."

Harper grimaced. "Unfortunately, I'm on my own. I never knew my father. He left when I was a baby. My mother raised me on her own."

Elizabeth's face had filled with kindness and admiration. "She must be an amazing woman."

Harper nodded sadly. "She was."

Elizabeth frowned. "Was?"

Harper sighed. "She died five years ago."

"Oh, you poor girl!" Elizabeth's expression showed genuine compassion. "You must have still been a child! Who looked after you, saw to your needs?"

Harper shrugged and looked away. She didn't discuss her past with anyone. It always made her uncomfortable. She didn't want to see the judgement in people's eyes. Or even worse, their pity.

"Do you have any relatives? An aunt? Grandparents?" Elizabeth probed gently, filling the silence.

Harper forced a smile. "No. It's just me."

Elizabeth looked genuinely appalled. "Oh, Harper! No family? I can't imagine." She spread her arms wide. "As you can see, I have multiple family members. I'm happiest when I'm surrounded by them. I can't imagine how difficult it must be for you to have no one."

"She doesn't have no one, Mom. She has me."

Harper sighed quietly with relief when Nicholas materialized with Elizabeth's drink. He handed it to his mother and then put his arm around Harper's shoulders and drew her close as if it were the most natural thing in the world. The action wasn't missed by Elizabeth. She gave them both an assessing gaze.

"I see. Well, I'm glad. Harper was just telling me she's an orphan."

Nick looked at her in surprise. "Yes, I remember you told me that not long after we met. I'm sorry I didn't ask anything more about it."

Harper shrugged uncomfortably. "I guess it didn't come up."

"But of course, there's your sister," Nick said.

Harper froze. She'd forgotten all about the fictitious sister. The one having a baby, no less.

Elizabeth frowned. "Oh, I thought when you said you had no family, you meant no family at all."

Harper thought furiously, but came up blank. Nick shot her a curious look.

As if sensing the couple had things to discuss, Elizabeth murmured her farewells and moved away. Harper watched her leave. She thought of all the things she knew about Elizabeth's husband and wondered how someone who seemed so thoughtful, kind and genuine could have been married to such an arrogant pig.

"Hey," Nick said softly. "Is everything all right?"

Harper forced a smile. "Yes, of course."

"I'm sorry about mentioning your sister. I didn't realize she was off limits. Do you speak to her often?"

Nick's words kept coming, hammering away in her head. That was the problem with lying. Unless, she came out and told the truth, she'd be forced to continue the subterfuge.

Oh, God. What am I going to do?

Nick continued to regard her closely, concern now shadowing his eyes. "Harper? It's all right. I understand if you don't want to talk about it."

"Why are you being so nice to me?" she cried. "I don't deserve it!"

"Of course you do. Besides, what's wrong with being nice?"

"Nothing. Nothing at all. I guess I'm just not used to being treated so kindly."

Nick's expression filled with compassion. "I don't know much about you, Harper, but anyone who was orphaned at such a young age has to have had some tough patches. With or without a sister."

A wave of guilt washed over her. "I don't have a sister," she blurted out.

His eyes went wide with surprise and confusion. "Of course you do. She's pregnant, remember? You're going to be an aunty."

Harper shook her head vehemently. "No, Nick. No, she's not. She doesn't exist."

His eyes narrowed in sudden comprehension. "What are you talking about?"

The ice in his tone tore her apart. She blinked back tears. "I lied, okay. I lied when I told you I had a sister."

He looked at her in bewilderment. "Why? Why would you do that?"

She sighed, feeling sick to her stomach. Still, now she'd started down this path, she was determined to see it through.

"If you cast your mind back to the conversation, you came up on me unexpectedly. You overheard me voicing my delight over something I'd seen on my phone. I was embarrassed about what I'd really been crowing about, so I told you I had a sister."

The confusion on his face deepened. "I still don't understand. Why wouldn't you just tell me the truth?"

She looked at him and yearned to tell him everything. But she couldn't. He'd hate her and she wasn't ready for that. Over the previous weeks, he'd come to mean more to her than she was prepared to admit. What she did know was that she didn't want to own up to something that would mean she'd never see him again.

"Please, Nick. Please just trust me when I say I wish I had. Things have gotten so complicated. I never expected…"

Her voice caught on a sob and to her horror, the tears she'd tried hard to hold at bay welled up in her eyes and began to slide down her cheeks. Nick looked instantly contrite.

"Oh, hell. I didn't mean to upset you. Harper, please don't cry."

The kindness and concern on his face was her undoing. She didn't deserve this beautiful man, but she desperately wished she did. She wished she could wipe out her hurtful memories and her hell-bent determination to seek revenge. Not for the first time, she wished things were different. Knowing she should walk away, but unable to get her feet to move, she was helpless to resist when Nick stepped forward and took her in his arms.

"Oh, baby!" he murmured against her hair. "What am I going to do with you?"

Harper tried to resist, but it was as useless as trying to hold back the tide. It felt so good to have someone to lean on after being on her own for so long. With a sigh, she rested her head against his broad chest and closed her eyes, savoring the notion of being safe and secure, if only for a short while.

The heat from Nick's skin seeped through her light dress. Her hands were clasped around his waist. She felt his heartbeat, strong and sure and rapid. Her pulse rate jumped in response.

She lifted her head and stared up at him. She'd always been petite. Even in her new high heels, he was head and shoulders above her. His blue eyes were shadowed with desire. His lips parted on an intake of breath.

Unable to stop herself, she came up on tiptoes and angled her head. She pursed her lips. Her eyes drifted closed.

Harper, don't do it! Don't kiss him! It's the worst thing you can do!

But she ignored the frantic voice in her head and did what she'd wanted to do for a long time. She touched her lips to his.

Fire shot along her nerve endings and centered in her core. She felt his momentary surprise, but then he tightened his arms around her and kissed her like a starving man. His mouth ravaged hers. He held nothing back. She met his explosive passion with passion of her own. It was the first time she'd kissed a grown man and it was like nothing she could have imagined.

His tongue pressed against her mouth, seeking entry. She opened it and his tongue swept inside. She clung to him and moaned, matching him kiss for kiss. Her body was on fire, burning with need. She'd never felt like this before. It left her feeling disorientated, out of control. She tightened her hold on him, afraid she might lose her balance if she let go.

That's how she felt. Off-balance. Desperate. Burning to get closer, to take this all the way.

This is madness! We're at a party! A baptism! There are people everywhere…

Slowly her thoughts penetrated the fog of desire that had overtaken her and she loosened her hold, letting go of his shirt, dropping back down on her heels. She stood staring up at Nick. They were both breathing hard.

Oh, hell. I can't believe I kissed him! What was I thinking? This is all so wrong…

Nick must have seen some of her inner turmoil on her face. He reached out and cupped her cheek.

"Harper. Don't. Whatever it is you're thinking, just… don't." His eyes pleaded with hers.

She recalled his words that girls like her were never interested in guys like him and she silenced the words of apology on her lips. What had just happened between them was magical, like nothing she'd ever experienced and no matter the consequences, she wasn't sorry and she wouldn't pretend otherwise.

"Okay," she breathed. "Okay."

Hope flooded his face. A little smile tugged at his lips. "Okay? Really? You're okay with it?"

Slowly, she smiled back at him. "Yes. I'm okay with what just happened. I didn't plan it and I don't know if it was wise or the stupidest thing I've ever done, but…I don't regret it."

His smile blossomed into something that snatched her breath away. The joy in his eyes was plain to see. A shaft of guilt threatened to ruin the happiness that surged through her. *Maybe it's time to re-think my plan?*

The thought jarred her. For five long years, she'd lived for the day she could bring Henry Craigdon to his knees. She hadn't been quite sure how she'd go about it, but she was certain her sheer determination to make it happen would mean she'd find a way. Now all of that had been turned on its end because of one incredibly sweet, desirable man.

What am I going to do?

Fortunately, there would be plenty of time later for her to sift through her feelings and work out what needed to be done. For now, she'd enjoy Nicholas' company and look forward to meeting the rest of his family. Decision made, a sense of calmness descended upon her. She reached for Nick's hand and threaded her fingers through his.

"Shall we head back to the party?" she asked.

Nick grinned. "You bet. I can't wait to show you off."

The rest of the afternoon passed in a blur of unfamiliar names and faces and several more glasses of wine. There was barbeque, canapés, music and lively conversation. To her surprise, Harper couldn't remember the last time she'd had so much fun.

Nick's family was incredible. She was a stranger to them and yet they welcomed her without a moment's hesitation. Along with Sophia, Nick introduced her to his brother Joel and Joel's fiancée, Sheridan. Then there was his sister, Isabella and her boyfriend, Raine. The two had only just become an item and were still the talk of the family, along with the possibility Isabella might be moving to Brisbane to be closer to Raine. It was a big decision and one Harper was sure

Isabella wouldn't make lightly. Still, the woman seemed to take it in stride and it was clear from the way she looked at Raine that she was prepared to make whatever sacrifice was necessary for them to be together.

"Having fun?" Nick asked, pulling her aside and planting a kiss on her mouth.

"Absolutely. Your family is great." It felt so natural. Kissing and laughing and holding hands. She still couldn't quite believe it.

Then Nick's expression darkened. "Speaking of family. Don't look now, but I should warn you, not all of them are great."

Despite his caution, Harper looked in the direction Nick was focused and immediately froze in shock. Christopher Barrington strolled toward them, a look of surprise on his face. He quickly concealed it behind a scowl.

He inclined his head in Nick's direction. "Nicholas. We meet again."

Nick put his arm around Harper and drew her close. He stared at Christopher in silence. In case the man hadn't gotten the message, he kissed Harper briefly on the lips, making it clear she was his. Christopher's eyes flared wide with surprise.

Harper's feet were rooted to the ground. She couldn't even bring herself to look at Christopher. Panic flooded her veins. She'd been having such a good time with Nick and his family, for a while she'd almost forgotten what had brought them together in the first place. Now Christopher could ruin everything.

Relax. He's not going to say anything. He's just as complicit in this as you are. If he rats you out, he'll have to admit his own part in this scheme...

Christopher's gaze raked her from head to toe. "Well, well, well. And who is this?"

Nick glanced at her. "Harper, I'd like you to meet my half-brother, Christopher Barrington. Christopher, this is Harper Wyburn."

Harper barely contained her shock. *His half-brother? Are you freaking kidding me?*

Aware that both men were watching her closely, with an effort, she smiled in Christopher's direction. "It's nice to meet you."

He eyed her sardonically. "And you, Harper Wyburn."

She stared at him and willed him with her eyes not to say anything. He looked at her knowingly and smirked before flicking his gaze back to Nick.

"There's no need to sugarcoat it, Nicholas." He turned to Harper. "I'm his father's bastard."

Harper gasped in shock. The crude language and its implications seemed inappropriate in such happy, light-hearted surroundings. And then realization set in.

Oh, God. Christopher was the son Henry had with another woman. I remember reading about it. It's clear he hates them. Christopher hates the Craigdons. I can see it in his eyes. The way he looks at everything with such disdain… He's played me and I didn't even know it…

She hadn't wanted to think about Christopher's motivation for buying the Craigdon secrets she'd been only too willing to sell. She hadn't wanted to look past the good fortune that she'd found someone willing and eager to be part of her scheme. Christopher had helped her achieve her goal. Now she realized his beef with Nick and the Craigdon family went far beyond what she could have imagined.

Destroying the Craigdons is even more personal for him than it is for me… Oh, God. What have I done?

She was suddenly terribly afraid of what Christopher meant to do. It was clear from the lost contracts that he'd used the information she'd supplied him to do significant damage. Harper could only hope the damage already inflicted wasn't enough to see the company Nick loved go under.

She might have started out with that goal, but now she'd gotten to know him, she realized she couldn't go through with it. He was innocent of the sins of his father. In fact, he was nothing like his father. He was loving, modest, caring, kind. He'd taken after his mother. Harper didn't know Elizabeth well, but from what she'd seen, Nick's mother was the opposite of the ruthless, arrogant pig that was her late husband.

Harper was ashamed to admit she'd judged them harshly and they hadn't deserved it. She didn't even know them and yet she was willing to destroy them over something none of them had done. Henry Craigdon was solely to blame for her mother's death. It wasn't fair to make his family pay. The only problem was, she'd already started down that path and Christopher knew all she'd done. It would kill Nick if he found out how she'd betrayed him.

Oh, God. Please help me. What am I going to do?

Chapter Twelve

Unable to stand there with the two men for another minute, Harper mumbled her apologies and said something about needing to use the bathroom. Without waiting for a response, she dashed toward the house and made her way inside. Priceless artworks lined the walls of the opulent living room that opened up onto an even more impressive formal dining room. She could tell at a glance the highly buffed wooden table could comfortably seat twenty.

Spinning on her heel, she went in search of a bathroom and finally found one beside a smaller, cosier room that contained comfortable sofas, pale-colored soft furnishings and an array of family photos on an antique dresser. She glimpsed a grand piano right before she turned away and took refuge in the bathroom.

She locked the door behind her. Leaning on the sink for support, she stared at herself in the mirror. Her cheeks were flushed, her eyes were wild. She breathed like she'd run a marathon. She couldn't believe the man she'd been selling secrets to had an agenda of his own.

Stupid! Stupid! Stupid! You should have asked why he was so willing to pay a fortune for that information! You should have suspected he was up to no good. No one paid thousands of dollars for information they had no intention of using...

She was wracked with guilt. The truth was, she'd *wanted* Christopher to act on the information. She'd *wanted* McClintock Properties to outbid the Craigdons. She'd *wanted* to bring Nick and his company down.

But that was before. Before she'd gotten to know him. Before she'd met his family. Before she realized they were as good and decent as anyone could hope for. Now she felt sick at the thought of what she'd set in motion. Craigdon Enterprises had suffered a serious financial blow and it was all her fault. Worse still, she wasn't at all sure she could trust Christopher to keep his mouth shut about it.

Knowing she couldn't hide out in the bathroom forever, Harper splashed some water on her face and patted it dry with the hand-embroidered linen towel that sat on the counter. She opened up her purse and touched up her makeup. Satisfied the turmoil inside her had been brought under control, at least on the outside, she opened the door and left. She'd barely taken two steps when she almost collided with Sophia.

"Oh, I'm so sorry!" she cried, managing to sidestep Nick's sister just in time.

Sophia smiled away her apology. "No harm done. I should have been looking where I was going. How are you enjoying the party?"

Until a few moments ago, I was having a lovely time…

She kept the reflexive response locked tightly behind her closed mouth and managed a strained smile. "It's great. I've met so many lovely people. Everyone's so friendly and sweet."

To Harper's consternation, Sophia linked their arms together and led her into the room she'd passed on her way to the bathroom. Unlinking their arms, Sophia sat down on a pale-gray sofa and patted the seat beside her.

"Sit with me for a while. I feel like we got off on the wrong foot. I want to fix that."

Despite her inner turmoil, Harper laughed. "Don't be silly. It's my fault for thinking you were Nick's wife."

"Ah, but I've been such a pest these past weeks. I've been annoying Nick no end. A real fishwife."

Both of the women grinned. All of a sudden, it felt like they were confidantes, even friends. Harper felt herself relax. She guessed she and Sophia were close in age. For a brief moment she wondered what it would be like to have a sister. A real sister, not a made-up one. Someone like Sophia.

Sophia sighed. "It's just that I've been so out of sorts since Dad died." She threw Harper a sideways look. "I assume Nick filled you in on that?"

"Yes," Harper managed.

"I still don't understand why he did it! Why he treated some of us so unfairly! Isabella was left twenty million dollars! I was left enough to cover my student loans. How is that fair?" she cried.

Harper sympathized with her. "It isn't."

"Darn right, it isn't. I'm so mad at him! I want to yell and scream and shout at him. I want to throw things at his head. I want to demand an explanation! But I can't do any of those things and I think that's why this has been so hard. He'll never be able to make things right or give me an explanation."

She sighed. "This anger that's eating me up inside is wasted. What good can it do? Nothing's going to change. It only makes me feel worse… And then I take that out on my family. Unfortunately, Nick's been the main one in the firing line."

"Nick understands. He has broad shoulders. He can take it. Besides, I know for a fact he cares very much about you. He doesn't like to see you upset."

Sophia shot Harper a grateful look. "Thank you. I can see what my brother sees in you. You're easy to talk to."

Harper looked away, suddenly uncomfortable. "I'm just his EA."

Sophia's expression turned speculative. "Uh, uh. I'm not buying it. Nick's never brought a woman home before. He wouldn't have done so now if you weren't important to him. He really likes you, Harper. I hope you feel the same."

Sophia's probing gaze only increased Harper's discomfiture. She clenched her hands into fists and tried not to squirm on the couch.

As if I didn't feel guilty enough…

Sophia continued to regard her expectantly, waiting for Harper's answer. With nerves tightening her stomach, she managed to clear her throat.

"Um, of course. Nick's a great guy. There's plenty to like."

Sophia's face fell with disappointment. "Oh, so it's like that, is it? You don't like him like that?"

Panic surged through Harper. She wasn't ready for this conversation. She'd just kissed Nick senseless and yearned to do it again, but she still wasn't ready to admit he meant way more to her than she was prepared to accept. Especially not to his sister. She palmed Sophia off with another vague response, hating herself.

Sophia regarded her somberly. "If that's the case, you need to be honest with him. I know my brother well. He likes you, Harper. He likes you a lot. I wouldn't be surprised if he already thinks he's in love with you. If you're not on the same wavelength, you need to tell him. And soon. Let me warn you, I'll never forgive you if you break my brother's heart."

The fierceness in Sophia's expression should have taken Harper aback, but all she could think was how lucky Nick was to have such a loving, supportive family. It was clear they had his back. For a brief moment, she felt sorry for herself, given that family love and loyalty was something she hadn't experienced for a long time.

Tears of self-pity pricked her eyes and she hurriedly dashed them away. With muttered excuses, Harper got up from the couch and quickly made her escape. She found Nick standing by the pool, talking to a couple who stood with their arms around each other's waist. The man looked enough like Nick that he had to be another brother. As she approached, Nick looked up and saw her. He smiled. The happiness in his eyes made her heart clench.

He's so beautiful, inside and out. So sweet, so kind, so caring... He's everything I could ever want... And now I've ruined everything. He'll never forgive me if he finds out what I've done...

She forced a smile and pecked him on the cheek. He reached for her hand and took it in his, holding it firmly.

"There you are! I thought I might have to send a search party."

With an effort, she managed to return his smile. "I was just talking to Sophia. We were bonding over her phone calls."

Nick groaned with exaggeration. "Good Lord!" His grin encompassed the others. "Harper, I'd like you to meet my brother, Callum and his fiancée, Grace. We were just talking about the affordable housing proposal I'm hoping to take to the board."

Harper shook hands with them and murmured greetings. "It's a great proposal," she replied, giving Nick's hand a squeeze.

"We think so too," Callum said, his eyes lighting up with enthusiasm.

"Callum is in the process of refurbishing and extending the soup kitchen where I work," Grace explained. "He's also building affordable housing apartments on the floors above, in order to provide temporary accommodation for the homeless. I'm not sure if you're aware, Harper, but there's a real shortage of affordable housing in the city."

Harper nodded, her mind instantly awhirl. She knew all about overflowing shelters and places where the demand was always greater than what was available.

"It sounds very admirable," she managed. "Do you have government backing, or have you secured private investors?"

Grace and Callum shared a tender look. "Earlier this year, Callum inherited a sizeable sum of money from his late father's estate. It was in the vicinity of ten million dollars. He's putting all of that money into the soup kitchen and the accommodation."

Harper looked at Callum in surprise and admiration. "That's very generous of you."

He blushed. "It isn't just me. My cousin Flynn also donated his inheritance. A million dollars. It all adds up."

Harper nodded, impressed. "It certainly does. Wow. I've never met anyone so generous. To use your entire inheritance for the betterment of the less fortunate… That's amazing."

Nick chuckled. "Callum was destined for the priesthood before he met Grace. That's where he gets his charitable heart."

Once again, Harper stared at Callum in surprise. She couldn't believe how good and kind and thoughtful he was. She was beginning to believe it was only Henry who'd been completely and utterly selfish with little or no regard for anyone else.

"You must come and visit Jennifer's Kitchen and see for yourself," Grace said.

"Yes," Callum reiterated. "Please do."

"You should go," Nick urged, smiling at her. "Sophia volunteers there at least once a week. It would give you a chance to get to know her better. You two might one day even be friends. She's around your age, you know."

"We could always do with an extra set of hands," Grace added.

Surrounded by eager, expectant faces, Harper reluctantly agreed. "Okay," she laughed. "I'll come." She wanted to do something to support both Callum and Grace and all that they were doing for the less fortunate, and she also wanted to please

Nick. The only thing that held her back was the fear she might run into someone from her past.

Her mind had snagged on the words "Jennifer's Kitchen." Harper and her mother had spent many years eating at soup kitchens around the city, including that one. After a while, the regulars got to know one another. Though she hadn't been there for a long time, that didn't mean she wouldn't recognize anyone, or be recognized. It was enough to fill her heart with dread.

The sun was low in the sky when Nick drove her home. They covered the miles in silence. Every now and then he'd shoot her a glance, but she deliberately ignored the question in his eyes.

"Are you all right?" he finally asked.

"Of course."

"You're very quiet. You've been that way ever since we talked to Callum and Grace about the soup kitchen. Are you sure you're okay?"

She gave him a strained smiled and reached over and squeezed his hand. "I'm fine. Just tired. It's been a big day and I have work tomorrow."

"Are you worried your boss will ride you too hard?" he teased.

She gave him a small smile. "I have the best boss in the world."

He blushed at her compliment. When he pulled up outside the complex where he'd collected her from earlier that morning, he put the car into park and switched off the ignition. As if it were the most natural thing in the world, he turned and took her in his arms.

His kiss was soft and gentle, questioning, reaffirming, all in one. She kissed him back, but then slowly pulled away. He gazed at her with a hopeful look in his eyes, but she shook her head.

"I'm sorry, Nick. I'm beat. How about we call it a day?"

Disappointment filled his face, but he smiled graciously. "Of course."

He climbed out and went around to her side of the car. Opening the door, he helped her out.

"Thank you for a lovely day," she said sincerely.

"I'm glad you enjoyed yourself."

"I did. A lot more than I thought I would. Thank you for inviting me." She went up on her tiptoes and pecked him on the lips. "I'll see you tomorrow."

He grinned. "Don't be late."

With that, he went back around to the driver's side and climbed behind the wheel. She waited for him to pull away from the curb and join the stream of traffic before turning her back and heading toward her studio a couple of blocks away. As much as she wanted to invite Nick in, she had to deal with Christopher first. She wasn't sure how she could make up for the damage she'd already caused, but she'd make sure Christopher knew she was done.

Her main fear was that he might not accept her decision. This time, he'd chosen to play along and remain silent, but for how long? What he knew about her could destroy her if he chose to share it with his half-brother. If he did, any possibility of a relationship with Nick would be doomed before it had a chance.

Chapter Thirteen

Nick had purposefully kept his office door open so he could have a clear view of Harper from where she sat at her desk. She'd greeted him happily enough earlier that morning, but there had been no kisses or anything else that suggested their relationship had moved past the level of boss and employee.

He was disappointed, but he understood her need to keep some distance between them. After all, they were at work. There were others around them. And even though Nick didn't give a toss who knew he had the hots for his EA, it was obvious Harper wasn't prepared to make their relationship public.

He glanced at his watch. It was going on eleven. He wondered if Harper would still be willing to go to Jennifer's Kitchen with him. She'd promised Callum and Grace the day before that she would, but things were different between them in the office in the light of a new day. It was like a wall had gone up between them. He didn't know if it were just for the benefit of the other staff members in the office or if something else was going on.

He'd been disappointed when she hadn't invited him in to her apartment. Not that he'd expected her to, but it would have been nice, a further cementing of their relationship. Being a virgin, the thought of having sex with her filled him with equal parts yearning and terror. What if he messed up? Came too quickly? What if she didn't come at all?

There were so many pitfalls to negotiate. In a way, he was relieved she hadn't invited him in. Still, it would have given him some confidence that maybe they could be a couple, that she felt the same way as he did. But she'd farewelled him on the street and he'd had to be content with that. He'd spent a restless night, tossing and turning, wondering what it all meant.

The only thing to do was to ask her, and if he were as confident as his siblings, he might have done just that, but he'd never been comfortable around women and more especially, a woman he was fast falling for. It was a dilemma.

And then she was there in the doorway, looking at him expectantly, and his thoughts flew away like dandelion seeds on the wind.

"Are we still on for the visit to Jennifer's Kitchen?" she asked.

Nick nodded eagerly. "Of course. Are you ready? If we leave now we should make it right before the lunch rush."

They went in Nick's Mercedes. He didn't know if Harper even owned a car. A lot of people who lived in and near the city didn't. The public transport was good enough to get where you needed to go most of the time. For Nick, he enjoyed the convenience of being able to go anywhere, whenever he wanted. There was no queuing in line, no waiting for a bus that was late.

But the main reason was because he also loved cars. He loved cars like some people loved their pets. It was his not-so-secret passion and one his family and friends ribbed him about with frequent regularity. After his latest trip to Brisbane, he'd lashed out and spent a decent lump of his inheritance on a 911 Turbo Cabriolet Porsche. He'd paid an extra six thousand dollars for the Carmine Red paint job. He was due to pick it up from the dealer later that day. He couldn't wait to take it out on the open road.

Glancing across at Harper, he wondered what she'd think of his new purchase. Though she always turned up for work nicely dressed, her clothes looked like they'd been bought from discount stores. Not that he was an expert in women's clothing, but her outfits certainly didn't look expensive. And there weren't that many of them.

She'd been with him more than a month and he was sure she wore the same black suit every day. In fact, the nicest dress he'd seen her in was what she'd worn to the baptism. Not that it mattered to him. Not everyone was lucky enough to be born into wealth. Her job as an EA paid well, but he didn't know about her other expenses. There were a lot of things he didn't know about her, including what had happened to her parents. He hadn't had a chance to quiz her further about that, but she was a captured audience in his car. He could ask her on the way to the soup kitchen. So he did.

"What happened to your parents?"

She turned briefly to face him. A frown marred the smooth skin of her forehead. "What do you mean?"

"You were orphaned at seventeen. That's very young to lose both of your parents. I was just wondering what happened to them."

She looked away and stared out the window. She was silent for so long he didn't think she was going to answer. And then she sighed quietly.

"I've already told your mother, so I guess it doesn't matter that you know. My father left not long after I was born. I've never met him. I don't know where he is."

"And your mother died when you were seventeen?"

Harper closed her eyes and blew her breath out on another sigh. "Yes."

"Wow. Cancer?"

"No. She died of malnutrition and pneumonia."

"Malnutrition? What happened?"

She looked at him with so much pain in her eyes, he wished he could take the question back.

"Don't worry. It doesn't matter," he said hurriedly, not wanting to cause her any more distress.

Whatever happened to her mother wasn't important. What mattered was that she knew how much he cared. He reached over and took her hand. He brought it up to his lips and pressed a kiss into her palm. He was pleased when she didn't pull back. Through the rest of the trip, he kept her fingers entwined with his.

There was already a queue outside the soup kitchen when he and Harper arrived. Nick found a parking spot around the corner and the two of them made their way there on foot. They entered through a rear door. Grace looked up from stirring a huge pot of spaghetti sauce and gave them a cheery smile.

"Hi! I'm so glad to see you! You're just in time!"

Nick kissed her on the cheek. "Where do you need us? We're here to help."

"Great. Unfortunately, Sister Mary-Catherine has taken ill with the flu and Sophia hasn't come in today, so we're shorthanded. If you could drain that spaghetti and pour it into those warming trays in the Bain Marie that would be fantastic."

"No worries," he replied and moved over to the stove.

"What can I do?" Harper asked, a little apprehensively.

Nick shot her a look of encouragement. She gave him a strained smile. Something that almost looked like fear shadowed her eyes. He wondered at that.

"You can bring the meatballs over here and we'll add them to the sauce."

Harper did as she was asked and then both of them took up positions behind the counter, serving spoons in hand. Callum arrived right before opening time and greeting them both with a wave and a smile, he headed across the vast expanse of the dining hall and opened the double doors. Immediately, a crowd of people swarmed in, all headed for the food.

Nick braced himself for mayhem, but to his surprise, the people organized themselves into an ordered line and waited their turn at the counter. Grace joined them in the serving line and greeted many of the patrons by name.

"Hello, Jack. How are you doing?"

"How's that sore hip, Dorothy?"

"You're looking better, Ralph. Did you get to the doctor?"

And on it went. She had a caring word for everyone and they responded in kind. After only a short time, it became obvious how much they loved her. It wasn't hard to work out why Callum loved her, too.

Nick glanced over at Harper. She had her head down and was concentrating hard on ladling meatballs into bowls. She barely looked at the patrons. Though she wasn't being rude exactly, she was far from the friendly personage he expected.

What's going on with her? She seemed so passionate about the need for cheap housing to help the very people who came to the soup kitchen and yet she's acting like she's somehow frightened of them, like they might attack her or something…

Which was plain stupid. She couldn't be thinking that. He was overreacting. But the more he continued to observe her, the more he was sure there was something up. Harper looked plain uncomfortable.

Unable to leave his post, Nick continued serving the spaghetti. Every now and then he glanced in Harper's direction. Her closed expression hadn't changed. With dogged determination, she continued to serve those waiting for a meal, but hardly ever interacted beyond a brief nod.

He didn't know what was going on with her, but he couldn't deny he was disappointed. He'd been raised to treat everyone as an equal, no matter who they were or their circumstances. He liked to think most people held that attitude, but it seemed Harper didn't quite know how to act around the patrons. She sure as hell wasn't interacting like Grace did with them. The knowledge troubled him.

Harper was on tenterhooks every moment someone new lined up at her post. Her heart beat fast and adrenaline surged through her body. Any minute she expected to look up and see someone she recognized, or worse—someone who recognized her. Being back in the soup kitchen also dredged up sad memories of the numerous times she and her mom had lined up for a hot meal. She thought she'd long-buried those distressful years, but apparently not. On top of that was her concern how Nicholas might react to the discovery she and her mom had once been homeless. She was almost sure he'd be sympathetic, but she wasn't ready to answer all the questions a discovery like that would generate.

So she kept her head down and severely limited her interaction with the patrons. Every now and then she caught Nicholas sending her a strange look, but there was nothing she could do about it. Silently, she prayed for the line to come to an end.

Eventually, it did and she breathed a sigh of relief. Setting the ladle down, she glanced around her and hoped they could leave. But Nicholas, it seemed, had other ideas. Already he'd moved out from behind the serving counter and was moving freely among the patrons. He talked to one, then another and another, sharing conversation, jokes and laughter. He seemed so natural, like he'd been mingling with society's less fortunate for years, and he didn't look at all perturbed by the ones who rebuffed him and looked at him with suspicion in their eyes.

It was obvious he treated everyone with respect and many responded in kind. After a while, even the most suspicious began to warm to him. Eventually he made his way back to her side.

"What are you up to?" she asked.

He smiled. "With the rush over, I thought it might be a good opportunity to talk to some of the people and ask them about what they need. I wanted to get some insight from the kind of people with firsthand experience about homelessness before I finalize my proposal."

She looked at him and was filled with warmth and admiration. The extent of his goodness and decency continued to surprise her.

"What a great idea. They've probably never been asked for their opinions, especially by the developer. Good job."

Nick merely shrugged as if what he'd done was of no consequence. "What better way to find out what they really need? After all, they're the kind of people I'm doing this for."

Her heart turned over at the earnestness on his face. He genuinely cared about the less fortunate and he wanted to see his project come to fruition. Were he in charge when she was a child, she doubted the cruel eviction would have happened, or if it did, that other affordable accommodations would have been arranged for the tenants who'd been displaced. It pained her that she might be the reason the board rejected his plan. Not only would Nick be prevented from doing something he felt so strongly about, many desperate, needy people would miss out.

"You're a special man, Nicholas Craigdon," she whispered.

His eyes widened in surprise. "Careful, Harper. That sounded very much like someone who likes me more than they're willing to admit."

She tried to laugh off the comment, but it came out

sounding more like a croak. Nick moved closer and put both of his hands on her shoulders. He drew her toward him and kissed her soundly on the lips.

She stared up at him. "What was that for?"

"Just because."

"Because why?"

"Because I wanted to. Is that all right?"

Her smile was slow in coming, but when it did, it stretched her lips wide. She'd never felt so happy. Here was a good man, a decent man. A man she could fall in love with. "Yes, that's all right."

To Harper's relief, as soon as the meal was finished, the dining room emptied of people until all that was left were the staff and a mountain of empty dishes. With a large plastic garbage bag in hand, Grace and Callum set about scraping plates and clearing the tables. Harper and Nick loaded the three, newly installed industrial dishwashers and then started in on the pots and pans that lined the counter.

They worked together in companionable silence. Harper washed and Nick dried. When the last of the pots had been put away in the storage room, Nick turned to Harper with a smile.

"We make a good team," he said.

She bit her lip against a rush of emotion. It wasn't the first time he'd referred to them like that. What she wouldn't give to have no secrets between them. To be two people who met through uncomplicated circumstances and who were free to be themselves and maybe fall in love…

"Thanks for all your help you guys," Grace said as she walked into the kitchen and flopped into a chair. "We had a good turnout today."

Callum took the seat beside her and shot her a tender smile. "You always have a good turnout. They love you and you love them. Anyone can see it."

Grace smiled softly at Callum's words and then looked at Harper and Nick. "Does anyone want a cup of tea or coffee? I could do with one, that's for sure." She made as if to stand.

Callum was instantly on his feet. "I'll get it. You stay there." He turned to Harper and Nick. "What about you two? Do you want something?"

"A coffee would be great," Harper said with a smile.

"Make that two," Nick chimed in. "In fact, I'll come and help you."

With that, the brothers moved toward the far end of the kitchen where the tea and coffee station had been set up. Grace shot a sideways glance at Harper. Something in the other woman's eyes made Harper tense.

"It was great of you to stop by today, Harper," Grace said in a conversational tone.

Harper managed a smile. "Thank you. I'm glad I could help. Do you normally have someone come in and do the cooking?"

Grace laughed. "No. I'm the one who does all the cooking. Usually I have some volunteers—Sister Mary-Catherine, for one, Sophia, a couple of university students. They come in when they can and help with the serving. Unfortunately they were all away today, so I'm really glad you and Nick came."

Harper shook her head in disbelief. "There are so many people who come here for a meal. I can't believe you cook for all of them."

"I love to cook and to be frank, none of the other volunteers have much talent in that department. If I didn't do it, I'm not sure where we'd be. Don't get me wrong, I appreciate their presence, but they're much better off serving." She grinned.

Harper grinned back, filled with admiration for the woman who sat across from her. "I don't know how you do it every day. They're so lucky to have you."

Grace merely shrugged and smiled. "I love doing it. And someone has to care. Too many people don't." She paused and then added, "I was watching you earlier, while you were serving. You seemed a little uncomfortable. There's no need to be wary of them. They're just ordinary people, like you and I. If you treat them as such, you'll be fine."

Harper started in surprise. She had no idea Grace thought she was fearful of the patrons. She hurried to set the woman straight.

"It's not that. I'm not frightened of them. It's just that I'd forgotten what it was like. It brought back a lot of sad memories and I—"

Harper suddenly stopped speaking as she realized what she'd said. Embarrassment burned her cheeks. She risked a glance in Grace's direction. The other woman merely nodded slowly, her eyes filled with compassion and understanding.

"I know exactly what you mean," Grace said.

Nick added milk and sugar to Harper's coffee, pleased that he'd remembered how she liked to drink it. He poured himself a long black. While he waited for Callum to take his turn at the coffee machine, he remembered his intention to talk to his brother about the letters he'd discovered in their father's safe.

"I've been going through some of Dad's papers," he said.

Callum looked mildly interested. "Find anything of interest?"

"There's a bunch of stuff in his safe. The one he had in his office at work. I found documents relating to the establishment of the Stella Taunton House for Widows and Orphans. It was set up at Dad's request."

Callum paused what he was doing and frowned. "That's the charity Dad left a huge sum of money to."

"Yes. Fifteen million dollars, to be exact."

Callum shook his head, looking perplexed. "I've never heard of them. It still escapes me what that's all about."

"Yeah," Nick agreed. "I didn't find anything else to enlighten us further. It might be one of those things we never get to the bottom of. Has the bequest been paid out?"

"Yes. In our capacity as executors of Dad's estate, the lawyers had Flynn and I sign the papers authorizing the transfer a few months ago. I assume the money has been handed over."

Nick took a sip of his coffee and then spoke again. "I found something else."

Something in the tone of his voice must have alerted Callum to the seriousness of what Nick was about to say. Callum regarded Nick warily. "What is it?"

"Have you ever heard of a man by the name of Daniel Gunning? He was—"

"Daniel Gunning? Of course I've heard of him. He was Grace's late husband. He worked at the City of Sydney Council as an urban planner in the years before he died."

"It seems he and Dad knew each other."

Callum shrugged. "Well, it's certainly a coincidence, but given Dad had extensive dealings with the council every time he sought approval for a new development, I guess it's not surprising."

Nick cleared his throat. "I think there was more to it than that."

Callum frowned. "What are you getting at?"

"I found a pile of letters passing between Dad and this Daniel guy. They're not dated, but some of them are in Dad's handwriting. There's no doubt he was the intended recipient and he responded in kind."

Callum's expression turned wary. "What did they say?"

"I think Dad was paying Gunning to expedite his development projects through the planning office. In particular, he was circumventing the need for a final engineer's report."

Callum's eyes widened. "Paying, as in *bribing*?"

Nick nodded. It was obvious from Callum's tone the news was as welcome to him as it was to Nick.

"Are you sure?" Callum asked.

"Pretty sure. The letters are damning. They're not dated, but I sorted them into some kind of order, going purely from the tone. They start out amicable enough as each party agrees to help the other. Dad offers Gunning a sum of money and Gunning agrees to issue occupation certificates without waiting for the engineer's final report. At some stage Gunning appears to have gotten greedy. He increases his demand for money. Dad wasn't happy." Nick shrugged. "I'm not sure if any of it's relevant, given both parties are dead, but I thought you ought to know."

Callum nodded, looking dazed. "Yeah. Thanks, mate. I appreciate you telling me. Listen, do me a favor and don't say anything to Grace. I need some time to process all of this and work out if she needs to know. She has a lot going on at the moment with the end of her rehab right around the corner and trying to get full custody of her kids. I'll… I'll just have to wait and see."

"Of course," Nick readily agreed. "You tell her or not tell her. Whatever you decide, it's fine with me."

Callum gave him a strained smile. "Thanks, bro. I appreciate it."

With that, they collected their coffee mugs and returned to where their women waited for them.

Chapter Fourteen

ick and Callum returned with the coffees and Harper did her best to shrug off her doldrums. Despite her best efforts, her mind kept straying to the dark times in her past that being back there in the soup kitchen, surrounded by people down on their luck, had re-ignited.

Oblivious to her tumultuous thoughts, Nick sipped his coffee. Silence fell between them. Nick broke it by inviting them all to lunch at his favorite Indian restaurant in the city.

"I can drive us all there, if you like," Nick offered.

Callum and Grace looked at each other and shook their heads. "Thanks, Nick, but we still have a few things to do here before we finish up."

Nick glanced at Harper. "We can stay a bit longer and help, if you like."

"No, that's fine," Grace replied. "I have to go over tomorrow's menu and make sure I have enough supplies. Boring stuff, but unfortunately it needs to be done."

Nick turned to Harper. "What about you? Do you fancy a hot curry?" He followed the question with a wink.

Harper's heart skipped a beat and then her pulse took off at a gallop. As much as she was aware of the concerned glances Nick had shot her way during the lunch hour, she wasn't ready to bring an end to their time together. With nothing pressing waiting for her at the office, she nodded her assent. "Sounds great."

Nick's eyes flared wide with pleasure and they soon made their farewells. He hurried Harper to his car.

"Aren't you lucky you have such an easy-going boss?" he teased as they climbed in. "I won't even dock your pay."

"Hey!" she said in mock outrage. "I've just donated my time to the poor. Surely that deserves some recognition."

"Absolutely." He grinned. "That's why I'm taking you to lunch. You worked hard at the soup kitchen. The least I can do is feed you."

He gave her a probing look and she knew her reticence with the patrons hadn't gone unnoticed. Still, she had no answers for him. At least, none that she was prepared to give.

They arrived at the restaurant and Nick opened the door for her and waited for her to enter. The room was tastefully decorated with traditional Indian furnishings and the smell of curry immediately permeated the air.

"I hope you like curry," Nick teased.

Harper laughed. "I *love* curry. The hotter the better."

"A woman after my own heart."

He said the words lightly, but all of a sudden the air between them seem charged. Images of their passionate kisses at the party flooded Harper's mind. From the look on Nick's face, he was remembering the same thing. Her mouth parted on an intake of breath. Nick's gaze zeroed in on her lips. Her pulse raced. She could almost feel the sweet pressure of his mouth on hers.

"Harper—"

"Mr Nick! Great to see you! Your usual table?"

The arrival of the restaurant owner broke the tension. Harper tore her gaze away from Nick's. Her cheeks heated with embarrassment. Nick recovered more quickly.

"Arjun. It's good to see you again. This is Harper."

The gray-haired Indian man regarded Harper with interest. He looked at Nick with laughter in his eyes. "Your girlfriend?"

Nick glanced at Harper and then back at Arjun. "Yes."

Arjun's grin widened. "Good. Your girlfriend. Very good."

Harper ducked her head and avoided eye contact. Though she wasn't offended to be introduced as Nick's girlfriend, she wasn't sure she was ready to take on such a title. There were still so many secrets between them. The more she went along with the subterfuge that everything between them was fine, the harder it was going to be to tell the truth…and risk breaking Nick's heart.

Arjun took them to a table near the window that looked out on the street. The place was clean and tidy and had atmosphere, but it was far from the sophisticated dining establishment she might have guessed someone of Nick Craigdon's status would eat. There were no celebrities in the corners. No bloggers on their phones. In fact, apart from a middle-aged couple a few tables over and two women behind them, they were alone.

Her impression of him kept being turned on its end and it continually surprised her. He was nothing like the man she'd imagined. The truth was, she'd imagined him to be exactly like his father. But he wasn't. And those differences made everything so much more difficult.

"So, what are you doing tonight?" Nick asked.

"Tonight's my night at the youth club," she replied.

He smiled. "Ah, the youth club. I've been thinking…"

She looked at him expectantly.

"I don't want you to think I'm interfering, but I was wondering how you'd feel if Craigdon Enterprises came on board as your major sponsor?"

She stared at him in surprise and disbelief. "Really? You really want to do that?"

Nick shrugged and looked a bit embarrassed. "Why not?"

"Oh, my goodness!" she cried, suddenly overwhelmed. To her horror, her eyes filled with tears.

Nick's expression immediately filled with concern. "Harper! Please, don't get upset! I thought this would make you happy!"

"Of course it makes me happy!" she managed. "I'm so happy, I could cry!"

A smile of relief gradually washed over his face. "Really?"

"Yes! Really! I could kiss you right now!"

He grinned. "Don't let me stop you."

Needing no further encouragement, Harper threw caution to the wind and pushed back her chair from the table. She stood and went around to his side. Taking his head between her hands, she kissed him soundly on the lips.

She should have known one kiss wouldn't be enough. The moment her lips touched his, she was on fire. Nick kissed her back with just as much enthusiasm and it was only the sound of the waiter discreetly clearing his throat that brought her back to her senses. Blushing, she ducked back in her seat. Nick looked at her with love and laughter in his eyes, completely unapologetic.

"Are you ready to order?" Arjun asked, his eyes sparkling with good humor.

"Absolutely," Nick declared. "We're starving, aren't we Harper?" He followed the comment with a wink that had her blushing again.

Oh, my goodness! I'm falling hard. What am I going to do?

The curries were as good as Nick had promised and Harper's stomach was bursting when she finally set down her fork.

"Oh, Nick. That was *soooo* good," she said.

"There's more left, if you want some."

She put her hand on her bulging stomach. "Thank you, but no. I couldn't eat another bite."

Nick smiled. "What time's your class at the youth club?" he asked in a conversational tone.

"It starts at seven, but I like to get there a little earlier to set up. Why? Would you like to come?" she joked.

"As a matter of fact, I would."

She blinked in surprise. "Really? I mean, you don't have to. Just because you've offered to sponsor us, doesn't mean we expect you to give up your time to visit. I'm sure Marty will call you himself and thank you."

"I want to come. This is something that's important to you. I'd like to be a part of it."

His words filled her with warmth. Beyond her mother, she couldn't remember anyone ever caring for her like this.

Is there no end to this man's sweetness?

She looked at him tenderly. Here was a man she could fall in love with, if only she let herself. If only she didn't have history with his father. If only she hadn't betrayed him in the most awful way. If only…

She swallowed a sigh and forced a smile. She was tired of all the "if onlys". Right now, she wanted nothing more than to enjoy this time in the company of a man she held in high regard and forget about her worries for a while, including all the reasons why she should get the hell out of Dodge and turn her back on Nicholas Craigdon forever.

Nick found a parking space right outside the warehouse that served as the premises for Marty's Youth Club. He turned to Harper with a smile.

"Beats the train, right?"

She smiled back. "Absolutely."

He hadn't been sure how she'd react to his request to visit the youth club, but to his relief, she'd taken it in stride. He'd even hazard a guess that she was surprised and pleased with his interest, and especially with his offer to come on board as their major sponsor.

They climbed out of his car and headed toward the entry doors hand in hand. It felt so good and so natural. He wanted to hold hands with her forever.

Whoa! Steady, Nick. You barely know this girl.

It didn't seem to matter. Where Harper was concerned, he'd fallen head-over-heels in love. Though he'd never been in love before, he was sure this nervous, can't-think, twisted-up-inside feeling he got whenever Harper was around was definitely part of it. Along with the fact he thought about her all the time.

When they were apart, he thought about what she was doing and where she might be. When they were together, he wanted to be as close to her as he could be—talking to her, laughing, arguing—whatever. It didn't matter, as long as they were together.

All he had to do was convince her to take a risk on him. He hoped he could get her to fall in love with him. She'd already told him it was possible. He intended to turn that possibility into something that was real.

Inside, the warehouse had been converted into something that resembled his old high school gymnasium. White-washed walls in need of cleaning and a concrete floor that was cracked and stained indicated the lack of love the warehouse had been given over the years, but it was definitely fit for the purpose.

A boxing ring had been set up in the middle of the room. A couple of teenage boys were gloved up and sparring. A grizzled looking man with a head of white hair and bright blue eyes stood outside the ring, encouraging them on.

"That's Marty," Harper said, nodding toward the man.

In addition to the boxing ring, there was also an area that was obviously used for judo. A handful of young children dressed in judo outfits were doing warm-ups. Further along, there were trampolines, rings and vaults set up for budding gymnasts. Harper waved toward a woman who was helping a young girl to climb up onto the vault.

In the far corner of the room, rows of wooden tables and plastic chairs had been set up, reminiscent of a classroom. He could tell from the way Harper lit up that this was where she taught.

"So," she said, turning to face him. She thrust her arms out wide. "What do you think?"

He looked around and nodded. "I like it. Everyone has their own space, but it all comes together well. When do your classes start?"

"In about ten minutes. The girls should start arriving soon. I need to get the supplies out of the storeroom before they get here."

"Do you need a hand?"

She flashed him a smile. "That would be great."

"I'd like to meet Marty at some stage," he said as they headed toward a cupboard that stood against the wall.

"Of course. I'll introduce you after classes finish. It won't be quite as hectic, then." She opened the cupboard and began pulling out large ice cream containers filled with things such as hairbrushes, combs, clips, ribbons and hairspray. A few more containers overflowed with makeup—eye-shadow palettes, lipsticks, pencils and some other things he couldn't identify.

"What's that?" he asked, pointing toward a metal contraption.

She grinned. "Don't tell me a man of your age and education doesn't know what an eyelash curler looks like?"

He grinned back, loving this lighter, teasing side of her. It seemed being in the youth club brought out the best in her.

They'd hardly set out the containers when a dozen or so teenage girls and young women drifted in. They all greeted Harper enthusiastically before shooting him frank glances filled with avid curiosity. Harper called the class to order. She looked at Nick with a question in her eyes.

"I'll just take a seat at the back. You won't even know I'm here."

The girls quieted, but every now and then, they threw glances at him over their shoulders and giggled. Eventually, Harper stopped.

"Okay, girls. Listen up. I forgot to introduce my friend. My bad. And it's obvious that until I do, you're not going to hear I word I say. Am I right?'

There was a general chorus of agreement and plenty of giggles. Nick grinned and ducked his head, feeling slightly embarrassed from all the attention. It wasn't something he was used to.

Harper looked at him and winked. "Girls, please say hello to Nicholas Craigdon."

As one, Harper's students turned and faced him, giving him murmured greetings and wide-toothed smiles. Nick gave them a grin and a wave. After that, the girls settled down and paid attention to everything Harper said. They were enthusiastic about giving everything a go, and it was hilarious listening in on their conversation. Nick had grown up with two sisters, but even he didn't know what the girls were talking about most of the time. For him, it was like listening to people talk in a foreign language.

Apart from teaching them new hairstyles and the difference between applying makeup for the office and makeup to wear out at night, Harper also talked about the importance of good posture and in particular, the way they carried themselves. Apparently the girls had been given these lessons in previous sessions, but most were more than willing to practice the moves again.

There was much laughter as the girls walked up and down the aisle between the rows of tables. Harper had the girls put books on their heads. Every now and then, a book went tumbling and the girls burst into giggles. The mood was light and friendly and everyone was having fun, but Harper was also managing to teach the girls skills that would help them throughout their lives.

A burst of admiration rushed through him, leaving him tingling with warmth. The more he got to know her, the deeper he fell in love. She was everything he wanted in a woman and there was still so much he didn't know. He wanted to spend a lifetime getting to know her, loving every facet of her being.

But does she feel the same? Will she let me love her like I want to?

Harper tried hard to stay focused on her class, but with Nicholas seated at the back and looking more gorgeous than any man had a right to, it was difficult. Every now and then he'd send her a goofy grin. She could understand how her girls were so distracted. Eventually, she'd had no choice but to introduce him. No doubt as soon as he left they'd pester her about whether he was her boyfriend, and how long they'd been dating and whether they were in love… She wasn't sure how she was going to answer those questions. It was a good thing, she had some time up her sleeve.

True to his word, he'd kept quiet but that didn't help much. His mere presence was enough to cause a stream of constant giggles in her girls who were normally much more reserved. They kept stealing glances at him and whispering behind their hands. Every time he looked at one of them, they blushed.

She knew exactly how they felt. Ever since they'd met, she'd felt unsettled. Despite her reason for being there, she'd been taken aback by his good looks and his sweet nature and it didn't matter how many times she told herself that none of that mattered to her quest, it kept interfering with the way she felt about him over and over again.

He'd been treated badly by his father, apparently for most of his life, and yet instead for being bitter and twisted, he demonstrated understanding and compassion. She could tell his father's treatment had hurt him, but he hadn't let it define him and now that he'd been given the opportunity to run Craigdon Enterprises, it was obvious he wanted to put his own stamp on it. In fact, if he wasn't Henry Craigdon's son, he'd be her perfect man. The irony wasn't lost on her.

As they took a break, Nick got up and began mingling with the students. His easy laughter rang out over their excited chatter. He was as comfortable with them as he was with the rich guests at a family celebration. As good and kind and non-judgemental as he was with the patrons of Jennifer's Kitchen.

The flurry of emotions he instilled in her were both uplifting and confusing. She liked him so much, way too much. But he was the son of her sworn enemy. There were lines that couldn't be crossed, no matter how much she might want to. Not unless she was willing to turn her back on the promise she'd made to her mother.

Oh, Mom. I wish you were here so you could give me some advice! What would you do if you were in my shoes? On one hand, I'm finally in a position to get my revenge. The same revenge that has kept me focused all these years. On the other hand, there's a man who is beautiful inside and out. A man who cares about me. A man I could love...

It was a quandary and one she didn't have any answers for. All she could do was go with the flow and see what developed. In the meantime, she'd definitely contact Christopher and make sure she was out. There would be no more stolen secrets or money changing hands. And that was that.

Chapter Fifteen

Nick wasn't surprised by how much he enjoyed himself seated at the back of Harper's class. Time he spent in her company was always good. He liked the professional, efficient way she conducted herself in the office, but he also liked this Harper: caring, light-hearted and relaxed. If he hadn't already made his mind up, after the session, he would definitely have been on board with the financial support required to keep the youth club running.

As the class came to an end and the students began to disperse, Harper came toward him. The smile she wore turned his heart upside down with nerves and an overwhelming desire. It was a bit scary how hard and fast he'd fallen for her.

"So, what did you think?" she asked.

"You were great," he replied truthfully. "I can see why they keep coming back. They're treated fairly and with respect and everyone has a good time. On top of that, you're teaching them skills that will stand them in good stead for the rest of their lives. It's a win for everyone."

She blushed under his praise and remained silent. Her humility further endeared her to him. It was obvious she didn't volunteer her time there for the accolades or the recognition. She genuinely cared about the kids who came through the doors.

"Let me introduce you to Marty," she said. "He's going to be thrilled when I tell him about your willingness to support us." She frowned momentarily. "You're still willing to come on board, aren't you?"

"Of course. It would be an honor to have the Craigdon name associated with the club."

Once again, she beamed at him and his insides turned to mush.

Oh, I'm a gonner, for sure… Let's hope she learns to love me the same way…

He scowled. Just because his father rejected him didn't mean he was unlovable. She just had to get to know him better, get over the complications that were holding her back and let herself fall in love. It was as simple as that.

After helping her pack up the containers of supplies and stowing them away in the cupboard, he followed Harper to where the elderly man he'd spied earlier near the boxing ring was packing away the gloves.

"Marty, I'd like you to meet a friend of mine." Harper gave him a quick glance. "This is Nicholas Craigdon."

Marty held out his hand toward him and Nick gave it a firm shake. "It's nice to meet you, Marty. You're doing great things here for those kids."

Marty ducked his head and muttered something unintelligible.

Another modest person, just doing all this for the kids…

Harper shot him another glance and this time she accompanied it with a grin. "I brought Nicholas along tonight because he wanted to see for himself what we did here and why it's a great idea that he come on board as our major sponsor."

It took Marty a few moments to comprehend what Harper had said. And then his eyes widened in shock. He turned to Nick, his mouth gaping.

"Sponsor? You're going to be our sponsor?" Tears glittered in the old man's eyes.

This time it was Nick who felt the urge to duck his head. "Yes, sir. If you'll have me."

"Have you? Good, Lord! You're going to save us from closing!" And then Marty threw his arms around Nick and hugged him.

Choked up with emotion, Nick could barely murmur a word, but it seemed words weren't necessary. Harper moved closer and hugged him, too. The feel of her soft breasts crushed against his chest filled him with instant desire.

Harper smiled softly and spoke to Marty. "Nick's company's prepared to supply us with everything we need, including cash to cover the rent and utilities. Isn't that great?"

"I can't believe it!" the old man said, his voice husky with emotion.

"He's our guardian angel, isn't he, Marty?" Harper said. She looked back at Nick with such gratitude and love he felt the burn of tears prick his eyes. He laughed a little awkwardly to cover his emotion.

"I don't know about that. What I can say is, I'm impressed with what you do here, Marty. You and Harper and the rest of the volunteers. I was fortunate to grow up in a wealthy family, but I was well aware there were plenty of kids who didn't. If I can help even a few of them live a better life, then I'm all for it."

"God bless you, Nicholas Craigdon," Marty rasped, his eyes once again tearing up.

When everything had been packed away and the floor swept and the lights switched off, Marty locked the door behind them and bid them a good night. Nick walked with Harper to his car. He opened the door for her and waited for her to climb in before closing it behind her. Then he went around to the driver's side.

"This is a nice car," she commented, running her hand over the wood paneling and leather seats. "Why didn't you drive it to Brisbane that time?"

He chuckled as he started the ignition. "Because then I wouldn't have been able to drive the Porsche."

She smiled and shook her head. As he pulled out into the traffic, a comfortable silence fell between them.

"You were great tonight," he said softly. "Those girls look at you like you're their hero."

She laughed self-deprecatingly. "I don't know about that."

The emotions he'd been battling all night welled up in his chest. He stared at her, his gaze intense. "I do."

She held his gaze and her eyes flared wide at something she saw in his eyes. His gut clenched with an answering need.

"Harper…"

Her mouth opened on a silent intake of breath. She nodded once. It was all the encouragement he needed. Hoping he'd read her signals correctly, he pulled over to the curb. With only the slightest hesitation, he took her in his arms.

To his relief, she met him halfway and molded herself to his body. Though it was awkward with the gearstick between them, somehow they made it work. His lips moved over hers, kissing and tasting and searching. She kissed him back with just as much passion and then she opened her mouth. His tongue slipped inside and he tasted her sweetness, deepening the kiss until they were both breathless. When at last they pulled apart, they were panting.

His body burned with a desire so hot he thought he might combust. His cock was hard, almost painfully so, but he wasn't going to rush her. He didn't know how experienced she was, but whether she was or wasn't didn't matter. This was about him and Harper and he was going to make sure it was perfect.

Slowly, he took her hand and pressed it against his erection. "I want to make love to you," he rasped.

From the light of a nearby streetlamp, he saw her eyes widen. Surprise and desire warred in their depths and then she tightened her hand around his cock.

"I want to make love to you, too."

As if he couldn't get any harder, another surge of blood rushed to his groin. He groaned. "You don't know how long I've waited for you to say that," he said.

Her answering smile held a little uncertainty. He frowned. There was no way he was going through with this if she wasn't on board all the way.

"Harper? What is it?"

She compressed her lips and then stared down at her lap. Her fingers released his cock. "The thing is… I've never done this before."

Her words came out in an embarrassed rush, but he barely noticed. His heart filled with joy and relief.

"That's good. Because I haven't done this either."

She stared at him in disbelief. "You haven't?"

He shook his head. Ordinarily, he'd be embarrassed to admit his lack of experience, but with Harper it was different. He was glad she was going to be his first and he was even more pleased he'd be hers.

We're made for each other, Harper. Don't you see? Now all I have to do is get you to love me…

He pushed the thought aside and concentrated on the present. Harper was there right beside him and wanted him as much as he wanted her. For now, it was enough.

"My place is closer. Is it all right if we head over there?" he asked.

She nodded and scooted a bit closer. Shyly, she reached for his hand. With their fingers entwined, Nick negotiated the traffic and before long, pulled up outside his apartment. He tried to remember if he'd left dirty dishes in the sink or whether he'd picked up the clothes that were usually scattered around the bathroom. And then he let those worries slide. Hopefully he'd keep Harper so engrossed with his loving, she wouldn't even notice.

Though his heart raced, he managed to remain outwardly calm. He took her hand and led her up the short flight of steps to his first floor apartment. She followed him through the door and dropped her handbag on the kitchen counter. A quick glance assured him he'd indeed cleaned up the kitchen after his last meal.

And then she stepped into his arms as if it were the most natural thing in the world. He forgot all about dirty dishes and scattered clothing and drew her up against him. Their lips met in a fiery kiss, filled with pent-up passion. Her arms crept up around his neck and his hands cradled her ass. He pressed her against his raging cock and the feel of her was like nothing he'd ever experienced. Even the time he'd engaged in heavy petting with Katrina all those years ago, couldn't compare with this.

The difference was, because he was in love with Harper Wyburn. She wasn't just a woman he was attracted to. She wasn't just someone he wanted for the night. He'd fallen in love with her and he wanted her by his side for all time.

The strength of his feelings were hard to fathom and no doubt his siblings would question their legitimacy. He could almost hear their responses.

It's just sex, Nick… It's because you've never had a woman… It's lust, Nick. Pure and simple. Don't confuse lust with love…

But he wasn't having any of that. So, he was a virgin. He'd never known what it was like to make love to a woman all the way. But what he felt for Harper went way beyond any of that. He loved her, yes. But he also wanted to cherish her, to protect her, to make her laugh. He wanted to share his life with her.

Of course, it was way too soon to tell her any of that. He didn't want to scare her off. Right now, all that was important was that they love each other in the most intimate way there was. With that thought in mind, he lifted her slight form in his arms and strode down the hallway toward his bedroom. She curled up against him with her arms around his neck, pressing sweet kisses along his jawbone.

Rock-hard and aching, he lowered her gently to the mattress, glad that he'd taken the time to make his bed before leaving for work that morning. Not that Harper appeared to notice. He leaned over and switched on the bedside light and saw that she looked at him with eyes that were wide with wonder and anticipation. It was enough to send a nervous burst of adrenaline through his veins.

Please, don't let me disgrace myself. Please, let it be good for her...

With a determined effort, he pushed aside the negative thoughts and focused on doing all he could to make it an amazing experience for both of them. Lying on his side, he slowly ran his finger over her chest, circling one of her breasts. He eased the buttons from her blouse, one at a time, until they were all undone. Then he spread her blouse wide and stared at her breasts.

She wore a plain white bra. Unable to help himself, he reached out and cupped her breast in his hand and squeezed it. Her mouth parted on an intake of breath. His hand moved lower and he went to work on the button and zipper of her skirt. Then, after sliding it slowly down her hips, he tossed the skirt over his shoulder and stared down at her in wonder.

"You're so beautiful." His voice was hoarse with desire.

She made a move as if to cover herself, but he stopped her. "Don't. Please. Let me look at you."

She continued to look embarrassed, but he quickly put her at ease by climbing off the bed and tugging off his clothes. Within moments he stood before her naked, letting her look her fill. Her gaze started at his shoulders and slowly made its way down. Across his chest, his stomach, before pausing at his cock that stood thick and proud.

And then he couldn't stand it any longer. He had to touch her. He climbed back on the bed. She sat up on her haunches and reached around and unclasped her bra. Her breasts sprang free, snatching his breath. He reached out and flicked his fingertips over one of her nipples. She gasped.

Following her down onto the mattress, his hand moved between them, across her taut stomach and lower. His fingers slid beneath her cotton panties and found her most sensitive flesh. He stroked the silky, wet folds. She made little murmurs of desire and moved against his hand. Even better, she encouraged him with her words.

"Oh, Nicholas. That feels so good. Oh, God. That feels amazing."

He stroked her until he could stand it no longer. His cock was throbbing and hot. Kissing his way back up her body, he reached over and pulled out a condom from the box in his bedside drawer. He wasn't sure why he even had the box. He'd had no sure plans to use them. But now that Harper was here, in his bed, he was glad they were there.

A little awkwardly, he sheathed himself and then returned to her side. She reached for him and pulled him down on top of her, sighing with pleasure as he settled his weight upon her. Once again, he kissed her.

With lips fused together and tongues entwined, they drove each other wild. When he was almost at the brink of no return, he slid down her body and positioned himself between her legs. She stared up at him with such desire, it was almost his undoing. Slowly, carefully, he eased himself inside her.

She was so warm, so wet, so tight. It was like nothing he'd ever imagined. He pushed a little harder and met resistance. She tensed beneath him.

"I'm sorry," he gasped. "I don't want to hurt you."

"It's fine," Harper assured him. "Don't stop."

She clung to his shoulders, urging him on. He flexed his

hips forward. All of a sudden, the resistance gave way and he slid all the way into her warmth. Both of them gasped simultaneously.

And then he began slowly moving. Harper's eyes closed. She moved in rhythm beneath him. The pressure inside him was building and it appeared she was just as affected. Her grip on him tightened and her fingernails dug into his back. She urged him on with little whimpers and then she cried out.

He opened his eyes and watched the wonder explode across her face. It was enough to send him toppling over the edge, falling, falling into the most wonderful abyss. He stared down at her in disbelief. She looked up at him, a satisfied smile on her face.

"That was amazing," she murmured.

Nick had never felt so good, or so powerful. He'd done it. He'd made love with Harper and he was pretty sure it was as good for her as it had been for him.

Moving onto his side, he drew her close and whispered against the softness of her hair. "I love you."

Chapter Sixteen

Harper was back at work the next day trying her best to keep focused on the pile of draft letters Nick had left on her desk that needed amendments. He was already ensconced in his office when she arrived and she had yet to set eyes on him. The thought of seeing him again after the way they'd parted late the night before, filled her with nerves.

She'd managed to get through the first five letters, but it was slow going. Her thoughts kept returning to the night before and the wonder of making love for the first time. Though she had nothing to compare it to, she could only guess that it didn't always feel like that. She suspected it had everything to do with Nick. He'd made it so incredible for both of them. Even more special was the fact it was the first time for him, too.

Knowing there had been no one before her had helped to ease her nerves. He was as new and inexperienced as she was. Both of them acted on instinct and a desire so powerful it had blown her away. But then he'd told her he loved her and her world had come crashing down…

Even now, she was wracked with guilt. From the moment Nick uttered those fateful words, they sat heavy against her chest. She hadn't responded. She hadn't been capable of saying anything at all. Nick's expression had gone from one of peace and fulfilment to a quiet hurt, and she was the one responsible.

She ought to be thrilled Nicholas Craigdon was in love with her. He was a beautiful man, inside and out. She couldn't ask for someone better. But he was the son of her sworn enemy. She'd vowed to bring him down. If he ever found out what she'd been up to, he'd never speak to her again. It was no basis for a relationship. Too bad she hadn't thought of that before she slept with him.

Still, she refused to regret what had happened between them. No matter how the future turned out, she'd always have that single magical night to remember. Something to look back on during the cold, lonely nights that stretched out before her, like the vastness of the desert. *If only…*

The phone in her handbag rang, interrupting her depressing thoughts. She reached down beneath her desk and brought the phone up where she could see the screen.

No caller ID.

Someone who had her number, didn't want her to recognize them ahead of answering. She deliberated a moment before pressing TALK, but finally did.

"Harper Wyburn."

"Dear Harper. How good of you to take my call."

The irritating tones of Christopher Barrington filled her ear. Her stomach somersaulted with dread. She hadn't yet found the courage or the opportunity to tell him she was through with selling him information. Now she had no choice.

"It was so unexpected running into you at the baptism. I didn't realize you and my half-brother were so close."

The man's snide tone grated on Harper's ear. Still, she knew how difficult Christopher could make things between her and Nick if he breathed a word about what she'd done. With gritted teeth, she lied.

"We're friends. That's all."

"Huh! It didn't look that way to me. In fact, the two of you looked very cozy. *Way* more than friends."

Harper bit her lip. She didn't know what Christopher had seen, but it was obvious he wasn't buying her friends routine. She decided her best move was to go on the attack.

"If you have nothing important to say, I'm going to hang up. I have plenty of work awaiting my attention."

"*Tut, tut, tut.* No need to get all snooty." And then his tone changed. "I want more information," he demanded.

"I'm sorry. That's not going to happen."

"I don't expect it this minute, but as soon as you get your hands on something of value, you let me know. The information you've supplied previously was gold. Exactly what I'm talking about. Why do you think I've been so willing to pay you so well?"

"I'm sorry, Christopher. You misunderstood. There will be no more information. Period. I'm done."

"You're done when I say you are," came the cold reply. "I'm in control here, and don't you forget it. I want that information. Don't make me do something I might regret."

Harper felt a frisson of fear. She'd always known it was reckless not to ascertain the motivation behind Christopher's eagerness to be part of her plan, but she'd never guessed it might be dangerous.

Surely he won't actually hurt me? No, of course he won't. It's all talk. He's just trying to frighten me into giving him what he wants…

"Meet me at The Venue," Christopher demanded. "We'll talk some more. I'll be there at one. Don't be late."

Harper frowned at the mention of Nick's favorite café, but then shrugged it off as coincidence. It was the café closest to the Craigdon offices. Probably the reason Nick favored it so much. It was also within walking distance of McClintock Properties.

Giving Christopher a single word of assent, Harper hurriedly ended the call and dropped her phone into her handbag. For the rest of the morning, she was on tenterhooks every time the phone rang. At one stage, Nick came out of his office and dropped some files on her desk. She nearly jumped out of her skin.

He frowned. "I'm sorry. I didn't mean to startle you."

"I-it's okay," she stammered. "I was…thinking about something else. I didn't realize you were there."

"Are you all right?" he asked, concern flooding his face.

She managed a tight smile. "Of course."

He continued to regard her uncertainly. By tacit agreement, they left the issue of last night alone. Eventually Nick nodded. "Well, if you're sure. I just gave you some files on the latest projects we're tendering on. Have a look over them and let me know what you think. Let's hope we have better luck with these than I've had with the last few."

"Of course. When do you need them?"

"As soon as you can get them to me. Is that all right?"

"Sure. But I need to go out during my lunchbreak. Is that okay?"

"Of course. I'm going to order in a sandwich and have it at my desk. I'll listen out for the phones." With that, he headed back to his office.

As much as Harper knew at some point they had to discuss what happened between them, in particular Nick's declaration of love, she was glad they weren't going to do it right now. The office wasn't the place for that kind of discussion.

She tried to concentrate on her work. The hands of the clock on the wall in front of her seemed to move with excruciating slowness, but eventually the time she'd agreed to meet Christopher arrived. A few minutes before one, she got up and went to the bathroom and refreshed her makeup. She smoothed out the wrinkles in her suit. She didn't care what

Christopher thought of her, but if she was going to war, she was going to show up looking her best.

Leaving the bathroom, she avoided passing by Nick's office and headed toward the lifts. She hoped he didn't change his mind about ordering in a sandwich. The last thing she needed was to run into him at the same café where she'd agreed to meet his half-brother.

Christopher was already seated when she arrived. A mug of coffee sat in front of him. He asked her if she wanted anything, but she declined. With her stomach churning the way it was, there was no way she could order anything.

Christopher gave her a slimy, insincere smile. It reminded her of a snake's.

"Thank you for meeting me," he said with false courtesy.

"I wasn't aware you'd given me a choice," she replied.

"*Tut, tut*, Harper. We all have choices. Some more than others, but no one's without options. For example, you were the one who chose to steal secrets from your employer and sell them to the highest bidder. It was just lucky I came along. If it hadn't been for you, I would never have known anything about those Craigdon bids. Thanks to you, *my* boss is extremely happy. He's thrilled to have beaten Craigdon to so many lucrative contracts. He's even given me my own office. Can you believe that?" He smirked.

Harper gritted her teeth. She had no one to blame but herself for being in this predicament and she had no need of the reminder. She might have initiated all of it, but she was done with playing Christopher's games. Even more so now, with Nick's declaration of love still fresh in her mind. Determination straightened her spine.

She leaned forward and narrowed her eyes at the man seated across from her. "Congratulations on the office. Enjoy it while you can. You'll get no more information from me. I've given you all you're going to get. This ends now. Got it?"

To her annoyance, he merely laughed. "Oh, Harper! You're such an innocent! A babe in the woods!" A second later his pleasant demeanor evaporated and he stared at her with such contempt, a shiver ran down her spine.

"I've told you before. This ends when I say it does. You'll continue to give me information and I'll continue to deposit very generous sums of money into your account. We both win. What's not to like?"

"I've provided you with enough. Craigdon Enterprises has taken a decent hit."

Christopher's answering bark of laughter was completely devoid of humor. "A decent hit? You think a few hundred million dollars can hurt a company like that? You're more naïve than I guessed. Either that, or you're stupid."

She tensed with shock and anger. Her resolve hardened into steel. "You've underestimated me, Christopher. The only stupid decision I made was to involve you in my plan. Now, get this through your thick head. We're done. Finished. Over. You can't get access to that information without me and as of now, I'm out."

She thought of Nick's affordable accommodation plan which was now in jeopardy and prayed she hadn't called a halt too late. She hoped it were true, that Craigdon Enterprises could survive the direct hit to its bottom line. A hit that would never have happened if not for her desire for revenge.

All of a sudden, the enormity of what she'd done hit her. Her shoulders slumped in defeat. The cost of avenging her mother had become too high.

I'm so sorry, Mom. I can't do it. I thought I could, but I can't. Please forgive me…

Christopher leaned across the table. As if sensing her weakness, his eyes gleamed with malice. She shivered in fear and glanced around the café to reassure herself they weren't alone.

"You think you're so clever," he snarled. "You're nothing! What do you think your precious Nicholas will think when he discovers you're the one who's been selling him out? Don't you know how low his self-esteem is? He was Henry Craigdon's son and yet he was treated no better than the lowliest of the staff. I should know. The old prick treated me even worse. At least he didn't try and sleep with my girlfriends. That would have really screwed with my head, just like it screwed with Nick's."

Harper stared at him in shock. "What are you talking about?"

Christopher's answering chuckle held no sign of amusement. "Good old Henry! Always needing to prove himself the stud. He had so many women, everyone lost count. But apparently that wasn't enough. He used to proposition Nick's girlfriends. The ones he brought home. Not that there were many. I don't blame Nick for keeping them away from that man. He was grotesque!"

Harper continued to stare at Christopher, her mouth gaping in shock. Surely even Henry couldn't have been as depraved as that.

She threw Christopher a challenging look. "I don't believe you."

Christopher merely shrugged, unperturbed. "I couldn't care less if you believe me, but I tell you, I came across them myself. Nick and his girl were making out in the cabana. Henry discovered them there and suggested the girl might get more satisfaction from a real man. You can imagine what that did to Nick."

Harper stared at Christopher in disbelief. She could picture Nick, devastated and humiliated by his own father. It filled her with digust. No wonder he lacked confidence around women! And yet, last night had been so wonderful, more than she could have ever dreamed...

She thought of Henry and fury ignited in her veins. She wished she'd done him some violence when she'd had the opportunity. Now it was too late.

"Is that why you're so keen to break the Craigdons? Even though they're family?"

Anger flashed in Christopher's eyes. "They're no family of mine! I'm his oldest child and yet Henry left me nothing in his will. *Nothing*! Craigdon Enterprises should have been mine! Now I'm stuck taking crumbs from the competition. How do you think that makes me feel? That my own father didn't think I was worthy of his love, of his consideration? I tell you what, it eats you up inside. Just like it's been eating Nick up."

His breath came fast, but he wasn't finished. "The two of us are a lot alike. We were both treated as pariahs by our father. Nick came off slightly better than me, but not by much. And now he's going to discover the girl he trusted, maybe even gave his heart to, has betrayed him. She smiled at him and wiggled her ass and pretended to like him, while all the time she's been selling him out for thirty pieces of silver. How do you think he's going to feel, Harper?"

Harper felt sick. Any minute she might vomit, right there at the table. Unwittingly, she'd played a part in a much bigger plan. She'd acted for noble reasons, but now it looked like an innocent man's life would be destroyed, along with the company he loved. She looked at Christopher, at the hurt and the hate etched into his face, and felt a chill down her spine.

What in God's name have I done?

Chapter Seventeen

Nick looked at his half-eaten sandwich. Though he'd ordered it in from his favorite café where the food was usually tasty and fresh, it wasn't doing it for him that afternoon. He guessed his discontent had something to do with the fact Harper had gone out for lunch.

Usually she sat at her desk, like he did, and ate a sandwich. Occasionally one of them would go downstairs and bring back coffee for both of them. More often than not, they dined alone. After what they'd shared the night before, he was hurt she hadn't wanted to have lunch with him. Now he couldn't help but wonder if she were meeting someone.

Of course, there was always the possibility she was avoiding him. Though he didn't regret telling her he loved her, a big part of him had hoped she'd say it back. He'd known she wasn't at the same stage in their relationship as he was. She'd told him things were complicated. It was just, after making love together, he'd hoped she might have changed her mind.

Now she'd gone out for lunch. Of course, she was allowed to take her lunchbreak wherever she pleased and if that included having lunch with a friend that was fine, too. It was none of his business who she had lunch with. Only, he *wanted* it to be his business.

He wanted to have the right to ask her. Or even better, have her want to offer him the information. That's what real couples did. They called each other, talked about their day and shared their plans, even if it were only where and with whom they were going to lunch.

But that was the problem. He and Harper weren't a real couple. They might have been as intimate as two people could be, but it seemed, for her at least, nothing else had changed. He wasn't exactly experienced in the ways of relationships, but he was pretty sure both parties shared way more than he and Harper had after what they'd done. There was no way she'd faked enjoyment over their lovemaking.

Or had she? How would he know? Women had been faking orgasms since time began. He hated that his confidence around women had taken such a battering that now he wasn't sure if Harper had faked her level of gratification, too.

Thanks, Dad. You really did a number on me. It's a wonder I have the confidence to approach a woman at all...

And then he cursed aloud and damned his father to hell. It was time he put all the bad shit behind him and look forward to a future he carved out himself. No longer did he have to pander to his father, to hang around and wait for the smallest scrap of praise. He could make his own decisions, choose his own destiny. Starting with Harper.

He'd go out and look for her. No doubt he'd find her at The Venue. It was the nearest café to work and the place where most of the Craigdon employees chose to eat. If he didn't find her there, he'd come back to the office and wait. She'd be back within the hour, after all. Not so long in the scheme of things. Especially for what he had in mind.

He wanted to bring everything out in the open, lay himself bare again and ask her to do the same. He wanted a commitment from her. At least an acknowledgement that they were a couple. He understood her reticence about making their relationship public in the office, but it was time to make a declaration. They couldn't share what they had last night and then continue on as if nothing had changed. His world had been turned upside down by her loving. He wanted to make sure she felt the same and even though he wouldn't rush her, he needed to know the end goal was the same for both of them, regardless of how long it might take for her to get there.

Shrugging into his jacket, he stepped out of his office. He looked across at Harper's desk. It remained unoccupied.

She's still out…

Increasing the length of his stride, he headed toward the lifts. A sense of urgency flooded through him. Now that he'd made up his mind to talk all this out with her, he wanted to get it over with as soon as he could.

Let's hope she feels the same way…

Reaching the bank of lifts, he pressed the DOWN button and waited impatiently for the lift to arrive. All the time, his thoughts were consumed by Harper and how she'd react when he summoned his courage, took a leap of faith and offered her his heart forever.

Christopher sat across from Harper and gloated. He had her exactly where he wanted her and it was all her fault. She was the one who'd come to him with her plan to steal Craigdon secrets. He'd merely provided her an outlet and she'd been well compensated along the way. It had been a terrific plan to thwart the Craigdons and he hadn't even come up with it himself. Harper suddenly pushed away from the table and stood.

Christopher smirked. "Where are you going?"

"I have to get back to work."

"So industrious, Harper. Your commitment to Craigdon Enterprises is admirable."

She didn't respond to his needling. Instead, she turned and headed for the door. Quickly, he pulled some money from his wallet and tossed it down on the table before following her out. She was already ten yards down the footpath before he caught up with her. He reached for her arm and spun her around.

She gasped. Anger mixed with fear flashed in her eyes. "Let go of me!"

Good. I'm glad she's scared. She ought to be scared. If there's one thing I inherited from my father it's his ruthlessness…

Christopher narrowed his eyes menacingly. "Don't forget, we have a deal. You need to deliver or you're toast! Do you understand?"

She stared back at him defiantly. He secretly admired her courage, no matter how misplaced.

"You're the one who doesn't understand," she spat. "Haven't you been listening? I already told you. We're finished."

Christopher opened his mouth to refute her statement and then looked across the road and saw Nick waiting to cross at the lights. A swift stab of pure glee went through him. He couldn't have timed it more perfectly. Ignoring Harper's angry gasp, he pulled her into his arms. With his head so close to hers his lips brushed her ear, he spoke.

"Remember what I said. If you let me down, I'll destroy you. Mark my words." With that, he released her. He was sure his glee-filled chuckle followed her all the way down the street.

From his vantage point across the other side of the road, Nick spied Harper and Christopher together and froze. His mind refused to accept what he was seeing.

What the hell? What's Harper doing in the arms of my half-brother? No, I must be mistaken…

But when Christopher lifted his head and released her, there was no mistaking the woman who a few seconds earlier had been in his arms. Without a word, she hurried away down the street.

Shock and rage like Nick had never known poured through his veins. What was she doing with Christopher? Harper was his! *No! No! No!* And then his half-brother turned and looked him squarely in the face and gave him a mocking salute.

Incensed, and heedless of the traffic, Nick charged across the road, dodging cars and a barrage of horns as he made his way to Christopher. On the verge of losing control, he raced angrily up to his half-brother and grabbed him by the shirt front, almost lifting him off the ground.

"What the hell is wrong with you? Why were you with Harper?" he cried.

Infuriating Nick even further, Christopher merely smiled. "*Tut, tut,* Nicholas. No need to be so touchy. I didn't know she meant so much to you."

"Of course you did!" Nick shouted. "You just can't help yourself. You want to destroy any Craigdon who crosses your path. I heard what you did to Grace. You nearly tore her and Callum apart. And Joel and Sheridan. You did your best to come between them, too. You stuck your nose into Isabella's business. Now it's my turn. Get over it, Christopher! I'm sick of it!" he roared.

"My family's been nothing but kind to you, but it's never enough. We can't undo the past. We can't undo the things done by our father. He was mean and nasty and sometimes he was downright despicable. You won't get any argument from me. But what he did and how he ran his life has nothing to do with the rest of us and it sure as hell has nothing to do with me! Stay out of my way and keep your fucking hands off my woman!" With that, he gave his half-brother a mighty shove.

Christopher stumbled, but quickly regained his balance. Nick's breath came fast. He was so angry, he felt like he might combust. In contrast, Christopher appeared entirely unruffled by Nick's outburst. His half-brother took the time to straighten his clothing and looked at Nick in such a condescending way, it set Nick's teeth on edge.

"You're right to want to hold on to her, that's for sure," Christopher said in a conversational tone. "She sure is one hot pussy. And boy, does she know how to suck cock."

Nick stared at his half-brother, aghast. In that moment, he'd never hated anyone like he hated Christopher. A red haze filled his vision. Filled with bloodlust, he charged toward the man.

With his head down, he took Christopher in the belly. The two of them went down. They hit the pavement hard. Fists flew. Nick felt a burst of satisfaction as his fist connected with Christopher's cheek, splitting it open. And then Christopher got a good hit in against Nick's ribs and he grunted in pain.

Eventually, they both ran out of steam as the pain began to set in. Christopher got to his feet and throwing Nick a final look of disdain, he took off. Breathing hard, Nick stared after him, hurting and feeling desolate. He didn't want to believe a word Christopher said about Harper, but he'd just seen the two of them together. They'd been standing close. Way too close for two people who hardly knew each other.

Then he remembered all he knew about his half-brother. Nicholas understood better than anyone how difficult it was to grow up feeling his father's constant disapproval. Christopher had been treated even worse than he had. It had left his half-brother with a chip on his shoulder the size of a fifty-story building. Christopher had gone through life doing his best to make things difficult, to cause trouble wherever he could.

Was that all this was? Christopher trying to cause trouble? He knows how much I like Harper. What better way to hurt me than to get me to believe he's been with her? Last night, it had been obvious she was a virgin, but what if she's done other things, things with Christopher?

Then he thought about Harper. She'd done nothing to break his trust. She'd been open and upfront and honest. She'd told him she was a virgin. At the time, she hadn't known he was, too. It had taken her courage to admit her inexperience. She'd also laid bare the sad circumstances of her childhood. She didn't even know her father. Then her mother had died when she was seventeen. She'd been forced to fend for herself. Okay, so she hadn't given him all the details, but he was sure she would one day, when the time was right.

No, he needed to give Harper the benefit of the doubt before he passed judgement. He'd ask her if she'd seen Christopher since the party. If she lied, then he'd know something was amiss. If she told him the truth, then all would be well and he could tell her again how much he loved her and how he was willing to wait for her, for as long as it took.

Harper headed straight for the bathroom as soon as she returned to the office. She was still shaking with anger and her mind was in a tailspin. Now she knew just how personal Christopher's vendetta was against Nick and Craigdon Enterprises, there was no way she could continue with her plan. Christopher Barrington was dangerous. Although she didn't know him well, she was horribly afraid he was a man who didn't make idle threats.

Oh, God. What am I going to do?

Thankfully, the bathroom was empty when she got there. Setting her handbag on the counter, she bent over the sink and splashed water over her face. Her cheeks were pale and her eyes were wide. Her hands were still trembling from the run-in. Every time she thought about the threat Christopher had made, fresh fear flooded her veins.

One thing was certain: If Nick found out, he'd never forgive her. Nick who was genuine and decent and kind.

Nick who wanted to help people like her, vulnerable people, disadvantaged people, people who'd been homeless. And she'd betrayed him.

Christopher had threatened to destroy her. And he could. She was just an EA with little power and apart from the tidy sum she'd collected for the information—money that was now tainted—she was dependent on her job. She could even go to jail for selling company secrets!

Oh, God! Oh, God! Oh, God!

Her head ached from the relentless mantra that beat a tattoo inside her brain. She pressed her fingers against her temples in an effort to ease the pain. She needed to calm down. She needed to think. She also needed to return to her desk. It was long past her lunch hour. Nick would be wondering where she was. She had to pull herself together.

With a determined effort, she opened her handbag and refreshed her makeup, pleased to see the trembling in her hands had eased. She loosened her bun and ran a brush through her hair and then secured it once again on the back of her neck with pins. Satisfied she'd pass casual inspection, she left.

She noted Nick's office was empty as she passed by it on her way to her desk. He must have stepped out. Good. It gave her time to collect herself and get focused on her work. With that thought in mind, she tucked her handbag beneath her desk and took her seat. Pulling the keyboard toward her, she opened the file she'd been working on right before her lunchbreak.

She glanced at the pile of documents near her elbow. Nick had given her those to look over. Not so long ago, she would have been bursting with excitement at the valuable information they might contain and how much it would be worth to Christopher. Now the very thought of selling Nick out again turned her stomach and intensified the pain in her head. But her decision to quit with the deception didn't solve her problem of what to do about Christopher. If he went through with his threat, any chance she had of finding happiness with Nick would be shot to pieces—and that was the best scenario. She'd be lucky if he didn't press charges.

The *ding* of the lift caught her attention. She looked up in time to see Nick striding down the corridor toward her. Her stomach immediately took a nosedive and nerves swirled around inside her. With her heart pounding, she kept her attention focused squarely on her computer screen, praying Nick wouldn't stop to chat. Unfortunately, her prayers weren't answered.

"How was lunch?" he asked, coming to a halt beside her work station.

She managed a strained smile and kept her gaze on the screen. "It was fine."

"I ended up going out, too. In fact, I ran into Christopher. You remember my half-brother? I introduced you at the baptism."

Harper fought to keep from reacting. It took all of her effort to maintain a calm façade. "Sure," she said as casually as she could manage. "I remember him. He was the one who described himself as your father's bastard."

Nick nodded. "Yeah. My dad had a relationship with his mother before my parents were married. Christopher's mother went on to marry Frank Barrington."

Harper pretended to be interested. "The mining magnate?"

"Yes."

He paused and for a moment she thought he was done. She returned her attention to the screen in front of her and began typing, hoping he'd get the hint. To her consternation, he spoke again.

"So, did you do anything exciting over lunch? Some shopping?"

Harper bit back a groan. She hated that she had to keep lying to him, but she had no choice. Until she worked out a way to get out of this mess, she had to keep her mouth shut and hope Christopher did the same.

She forced another weak smile. "Um, no. Nothing exciting. I just met a…friend for coffee. We…caught up about old times."

Nick frowned. Harper flicked a glance in his direction and was surprised to see anger flash across his face.

What the hell is that all about? Surely he can't be mad I met a friend for coffee on my lunchbreak?

There was a new tightness around his mouth. "So, an old school friend?"

Harper stared at the keyboard. "N-no, not a school friend."

His frown deepened. "An old flame? Someone I should be worried about?" The brusque laugh that followed sounded harsh.

"No, nothing like that," she hurried to reassure him. "He's a friend. No one important."

She felt Nick's hard stare upon her, but didn't elaborate any further.

Please, just go. You need to go. I can't stand it a moment longer. All the lies. So many lies…

This time her pleas were answered. Nick turned abruptly on his heel and strode toward his office. She watched him go and couldn't help but let out a sigh of relief.

This is killing me! How long am I going to have to keep this up?

She didn't know, and that was the worst thing of all.

Chapter Eighteen

Nick shut the door to his office with a decisive click and cursed long and hard. He'd given Harper a chance to come clean and she'd blown it. Even when he gave her the opportunity of telling him she'd been with Christopher. Instead, she lied and made up some story about meeting an old friend. It was bullshit. The only question he needed answered now was *why*.

Why did she lie to me about Christopher? What the hell's going on?

Was it possible she'd known Christopher even before Nick had introduced them? He thought back to their meeting at the baptism. He wished he'd paid more attention to the pair of them at the time. He cursed as his anger and disappointment grew.

It was obvious Harper didn't want him to know she'd met Christopher at the café. It frustrated Nick that he couldn't work out why.

What is she hiding? Why would she be meeting Christopher? What had they talked about?

And then later, he'd seen the intimate contact, where Christopher had taken her in his arms with his head bent close to hers. And then what he'd said to Nick, bragged about, in fact. Anger and pain burned holes in Nick's gut. He wanted to cry out in denial, shout that there was no way Harper had been with his half-brother. Christopher was a lying snake who said whatever he wanted in order to get a reaction. Nick couldn't take his word for anything. And yet there was a part of Nick, that part he thought he'd long buried, that reminded him of his shortcomings and the fact he could never get a woman like Harper. He could almost hear his father's mocking laughter…

With a cry of anguish, Nick threw himself down in his chair. He racked his brain, looking for some connection between Harper and his half-brother. And then he remembered Christopher worked at McClintock Properties. Their rival company. The same company they had recently lost several important contracts to.

He stilled as the possibilities seeped into his brain. *Oh, God. Please, no.* He could hardly bear to think about it. But now that the thought had occurred to him, he couldn't let it go. His mind went into overdrive. It was obvious Harper knew Christopher prior to the baptism. There was no way someone hugged a woman they'd only met once and the fact she wouldn't tell him about it made it even more suspicious.

How did Harper and Christopher know each other?

In a frenzy now, Nick dragged his keyboard toward him and tapped on the keys. He opened the Craigdon HR database and pulled up her details. There was scarce information. Only her name and address and the details of her temp agency. And then he remembered her telling him she'd worked for a property developer before. In the contracts office. With shaking hands, he dialed her agency's number and spoke to the woman on the other end of the phone.

"Hello, it's Nicholas Craigdon from Craigdon Enterprises. I'm looking for some information on one of your temps. Harper Wyburn. She's currently working in my office."

"Yes, Mr Craigdon, What would you like to know?"

"I'm seeking her past employment record. We don't seem to have a copy on file."

"One moment."

He was put on hold and tapped his fingers impatiently on his desk until the woman came back on the phone. It felt like years had passed before the woman spoke again.

"Sorry for keeping you waiting. I've checked Harper's file. She's one of our highly experienced secretaries. A very impressive work history for one so young. She's worked for a number of large companies, including the law firm Davis and Davis, and property developers McClintock's. I'll email you a copy of her full employment history, if you like."

Nick froze, his mind stuck on the word "McClintock's." Harper had been with him more than a month. In that time, despite the fact that relations between McClintock's and Craigdon Enterprises had thawed somewhat since his brother, Joel had begun dating Sheridan McClintock, in recent weeks he'd discovered they'd lost five significant contracts to that very company.

Has Harper been selling us out to the enemy? Does she have loyalties to McClintock's? Have I been duped?

And then an even more devastating thought occurred to him. Christopher worked at McClintock Properties. Harper must have known Christopher from before. Yet, when asked, she'd denied meeting with him.

Is Harper in cahoots with Christopher to destroy Craigdon Enterprises? Has she been playing me all along? Does she even like me at all? Has it all been an act?

The questions came thick and fast, each one with possible answers more devastating than the last. He didn't want to believe it, but the evidence was there for him to see. He cursed aloud and scrubbed his fingers through his hair. He was going crazy. He couldn't think. He needed to get out of there. He needed to talk to someone who might understand; someone who might be able to give him a different perspective.

He thought of Callum. His older brother had always been

the calmest of the Craigdon men. Callum tended to look at things from all perspectives and gave measured advice that could always be relied on. Grabbing his jacket, Nick shrugged it on and stormed out of his office. From the corner of his eye, he saw Harper look up from her desk. He didn't so much as glance in her direction. With his gaze fixed firmly in front of him, he made his escape.

Nick called Callum on his way out of the building. He wasn't surprised to discover his brother was at Jennifer's Kitchen. Heading to his car in the underground parking lot, Nick spun his wheels as he exited the building and headed east of the city. In less than ten minutes, he found a parking space in one of the side streets within walking distance of the kitchen and made his way there on foot. Once again, he entered through the rear door.

The lunch rush was over and the dining hall was empty. Grace stood beside the sink, washing pots and pans. Sophia was also there, loading one of the dishwashers. Both women looked up as he entered.

"What's the matter with you?" Sophia had never been one to mince words.

Grace was more circumspect. "Can I get you a coffee, Nick? It looks like you could use one."

Nick's response was short. "No, thanks. Where's Callum?"

"He's cleaning the bathrooms down the back."

Nick peeled away and strode across the wide expanse of dining room, weaving his way through tables that were now scrubbed clean. Chairs had been tucked neatly under the table, ready for the next meal. He was halfway to his destination when Callum appeared, holding a mop and bucket in his hands.

"Nick."

"Callum."

Just being in his brother's calming presence eased some of the pent-up anger that had been flooding Nick's veins. Callum came toward him. Setting the cleaning tools to one side, he closed the distance between them. He gave Nick a hug.

"What's happened?" Callum asked quietly and drew him back toward the kitchen. Grace and Sophia gathered round. Nick didn't care that they knew. They were family, after all.

With his chest tight with emotion, Nick took a big breath and started from the beginning. He left out the bit about making love, but admitted Harper had stolen his heart. By the time he got to the part about voicing his suspicions that she was working with Christopher against Craigdon Enterprises, Sophia made a sound of outrage and Callum's expression was filled with concern. Grace was the first one to speak.

"What do you know about her?" she asked quietly.

Nick shrugged. "Not much. She came to work for me through a temp agency. I didn't think anything of it. She was competent at her job and easy to get on with. She asked lots of questions and seemed genuinely interested in our work." His lip curled up in disgust. "Now I know why."

To his surprise, it was Sophia who came to Harper's defense.

"Don't jump to wild conclusions, Nick. Everyone deserves a fair hearing. From what I saw at the party, she seemed nice. How do you know this wasn't Christopher acting on his own? He hasn't made a secret of how much he despises the fact Dad handed his company over to someone else."

She paused and then added, "I saw the way you were with Harper at the baptism. You've just admitted how much you like her. I think she likes you a lot, too. I'd hate for things to fall apart between you because you charged in there all worked up and began throwing around accusations. Give Harper the benefit of the doubt. At least talk to her first."

Nick was quick to respond. "I've done that already, Sophia. Harper told me she'd met a friend for lunch. A *friend*.

Not Christopher. She could easily have told me he was the friend she'd met. But she didn't. Why would she lie about that?"

"I think she might have spent some time on the streets," Grace murmured.

Nick rounded on Grace in surprise. "What makes you say that?"

Grace shrugged. "I don't know. Something she said yesterday. It just made me think she was familiar with soup kitchens."

Callum nodded thoughtfully. "I think you're right."

"She told me she was orphaned at seventeen and put herself through school. She said nothing about being homeless," Nick protested.

Callum gave him a measured look. "Where do you think a seventeen-year-old with no parental support lives?"

Nick shrugged, uncomfortable with the line of questioning. He hadn't given any thought to how she'd done it. "I don't know. Maybe she went to live with family."

"Has she ever mentioned any family?" Grace asked.

Nick shook his head. "No. Yes. A sister. But then she admitted she'd made that up. The sister doesn't exist. But that doesn't mean she doesn't have any." Another wave of anger washed over him. "The thing is, she lied to me about Christopher. There's only one reason why she'd do that: to protect her involvement with him. She's been selling us out. It's obvious." He was filled with a sudden surge of determination. He narrowed his gaze. "And I'm going to do whatever I need to in order to prove it."

Nick left the soup kitchen with a full head of steam. He'd gone there hoping his family would convince him he was being ridiculous, that his suspicions had no foundation, but rehashing the whole situation had only cemented in him the certainty that Harper had purposefully deceived him for her own gain.

He was sure she and Christopher had developed a relationship while she was working at McClintock's. Then she'd taken the position at Craigdon, knowing full well the rivalry that existed between them. He didn't know which one of them had come up with the plan to steal Craigdon secrets, but it didn't really matter. The fact was, she was the one who'd had access to the confidential information and she was the one who'd passed that information on to their enemy. The depth of her betrayal filled him with pain.

He pulled into the underground parking area and left his car in his allotted space. Tearing off across the parking lot, he took the lift to the top floor. Striding down the corridor, he stormed past Harper's desk, relieved when he realized it was vacant. He continued on into his office and shut the door behind him. He threw himself into his chair and, with his elbows on his desk, cradled his head in his hands.

Why? Why did she go down this path? Is it all about money? What have I ever done to her that she wants this kind of revenge? Is there something I don't know about? Some deep, dark secret from my past? Or is she just as shallow and opportunistic as she appears?

He could well believe Christopher hatching up a plan to steal confidential information from Craigdon. Christopher had made no bones about the level of his anger at being overlooked in their father's will. If he'd struck up some kind of relationship with Harper, it was conceivable he'd found a way to hit back. And she'd obviously been a willing participant. She'd likely profited from the plan.

His head pounded. The very thought made his heart hurt. He hadn't wanted to fall for her, but he had. Her banter, her kisses, her sass. Her beautiful green eyes. He shut that thought down and focused on the problem. He needed to stop thinking about the pain of her likely betrayal. What he needed to do was to work out the extent of her treachery. He needed to set a trap.

Christopher's cheek throbbed where Nick had got in a lucky punch. He couldn't believe his normally mild-mannered half-brother had found the courage to hit him. And not just once! They'd gone at it like boys scrapping in the schoolyard. It would have been laughable if it didn't hurt so much. It was sure to leave a bruise.

Christopher hadn't realized until that moment how much the little EA meant to Nick. He'd seen them cozying up to each other at the party and that had been surprising enough. He couldn't remember Nick ever bringing a date to a family gathering. Still, to drive his half-brother to violence over a few throw-away comments about the girl was something else. He wondered what Nick would think if he knew his precious little Harper was selling out the company to its competitor. Christopher would love to be there when Nick made *that* discovery.

The problem was, though Christopher had no interest in climbing into Harper Wyburn's pants, he was certainly interested in the information she could provide. He'd earned serious accolades at McClintock's for his insight into the market, managing to snatch five contracts from under the nose of their main competitor. Zane McClintock had given him his own office. Even better, he'd recently been given a raise. Things were looking up for Christopher at McClintock Properties. He might even stay. All he had to do was convince Harper she needed to keep feeding him Craigdon secrets.

What he needed was a little leverage, something to get her to come back around to his way of thinking. She'd only worked at McClintock's for six months, but in that time they'd gotten to know each other reasonably well. She'd started in the typing pool, but her superior administrative skills had soon caught his eye and he'd promoted her to his secretary. He wasn't important enough to have his own EA, but she served just as well. Though they hadn't shared much personal information, he'd gleaned enough about her to know she was on her own and supporting herself. There had been no mention of any family.

It explained why she wore the same old suit every single day and though she tried hard to jazz up her outfit with a variety of blouses, he knew enough about women's fashion to know her clothes weren't expensive. Still, she couldn't have been earning a rip-roaring wage as a temp and she'd already told him she had only herself to rely on.

Her cheap clothes certainly didn't affect the standard of her work, or her eagerness to work harder than anyone else. She was often the last one to leave and was always the first one there each morning. She rarely took her break away from her desk. Instead, he often saw her eating a sandwich and an office-supplied coffee at her desk. There was much he admired about her, including her work ethic and her determination to do well. It was a rare find in one so young.

And then the temp job had come to an end and she'd moved on. He'd missed her in a vague kind of way, but only when he really thought about it. Mostly he missed her competence. He could hand her hours of dictation and she'd have it back on his desk in no time at all and it had barely needed any correction. A competent temp wasn't easy to find. She'd stood out in the crowd.

He'd been surprised and a little taken aback when she'd first approached him about giving him confidential information from Craigdon Enterprises. He hadn't even known that's where she'd ended up until she told him. Then she'd come right out and said she had a proposition for him. He'd asked her what she had against the Craigdons. She'd responded vaguely. When pressed, she told him she wanted to get back at Henry Craigdon.

"Why?" he asked, curious.

"Henry Craigdon was the reason for my mother's untimely death. She died after he evicted us and threw us out on the street. It was the middle of July. We had nowhere else to go. My mother had always suffered in the winter. She had bad asthma. It got worse when the weather turned cold. Living on the streets… Let's just say she didn't last long."

"How long?"

"Three years. She died at age thirty-five."

"Too young."

"You bet. And I lay the blame squarely on Henry Craigdon."

"Fair enough."

"That wasn't all."

"Okay," he said a little warily. Aware of his father's many failings, he didn't know what to expect.

"I tracked down Henry at his office. I lied to get my way in. When I told him about what had happened to my mother, he laughed in my face. Then he suggested we should set aside our differences and get to know one another better. It didn't take a genius to work out what he was referring to."

"You mean, he wanted to sleep with you?" Christopher asked bluntly.

"Yes."

"And did you?"

"What do you think?"

The outrage in Harper's voice appeared genuine. They talked a bit more. Harper then asked if he had an interest in joining forces. That plan had been coming together nicely. Harper had given him some golden information and he'd put it to good use. It was his suggestion that he pay her for her efforts. He was pleased with what he'd received and he wanted to keep receiving it. What better way to do that than with a monetary incentive? Particularly when he guessed money was something she needed. He didn't know any woman trying to get ahead in the world who wore the same suit day after day if she didn't have to.

But now it seemed she'd developed a conscience. Or perhaps she'd fallen for his quiet and humble half-brother. Nick certainly seemed to be taken with her. Whatever. Christopher didn't care why she no longer wanted to provide him with information, just that she did. He'd already been given a raise and an office of his own. A few more of those winning contracts and he might even be made head of his department. He wasn't particularly fond of his job at McClintock's, but he wasn't stupid. A promotion was a promotion.

He was also pleased by the thought of the possibility of bringing his late father's company to its knees, though he'd been careful to conceal that from Harper. She didn't need to know the deep-seated hatred he had for his father and the company that should have been his.

Imagine if the great Craigdon Enterprises is declared bankrupt? How wonderful would that be?

It would mean a blow to the potential windfall that would come his way when he managed to successfully sue the estate, but who really cared about that? His step-father, Frank Barrington, had always been generous with his money, particularly toward his children. Christopher was lucky to be counted as one of them, even though he'd been adopted.

The fact was, Christopher didn't need the money. That was never his motivation for bringing the lawsuit. It was all about seeking vengeance for the disgustingly nasty way his late father had treated him—both in life and in death. And now things threatened to fall apart. He couldn't let that happen.

Pulling out his phone, he typed Harper's name into a search engine. It didn't take him long to find her on Facebook. Though she gave details in her bio about living in the inner city, she didn't list her address. Still, he might be able to work out where she lived from some of her photos. A lot of people didn't put their mind to the kind of information they gave out when they posted pictures. They didn't think about the background. Street names, easily recognizable buildings, other familiar landmarks… They all served to form a picture of the person's location and with a bit of sleuthing, he was certain he could narrow down her place of residence.

Then he had a better idea. He'd call up that girl who worked in HR at McClintock's. He'd been sweet-talking her for the past few weeks. Cozying up to her in the café downstairs where most of the staff went for their daily caffeine fix. Paying her compliments. Giving her attention. It seemed to be working. They'd swapped phone numbers. Only yesterday she'd agreed to go out with him for lunch.

Sally was in her early twenties and was cute enough to capture his interest. She also had a wicked gleam in her eyes every time they flirted. He was intrigued. Up until recently, his *modus operandi* for meeting women had been online, but that had lost its shine. Now he was turning back to the old-fashioned way of doing it. So far it was working. Of course, he fully intended to use her for his own selfish needs, like he'd used plenty of other women. But right now, he needed her for a different service. He only hoped he'd done enough to get her onside.

She answered on the third ring. "Christopher! What can I do for you?"

He liked that she sounded a little breathless, like he'd taken her by surprise. "Sally, I was just sitting all alone at a table in The Venue and I started thinking about you. How about we set a time for that lunch date?"

He heard her excited gasp and could barely contain his smile of satisfaction.

"Any day's good for me, Christopher."

"Great. How about the day after next? Will that work for you?"

"Sounds great."

"Half-past twelve?"

"Perfect."

"Great. Listen, there's just one more thing," he added smoothly. "I had a temp working for me about a month ago. Harper Wyburn. She left a jacket in one of the lockers," he lied. "She wore it nearly every day she was here, so I'm guessing it means a lot to her. I was wondering if you could give me her address so I can get it returned to her."

"Oh, Christopher! That's so sweet."

"Oh, well, just trying to do the right thing. I know I'd appreciate it if someone did something like that for me."

"Absolutely!"

"So, can you give me her address?"

There was a pause and he wondered if he was going to get away with it. But then Sally whispered conspiratorially.

"I really shouldn't. Privacy laws and all that stuff. But it's not like I'm giving it to just anyone. You were her boss."

"Exactly. All I want to do is return her jacket."

"Hang on a minute."

He was put on hold and waited impatiently for Sally to return.

"Okay, here it is."

She gave him an address not far from the soup kitchen where Callum's fiancée worked. Christopher was familiar with the area. It wasn't that long ago he'd paid a visit to Grace Gunning there. Not that he needed to visit Harper's building to bring about his plan. Thanks to modern technology, he could do all that was required online and over the phone.

Plugging the address he'd been given into a database linked to the Land Registry Services, it wasn't long before he knew who owned her apartment. Now it was only a matter of some quick talking and some even quicker negotiating and he'd have Harper Wyburn exactly where he wanted her. At his mercy.

Harper sat at her desk and cast worried glances toward Nick's closed door. He must have returned while she was in the bathroom. She'd watched him storm out a couple of hours earlier and felt sick about that. She wasn't sure what she'd said to upset him, but it was clear she had. Ever since their discussion about her lunch meeting, his attitude toward her had changed.

Oh, God. What if he saw me with Christopher? He told me he'd run into his half-brother and I said nothing. What if he knows I lied?

The possibility had her frozen with dread. She should never have started down this path, despite the promises she'd made to her mother. She should never have gotten into bed with Christopher. She'd known from the outset he couldn't be trusted and she'd teamed up with him anyway. Now she was caught in a web of lies, one she'd contributed to willingly.

She knew if she allowed herself, she could fall in love with Nicholas. He was one of the good guys. He was too important to her for her to keep hurting him and he didn't deserve to pay for his father's sins. It was Henry who'd caused her family's suffering and he was dead. No matter how much it pained her, it was time to let that go…

But how am I going to explain to Nicholas before Christopher tells him?

There was no way she was providing Christopher with any more information, so it was only a matter of time before the man followed through with his threat. And then any hope of a relationship between her and Nicholas would be dashed forever.

She wanted to sob out her denial, but she had no one else to blame. Even worse than the pain that constricted her heart was the thought of Nick's hurt and devastation. Despite being born into a wealthy family, life hadn't always been easy for him. He'd had his fair share of hard knocks, including doing without the love and support of his father. That kind of inexplicable withdrawal of affection that a child should have been able to rely on could have devastating consequences and Nick had told her some of how that had affected him. It had broken her heart to hear him talking about his childhood and now she was about to compound that pain.

He's going to hate me. There's nothing I can say to make him understand. The best thing I can do is leave. Right now. Sneak away like a thief in the night, never to be heard from again.

No!

She didn't want to leave without giving him an explanation. She wasn't the kind of person who wreaked havoc and then snuck off without a word. She'd own up to what she'd done and she'd give Nick the reasons why and she'd hope like hell he believed her. If he didn't, she'd leave with her dignity intact, knowing she'd done all she could. Later, she'd have plenty of time to grieve over the fact it hadn't been enough.

Chapter Nineteen

Nick spent the night tossing and turning, his anger keeping any chance of sleep away. By the time the sun peeked its head over the horizon, he'd come up with a plan. If Harper was providing information to Christopher, there was one way to prove it—he'd feed her false information and see if she passed it on. He thought briefly of discussing the developments with Logan, but then decided not to bother. He'd wait until his suspicions had been confirmed with indisputable evidence and then he'd have the conversation with his cousin.

He'd come into the office early, before anyone else was around. He wanted the chance to prepare false tender documents. They had to look realistic enough that someone might fall for them. They definitely had to pass Christopher's inspection. Harper was new to the property development game, but the same couldn't be said for his half-brother. Christopher had worked in McClintock's contracts division for years. He wouldn't be easily duped.

The false bid was quite a bit lower than a real bid would be, but not too low as to ring alarm bells. No one was going to lose money, but for McClintock's to win the contract, they'd have to take a substantial drop in the profits they could usually anticipate on such a project.

By the time the office staff arrived, Nick was ready. He'd already had three cups of black coffee. His adrenaline was running high. His heartbeat was pounding. He buzzed Harper and asked her to come into his office. She opened the door and his gut clenched. Apart from the faint shadows under her eyes, she looked as composed and beautiful as ever. He watched her closely for some indication of guilt, but all he saw was her usual calm smile.

"Good morning, Nicholas. You asked to see me?" she asked in a bright voice.

It was all he could do not to snarl at her, but if he had any hope of pulling this off, he had to act as normal as possible. With an effort, he held on to his temper.

"Yes. I've prepared a bid for another property out at Badgery's Creek. I need you to type up the paperwork. There are also some contract documents I'd like you to look over and check that they're all in place."

"Do you want me to send them over to legal when I'm finished?"

"No. Bring them back to me." He wanted to give her time to do her dirty work before anyone else became involved. If he sent them to legal too early, he wouldn't be absolutely certain she was the only one with access to the confidential information.

She merely nodded in response and collected the paperwork off his desk. She looked at him briefly and smiled. "I'll have it to you by the end of the day." With that, she left.

He stared after her, aching with hurt and anger. She was so beautiful she made his teeth ache and while she smiled as if she didn't have a care in the world, his heart was breaking into a million pieces. He'd never felt her betrayal more acutely.

Still, he was prepared to give her this one last shot to clear her name. If McClintock's went in so low as to beat his false bid, and he could find out, he'd know for certain she was the culprit. And then they'd be done. He'd call her out for the cheat and liar she was and then make sure she was never hired by any reputable company again. Her professional life would be ruined and she'd only have herself to blame. She'd be lucky if he didn't press charges.

He wished the thought of getting even with her made him feel better, but it didn't. Instead, he felt just as hurt and disappointed and angry as he had the first moment he'd discovered the likelihood she was the traitor behind their failed bids. And here he'd thought she liked him. Really liked him. Was maybe even on the way to falling in love with him.

Ha! What a joke! He was a loser. Why had he thought anything different? No. No one could love Nicholas Craigdon. Not even his father.

Harper escaped back to her desk. The smile she'd fixed in place for Nick's benefit had disappeared as soon as she'd turned her back on him. The nerves that had eaten into her stomach since the day before returned in full force. It was obvious there was something up. Despite the fact he'd been courteous enough, she'd felt the tension emanating off him in waves. That worried her as much now as it had yesterday.

Does he know I lied about meeting Christopher? Is that what this is all about? Is it possible he's even joined the dots and decided I'm behind the company's failed bids?

Her belly took another nosedive at the thought. No, it was her guilty conscience overreacting. There's no way he'd have given her another confidential bid if he thought she was the mole.

Feeling slightly more in control, she started reading through the latest tender documents. The terms and conditions were much the same as all the other paperwork she'd reviewed. On the last page were the quotes for the job. They were significantly lower than the previous ones.

Have they bid so low because they're desperate to secure this contract? Are they struggling that much? Have I caused that much damage?

The knowledge Craigdon Enterprises was hurting financially from her actions filled her with another surge of guilt. Although it had been her intention from the outset to destroy Henry's company, that was before she'd met and fallen in love with Nick. That last bit gave her pause…

Am I in love with him? Really? Yes!

She'd never intended for that to happen, but she couldn't deny it was true. He had all the qualities she'd ever wanted in a man: He was kind, considerate, compassionate; smart, funny and oh so sexy. The fact he'd been Henry Craigdon's son wasn't his fault. She couldn't continue to blame him for what his father had done.

Now she'd probably ruined any chance she'd had for a relationship with Nick and she only had herself to blame. One thing was for certain: She wouldn't be providing Christopher with any more information. It might not be enough to save her relationship with Nick or even help the financial bind Craigdon Enterprises so obviously found itself in, but it was the right thing to do and she was more than at ease with her decision.

With that thought in mind, she scanned the contents of the tender documents and then began typing them up to deliver the revisions to Nick.

Grace Gunning stared out across the tranquil lawns of the Mind, Body and Spirit Wellness Center. The setting sun cast a beautiful array of purples and oranges and reds across the sky. She'd always loved that time of day.

She thought of how far she'd come since she'd first arrived

at the facility five months earlier. Fate had brought Callum Craigdon into her life and she could hardly believe her luck. A beautiful man, inside and out, she still couldn't quite believe he loved her and wanted to spend the rest of his life with her. Better still, he loved her children and was doing everything he could to help her get them back. Getting clean and finishing a six-month stint in rehab was part of the deal. And she was almost at the end. Only a few more weeks to go. Soon, they'd be married. Then they'd return to court and seek full-time custody of her children. She couldn't wait.

Her thoughts filled her with a surge of excitement. She turned away from the window and went to sit beside the man who would soon be her husband. Callum had been unusually quiet during his visit. Now she began to wonder why. For the first time she noticed the seriousness of his expression, the shadows beneath his eyes. A tiny sliver of dread trickled through her veins. Though she tried hard to maintain a positive attitude at all times, sometimes it wasn't possible. Like now.

She touched him gently on the arm. "You're very quiet. Is everything all right?"

Callum sighed. He reached for her hand and twined his fingers through hers. His somber expression didn't change. Another frisson of unease went through her.

"Talk to me, Callum. What's on your mind?"

"It's about Daniel."

She pulled back in shock. Her husband had been dead more than three years. "I... I don't understand."

Callum continued to regard her gravely. "Nicholas was going through some of Dad's papers. He found copies of some letters Dad had sent to your late husband. And letters showcasing Daniel's response."

A fresh wave of shock washed over her. "Letters between Daniel and your father? I didn't even know they knew each other."

"Dad was corresponding with Daniel in his professional role as the urban planner. Daniel was involved in some of Dad's development projects."

"Okay. I guess I can see that. What were the letters about?"

Callum sighed again and put his arm around her shoulders. He drew her close against his side.

"There's no easy way to say this. It seems like my father was buying off your late husband to fast-track Dad's developments. And Daniel seemed to be demanding more money in order to guarantee his continued cooperation."

Grace stared at him in disbelief. "You mean he was *blackmailing* your father?"

Callum shrugged, but she could see the possibility had already occurred to him.

"When did all this take place?" Grace asked.

"I don't know. Apparently there were no dates on any of the correspondence. I guess we could work out the approximate date from when the projects they refer to were lodged with the council, but it would only be a rough guess."

Grace thought of the huge debts Daniel had racked up before he died.

Is that why he was demanding a ransom from Henry Craigdon? So that he could pay back the money he owed?

"Do you think my father had something to do with Daniel's death?"

Callum's question shocked her all over again. "No! How could he? Our trip to the river was spontaneous, something we'd only planned the morning of Daniel's death. Your father couldn't have known about it. But…" Her voice petered off as another thought occurred to her.

"But, what?" Callum probed gently.

Grace blew out her breath on a sigh. "I'm wondering if Daniel was feeling the pressure. We both know your father wasn't a pushover. He had a reputation for being ruthless in business. What if he'd refused to pay more and threatened Daniel in return? What if Daniel's recklessness on the water that day was intentional?"

Callum frowned. "What are you saying?"

"I'm saying, maybe Daniel *wanted* to lose his life, was *hoping* for it. I remember how reckless he was that day. His skylarking seemed to have an additional frenzy to it, like he didn't care if he got hurt. Maybe he *intentionally* got himself tangled up in the rope?"

Callum shook his head. "You can't know that, Grace. We'll never know that. It's probably best not to think about it. No good will come of it because we're never going to have the answers. Presumably the police investigated the suicide angle at the time of Daniel's death?"

Grace nodded. "Yes. I remember them asking me about that, his mental health, whether he owed significant money and questions of that nature. When I asked them why they wanted to know, they told me they had to look at the incident from every angle, including whether or not Daniel had committed suicide."

So they looked into that and ended up ruling Daniel's death an accident?"

"Yes," Grace replied. She sighed again. Callum drew her into his arms and kissed her tenderly.

"I wanted to tell you because I thought you had a right to know," he said. "But whatever happened with Daniel and with my father, it doesn't change anything. I love you as deeply as I ever have and I can't wait to make you my wife."

She cradled his cheek and kissed him again. "Thank you for telling me. I don't want there to be any secrets between us. I love you so much. I feel like the luckiest girl in the world because I'm the woman who gets to marry Callum Craigdon."

Every time the phone rang, Harper jumped. She'd been doing her best to concentrate on her work, but it was a struggle. It had been more than forty-eight hours since her meeting with Christopher. She was on tenterhooks waiting for his call. And she was sure he would.

Previously, she'd provided him with valuable information at least once or twice a week. Likely, he'd be wondering if she was really going to stick to her decision not to give him anything else of use, or if she was all talk. He'd also be wondering how effective his threats had been.

She had to admit, she hadn't taken his threats lightly. She'd spent a restless night and when she finally did fall asleep, her dreams were punctuated with nightmares. She was being pursued down a dark alley by a faceless man. She didn't know who it was or what he wanted, but every time he drew close, the air was filled with menace. She woke from the nightmare breathing hard and lathered in sweat.

The phone in her handbag began to chime. With her heart in her throat, she drew it out and checked the screen. *No caller ID*. Her pulse went into overdrive. With a deep breath, she forced herself to answer it.

"Harper Wyburn."

"Harper. I'm so glad I caught you."

Christopher's tone was falsely bright. Immediately, icy dread filled her body and clogged up her throat. Suddenly she couldn't breathe.

"What? Nothing to say?" he continued.

With a determined effort, Harper pulled herself together. She couldn't afford to let Christopher know how much he rattled her. She needed to hold on to her courage and call his bluff.

"What do you want, Christopher? I've said all I'm going to say."

"Oh, but Harper. We have so much more to discuss. You

haven't called me with any information this week. You must have something to share."

Harper gritted her teeth and forced herself to answer. "No, Christopher. You're wrong. You and I have nothing to say to each other. Now, if you don't mind, I'm busy."

"*Tut, tut.* Don't be in such a hurry, Harper. Have you forgotten my promise? The one I made in the event you fail to come through for me? The one where I tell your beloved Nicholas exactly what you've been up to while you've been pretending to fall in love with him?"

Harper gasped in shock and outrage.

How does Christopher have any idea how I feel about Nick?

And then she remembered the party she'd attended to celebrate the Craigdon baptism. She and Nick had gotten up close and personal. It had happened in a secluded spot away from view of the other partygoers, but maybe Christopher had seen them? It was the only explanation. More worrisome was his renewed threat to tell all to the man she loved.

"And just in case you're suffering under some delusion that Nicholas won't believe me, let me remind you, he's my half-brother. We might not always see eye to eye, but he's known me all his life. He knows how bitter I am about how I was treated by our father. He commiserates with me. Who do you think he'll feel sorry for when I tell him you were the one who approached me with the idea of destroying Craigdon Enterprises. I was only along for the ride."

"You bastard!"

"Such language, Harper. It's unbecoming. You're only upset because I speak the truth and we both know it. When Nick finds out what you've done to him and his beloved company, he's going to be devastated. Pretty soon after that, he's going to hate you. I don't know if you realize, but Craigdon Enterprises is a pretty big deal. As the managing director, Nick has a fair bit of influence in the business world.

Once word gets out about your unforgivable breach of confidence, do you think you'll get any job in this city again?"

His tone had remained mild throughout, and somehow that made it even worse. He was so cool and calm and certain. One thing she knew, she couldn't afford to have her reputation damaged, or to lose her job.

The money Christopher had paid her was more than she could have made in a year, but it wouldn't see her through forever. Sooner or later she'd have to get another job and if Christopher had his way, it wouldn't be in Sydney. She'd be forced to leave and seek work somewhere no one had ever heard of her and she wouldn't be able to rely on references from previous employers. It would be like starting from scratch again.

Then there was Nick. Everything Christopher said was true. His revelations about her part in the scheme would destroy him. He'd suffered so many blows from people who should have loved him, whose support and loyalty should have been guaranteed. She wouldn't contribute to his pain by betraying him in the same way.

With a deep breath, she responded to Christopher. "I'm sorry, Christopher. It seems you didn't understand me the first and second and even third time. I'm not playing this game anymore. Yes, it was my idea, but that was to get revenge on your father. Nick's different. He's a good man. I'm not going to be responsible for hurting him any longer."

"That's too bad because I hold all the cards. Not only can I tell Nick about everything anytime I want, I also know where you live. What's more, as of three o'clock this afternoon, I'm now your new landlord. In fact, your lease comes up for renewal in a couple of weeks and I'm under no legal obligation to offer you a new one. What that means is, if you don't behave and do as I say, you'll find yourself out on the street... again."

Harper gasped in disbelief.

He's bluffing. He must be. There's no way he bought her apartment. That's crazy talk to try and scare her…

Slowly, the sound of the dial tone in her ear began to register. Christopher had hung up. Fear like she'd never known clutched at her belly, filling her with dread. It was one thing to threaten to tell Nicholas. But now she might be out on her ear. She had enough money to last her a little while, but what would she do after that? She needed that studio. Cheap accommodation was hard to find and in the long term she couldn't afford anything else.

Oh, God. Oh, God. Oh, God. What am I going to do?

Even as panic threatened to overwhelm her, she knew what she had to do. She was going to come clean to Nick, confess all. It was the only decent thing to do. Whether Christopher told his half-brother or not, it didn't matter. She was the one who'd planned and executed the destruction of a company Nick had given his heart and soul to. She was the one who had to own up. If that meant he hated her forever, then she'd have to live with that.

Tears burned behind her eyes at the thought of losing the only man she'd ever loved. If she could turn back time, she would. But that was fanciful thinking. As soon as she confessed all, their fledgling relationship would be over, destroyed by her own hand. Tears filled her eyes and slid down her cheeks. She cried for both of them. And then, with a stiffening of her spine and a surge of determination, she wiped away the dampness.

Right now. I'm going to do it right now, before my courage fails me.

With that, she pushed away from her desk and headed toward the closed door of Nick's office.

Chapter Twenty

Nick did his best to concentrate on the information displayed on the computer screen in front of him. He'd finally set aside time to dig deeper into the mystery of the millions of dollars Henry had paid out over the months before his death. With the help of a forensic accountant, Nick had managed to trace the money to a woman by the name of Stella Taunton. It was strange. The same name of the charitable trust Henry had set up and then bequeathed fifteen million dollars.

Who the hell is Stella Taunton?

Nick had yet to find out. As much as he wanted to focus on the mystery woman, he had more important things to deal with, namely Harper Wyburn. The trap he'd set would do the trick in flushing her out, but his heart hurt from what he was likely to discover. Despite Sophia's pleas to give Harper a chance, he was sure she was behind the failed tenders.

The only other people who'd been privy to that confidential information were the staff in his legal department and they'd been with the company for years. Why would one of them suddenly develop the need to give company secrets to their competitor? No, that didn't make any sense. It had to be Harper. The worst thing was, if his suspicions proved correct, he'd save his company, but his heart would be broken. When it came to relationships, he'd be a failure once again.

He scrubbed his hands through his hair. He wanted to cry out at the injustice of it. Then he remembered. This wasn't about him. He was a good and decent man. He tried to treat those around him with kindness and respect. No, this wasn't a reflection on him. It was all on Harper. The only thing he could be accused of was poor judgement when it came to women. He wasn't alone in that.

A tentative knock on his door broke through his tortured thoughts. He looked up in time to see Harper fill the open doorway. His heart clenched with pain.

God, she looks so beautiful, even with the fear and uncertainty in her eyes. If I needed any further proof of her guilt, I now have it. It's written all over her face. She knows I'm onto her. She knows our time together is over. We're done.

A renewed surge of anger went through him. "What do you want?"

He saw her wince at his harsh tone, but he didn't care. *He* was the victim here, the one with his heart broken.

"Um, Nicholas? Do you have a few minutes? There's something I need to tell you."

Here it comes... Oh, God, she's going to confess...

He was filled with dread. He couldn't bear to look at her, let alone respond to her request.

She seemed to sense his pain. She drew closer. She reached out for the back of the chair that stood opposite his desk and then seemed to think better of it. With her arms crossed over her chest, she turned slightly away from him and stared out the window.

"What I have to tell you is incredibly painful, as painful as it will be for you to hear it. I'm so sorry, Nicholas. I know that sounds so lame, but it's true. I never meant for this to happen! I thought—"

"What? That I'd be thrilled to discover you were selling us out to the enemy? That a woman I thought could be trusted was doing her best to sabotage everything I did? That's what you're about to confess to, right?"

Her head dropped forward in defeat. "Yes."

Hurt and anger coursed through him. "Do you know how long I yearned to be an integral part of this company? I gave every spare second of my life to Craigdon Enterprises! I always dreamed my father would one day recognize my potential and the passion I had to see his company become the very best it could be. And then Dad died and my birthright was stolen right out from under me.

"Oh, I don't blame Logan. He's as clueless as I am about my father's motives. But when Logan was generous enough to hand over the day-to-day running of the company to me, I was as happy as I could be. Craigdon Enterprises wasn't mine, but there's still a hope one day it might be. Logan has no interest in it. For me, this company's everything I worked for. Everything I wanted to be. And now you've tried your best to take all that away from me."

He glared at her, his breath coming fast. His chest hurt from the pain and disappointment of her betrayal. Not only with the company, but also with his heart.

"You know what hurts worst of all?" he continued. "The fact you pretended to like me. Pretended we had something special together. You even let me make love to you! And all so you could get closer to me, close enough so that handing secrets over to McClintock Properties was as easy as making a cup of coffee. Poor, stupid Nicholas. What a loser. So easy to fool. You must have gone home every night laughing at how easy it was."

He choked on a lump of emotion that had lodged itself in his throat. He wanted to hold on to his anger. Anger kept him from falling apart. But it was hard. So hard. He'd been betrayed like this before by the man who was supposed to love him and protect him. This time it was even worse because he'd come to care for Harper so deeply.

Her expression filled with remorse. Pain shadowed her eyes. He looked away and set his jaw, refusing to accept she felt any regret at all.

"Oh, Nicholas! I'm so sorry! You can't believe how sorry I am! Please, let me explain! I never intended to hurt you! It was your father I wanted to get back at. Your father ruined my life."

Nick turned his back on her. The desperation in her voice ratcheted up a notch.

"Please, Nick! You have to listen to me! This had nothing to do with you! I'd planned my revenge against your father. Then he died and my plans went awry. For a while, I didn't know what to do. Then I took a job at McClintock's and I learned about the rivalry between them and Henry's company. A new plan formed, but it had nothing to do with you. I swear! I didn't know who had inherited the company and I didn't care. This wasn't personal to anyone but your father."

"Take your sorry story to someone else, Harper. I've heard enough. You've admitted you came up with a new plan after learning of my father's death. You had every opportunity to let this so-called plan for revenge go and you didn't. Instead, you lined me up in your sights. I had nothing to do with whatever went on between you and my father, but that didn't seem to matter to you. Instead, you played me for a fool and I fell head-over-heels into your trap. I believed every lie you ever told me and I kept coming back for more." He made a sound of disgust in the back of his throat. "Hell, you must have been laughing your head off at my gullibility."

"No! Nick, please! Don't say that! It's not true! It wasn't like that!"

He turned and glared at her through narrowed eyes. "Do you deny you gave McClintock's confidential information about the Craigdon tenders?"

To her credit, she held his gaze without flinching. "No. I don't deny it."

"Did you profit from it?"

Once again, she didn't look away. "Yes."

His gut twisted. He looked at her in disbelief. Though it shouldn't have come as a surprise that she'd sold the information, it was just another blow to his heart.

"How much?" he snarled.

"Please, Nicholas! Don't look at me like that. It doesn't matter how much. It wasn't my idea to make money off it."

He gave a scornful laugh. "Oh, and I guess that makes it all better?"

"You don't understand why I did it! You don't know what your father did!"

"Leave my father out of this!" he shouted. "He might not have been a saint, but he had far more scruples than you. Now, clear out your things and get out."

Her face crumpled. Tears glimmered in her eyes. "You can't do this, Nick! Please! I love you!"

Nicholas froze. Once upon a time, her words would have filled him with indescribable joy, but now they left him cold. He refused to be moved by her words or her show of emotion. For all he knew, she could be faking them, like she'd lied about everything else.

"I never meant to hurt you," she said in a choked voice. "When I got to know you, I realized none of this was your fault and I couldn't continue with it. I told Christopher as much."

Nick felt another jolt of anger as his suspicions were confirmed. "Of course, Christopher. My beloved half-brother who never had any love for Henry, or this company. My, my, my. What a pair the two of you must have made. Making out… Trading stories about how much you hated the Craigdons." His lip curled up in disgust.

Harper's expression became more frantic. "No, Nicholas! Please, you have to believe me! It wasn't like that. In fact, that last tender you gave me, I refused to hand over to Christopher. He threatened me with all sorts of things, including eviction, but I didn't budge."

Nick stared at her in disbelief. "So all of a sudden you develop a conscience and you think that makes everything else all right? You have to be kidding! And how do I know it's true? You've lied so many times before. Why not now? For all I know, Christopher already has access to that information and has transferred the appropriate compensation to your bank account."

The longer he spoke, the angrier he became and the more hurt and betrayal twisted his insides. All of a sudden, he couldn't bear the sight of her a moment longer.

"Get out, Harper!" he cried.

She remained where she was.

"I said, get out!"

The anger in his voice must have finally gotten through to her. Pale and trembling, she turned and left the room. As she pulled the door closed behind her, he heard the sound of her sobbing. He hardened his heart.

She has no right to be upset. I'm the one with the broken heart. She and Christopher can go to hell…

To his relief, Harper wasn't at her desk when he emerged from his office a few minutes later. There was no way he could sit there after all that had happened. He had to get out. He had to talk to someone. Get the anger off his chest.

Just then, his phone rang. He pulled it out of his pocket and checked the screen.

Sophia.

To think Harper had once thought Sophia was his wife. It seemed funny at the time. He'd even been flattered that she was upset at the thought he was married. Now it just filled him with disgust. No doubt she'd been faking those feelings too, along with everything else. With a sigh, he answered the call.

"Soph. What is it?"

"Good afternoon to you too, Nick."

Nick grimaced at the reprimand in her tone. "Sorry," he mumbled.

"Don't tell me you're still upset at Harper? Did you talk to her like I told you?"

Trust Sophia to pick up on his mood. She might be a pain in the butt, but she'd always been perceptive and he knew she had his best interests at heart.

"Yes. She confessed."

He heard her sharp intake of breath. "Oh, no! I can't believe it! I thought she was so nice!"

"Yeah. Me, too,"

"Do you want to talk about it?"

He'd been headed out of the office with the thought of finding Callum, but now Sophia had offered, he realized he was just as happy to share what had happened with her. After all, she already knew some of what had been going on.

"Sure," he heard himself replying.

"I'm just pulling into the underground parking station. I'll meet you at The Venue in a few minutes. Is that okay?"

"Sure. See you there."

Nick was seated at a corner table away from the other patrons and had already placed orders for two coffees when Sophia came walking through the open front door to the café. She was dressed like she usually was in a designer outfit with matching accessories. He didn't want to think about how much it all cost.

Though she'd been largely overlooked in their father's will, she had access to a healthy trust fund set up by their mother, like they all did. Nick guessed she spent a fair amount of that money on her wardrobe. He felt a flash of sympathy for the man who might one day have to support her in the manner to which she was accustomed and then laughed the feeling away. Any man would be proud to call his little sister his wife. Not only was she beautiful, she was also smart and sassy and kind. All the qualities he used to think Harper had.

His mood soured at the thought. Sophia took a seat across from him.

"Hey, don't frown like that. It'll give you wrinkles," she gently chided after pecking him on the cheek.

He grunted in response.

"Come on, Nick. It can't be as bad as that."

He shook his head, feeling grim. "It's worse."

Sophia reached across the table and squeezed his hand. "How about you start from the beginning?"

Nick blew out his breath. "I thought about what all of you said, but I was still convinced Harper was behind the lost contracts. So I set a trap."

Sophia looked appalled. "Oh, Nick! What did you do?"

"Don't look at me like that," he said irritably. "All I did was provide her with documents containing a fake bid for a property I was looking to purchase. One out near the new airport. The property's legitimate. It's only our bid that's not. She's the only one I gave access to the information. If McClintock's end up getting that contract, they'll have to go in even lower than we did."

"I assume your bid was ridiculously low?" Sophia surmised.

"I wouldn't say ridiculous, but certainly much lower than what I would have normally submitted."

"So if McClintock's are successful, you'll know Harper gave them your information?"

Nick compressed his lips into a thin line. "Yes."

Sophia shrugged. "I guess as far as plans go, it's as good as any."

"Yes. The only thing is, it doesn't matter anymore."

Sophia nodded. "Because she confessed."

Just then, the waitress arrived with their coffees and they waited for the girl to move away before recommencing their conversation.

"Yes. She told me she was the one who'd given McClintock's the information about our bids. She's the reason we've lost millions of dollars in contracts."

Sophia took a sip from her coffee and sat back against her seat. "I'm still shocked. I really thought she liked you."

"So did I," Nick said grimly. He took a sip from his coffee, but barely tasted it. "And just as I suspected, Christopher was involved."

Sophia shook her head. "Oh, no. Not again. What the hell's the matter with him?"

"We both know he's always held a grudge against the family. It's been going on our entire lives. Dad's will was the final straw."

A silence fell between them. Both of them took refuge in their coffee. Sophia was the first one to speak again.

"You know, I kind of understand Christopher's motive for doing all he can to cause trouble for Craigdon Enterprises, but what did Harper get out of it?"

Nick felt a renewed surge of anger. "Money. Christopher paid her for the information."

"How much?"

"I don't know. She wouldn't tell me. She kept saying it wasn't important. That her real motivation was to get revenge against Dad."

Sophia frowned in surprise. "Dad? How would she even know Dad? He's been dead since February."

"Yes. She told me she'd known him from before. That he ruined her life. Who knows if she's telling the truth? She's lied so many times before."

"Wow," Sophia said thoughtfully. "Do you know how she met Christopher?"

"At McClintock's, is my guess. She worked there for six months before she came to work for me. I'm sure that's when the two of them cooked up this plan to fleece us of those contracts."

"So you think she deliberately angled for the job at Craigdons?"

"Yes. She needed to get on the inside in order for her plan to work. She had the perfect ruse as a temp. She could move between jobs without anyone thinking too much of it. I certainly didn't. I didn't even question where she'd come from until I began to get suspicious. Then I called her temp agency. They confirmed she'd worked for McClintock's."

Sophia continued to look thoughtful. "I've got to tell you, Nick. This plan seems to have been a long time in the making. There has to be more to this than money. What if she *did* know Dad from before? What if he did do something to ruin her life? I don't need to remind you how ruthless he could be at times."

Nick remained silent. He wasn't yet prepared to accept Harper might have a genuine grievance against his father.

Sophia persisted. "Remember what Grace said? She thought Harper might have spent some time living rough. You were the one who told us Dad had a practice of buying buildings that housed low-cost accommodation and moving the tenants out. Perhaps Harper's family were caught up in that?"

Slowly, Nick's anger receded. He wondered if Sophia was right. Harper had once told him about someone she'd been close to who'd been forced out of her accommodation when she couldn't afford the rent. He hadn't thought too much of it at the time, but now he couldn't help but wonder.

Did Harper have some other motivation for wanting to destroy Craigdon Enterprises? Had she been telling the truth?

Calmer now, he took another sip of coffee. He needed to fact check what Harper had told him. He'd already discovered documents relating to his father's Urban Renewal Program. He was sure he'd find other evidence in the company archives. He owed it to himself and to Harper to get to the bottom of what had happened. If he found no link to Harper or her family, he'd know for sure she was just another money-hungry person looking to make a fast buck and that she'd never cared for him at all. Better for him to know now, once and for all, then to be left wondering forever.

"Hey, I almost forgot my news."

He looked at Sophia. "What news?"

She grinned. "I have a job."

He chuckled. "You do?"

"Yes. A teaching job. I've picked up a maternity leave position at Mosman Primary School. It's not permanent, but it's a start."

He saw the excitement banked behind her eyes and grinned. "That's great news, Soph. I'm so happy for you."

She smiled wryly. "Yeah, well, I guess I should thank you. If you'd caved in to my demands and given me a job at Craigdon Enterprises, I would never have forced myself out of my comfort zone."

He shrugged. "No need to thank me. I'm just happy things worked out. When do you start?"

"Next week."

"Wow."

She smiled a little nervously. "Yes, wow."

"You'll be fine," he reassured her. "You're going to make a great teacher."

She shot him a grateful smile. "Thanks, Nick. You're the best brother, ever."

Back in his office, Nick thought about what Sophia had said about Harper. He owed it to her to get to the bottom of things. He also needed to bring Logan up to speed. It was Nick's responsibility to tell him the truth. It was a conversation he wasn't looking forward to, but as the managing director, the buck stopped with him.

With that thought in mind, he picked up the phone and called his cousin. The phone was answered on the second ring.

"Nick! What's happening?"

Nick could hear loud noises in the background. "Where are you?"

"I'm in the workshop. Sorry, my hands are covered in decking oil. I've got you on speaker."

Nick frowned. "Is there any chance you can get away this afternoon? I need to talk to you about something."

"Sorry, mate. I'm halfway through applying oil to the decking boards. Can it wait?"

Nick swallowed a sigh. He'd rather have the conversation face to face, but neither could it wait. He didn't want Logan to hear the news about Harper from anyone else. Nick wasn't yet certain about the extent of Christopher's involvement, but there was no guarantee he'd keep his mouth shut. If he thought he could cause trouble with it, he'd be just as likely to spill all.

"Look, it's about those contracts we lost to McClintock's. I found the leak."

"Who was it?"

"Harper."

"The temp?"

"Yes."

"Fuck. She was working for you! She had access to everything!"

Nick compressed his lips and remained silent as Logan vented his anger. And then Nick's uncle joined in the fray.

"Did you even check her references before you hired her, Nick?" Uncle Archie asked.

"She came to us through a temp agency, Uncle. They do their own checks."

"You're kidding?" his uncle continued, his voice filled with disgust. "You relied on an agency? What kind of show are you running? We'll sue the pants off them. And the temp."

"Dad. This is none of your business. You shouldn't even be listening in. This is between me and Nick. I can handle it."

"It doesn't sound like you can handle it and it doesn't look like Nick's competent enough to be in charge. I thought you were exaggerating when you told me he was useless, but now I see you were right."

Nick winced and then anger surged through him. He'd heard enough. He opened his mouth to defend himself, but Logan beat him to it.

"Dad! That's enough!" Logan's voice was steel. "Nick's more than capable of running the company. He's been doing it on his own all these months. I drop by for appearances sake and to keep up the subterfuge that I was actually needed there so you'd get off my back. And that's the truth."

There was a moment of stunned silence. When Uncle Archie spoke again, his voice was much more subdued. "Is that true, Nick?"

Nick replied without hesitation. "Yes."

"Then I owe you an apology. I'm sorry. It seems as though my son has been less than upfront with me. Anyway, that's between him and me. I'll talk to you later."

There was a moment of silence and then Logan spoke again. "You still there, Nick?"

"Yeah."

"I'm sorry. I should never have asked you to do that."

"It's fine. And I'm sorry about Harper. I should have known she was up to no good. I should have looked into her background. Turns out she'd worked for McClintock's before she came to us. She was in cahoots with Christopher. They banded together to bring our company down. I should have seen it."

"I don't blame you for not knowing. She's a temp. No one does a background check on a temp."

"Thanks, mate. I appreciate your understanding."

"I assume you fired her?"

"Of course."

"I guess that's for the best. Too bad it turned out like this, though. I thought she was nice."

Yeah. So did I…

Chapter Twenty One

Harper tried to keep her attention on the small group of students in front of her, but it was tough. No matter how many times she'd told herself to forget about Nicholas Craigdon, her mind kept drawing her back. She was in the middle of her etiquette class, this time with particular emphasis on preparing and dressing for a job interview, but her mind kept straying to her last conversation with Nick.

She hadn't seen him since he'd told her to leave his office. With tears pouring down her cheeks, she'd escaped into the bathroom. It had taken her quite awhile before she calmed down and was presentable enough to return to her desk. She was relieved to discover Nick was no longer in his office. While he was gone, she'd taken the time to clear everything out of her desk.

There wasn't much. She hadn't been there long enough to have much more than her personal coffee cup, a small potted plant and a framed photograph of her mom. She quickly tossed her few belongings into a bag. She logged off her computer. The tender documents Nick had asked her to type up still sat in a neat pile on her desk. She left them there. If he wanted them, he'd find them.

A fresh wave of hot tears burned behind her eyes and she

tried desperately to blink them away. It was just as she'd imagined. Nick despised her. She'd destroyed whatever love he might have had for her and she couldn't blame anyone else. Her need for revenge against his father had blinded her to everything else. Now she'd pay the price.

"Miss Harper? How is this?"

The excited question coming from one of her students brought Harper back to the present with a rush. She looked at the young Aboriginal girl who still had her hand up and walked over to where the girl sat. Her hair had been neatly brushed and twisted into braids. Her makeup had been carefully applied. The skirt and jacket she'd selected from the rack against the wall were a bit big and didn't match, but she still looked smart. She'd teamed it with a white blouse.

Harper smiled. "You look great, Cherie. I love what you did with your hair."

The girl blushed with pleasure. "I finally got it right! I did it exactly how you showed me."

"We're so grateful you want to help us," Sasha said quietly. She still hadn't mastered the art of braids, but she was trying hard.

Harper's heart melted. This was what it was all about. Helping those who needed it, who couldn't afford to get it from anywhere else.

And then one of the other girls looked at her and grinned. "How's your boyfriend, Miss Harper? Nicholas... Is he coming back for another visit?"

The girls immediately started talking about him.

"So dreamy..."

"Those eyes..."

"I wouldn't mind a boyfriend who looked like that..."

The comment was met with a round of giggles. It was all Harper could do to get them to quiet down. "Girls, please. You need to focus on your work."

"Aw, Miss. We're just joking," Cherie said. "Your boyfriend seemed really nice. Do you think he'll come and visit us again?"

Harper's answering smile was strained. "No, girls. I'm sorry. Nick and I broke up."

There was a chorus of murmured sympathies. Tears pricked Harper's eyes. The girls had only been coming to her class for the past seven weeks, but they already felt like family. Some of them were only a few years younger than she was. It made her wonder what it would have been like to have a sister.

Her thoughts turned to Sophia Craigdon. The two of them had gotten along so well at the party. It felt like they could be friends. After what Harper had done to Nick, she was sure Sophia would never speak to her again. Another sad consequence of her actions.

There was no point thinking along those lines now. What was done was done. She had to learn from her mistakes and put her past grievances behind her. Henry Craigdon was dead, and so was her mother. She needed to press RESET on her life and focus her efforts toward her future. A future that unfortunately no longer included Nick.

"How many more weeks do we have left, Miss Harper?" Sasha asked.

"One more after this. I'm thrilled that every one of you will graduate. You've all come so far from the girls who told me they didn't have a clue how to go about preparing for a job interview. Some of you were certain you'd never learn how to put on makeup and do your hair. Look at what you've achieved." She let her gaze rove over the assembled bunch of girls. They were all smiling in delight.

"I'm so proud of you all." She choked up and had to wait a moment before she could continue. "The next time you're called up for an interview, you'll know exactly what to do and

I bet you'll outshine all of your competition. How could you not? You've been trained by the best! You've been to the class of Harper Wyburn!"

"Yay!" They all cheered.

"Let's hear it for Miss Harper!" Cherie cried.

"Hip, hip hooray! Hip, hip hooray! Hip, hip hooray!" class members shouted in unison.

Fresh tears threatened behind Harper's eyes. "Thank you, girls. It's been a pleasure working with you."

It saddened her to know this was the last group of students she'd be teaching. After what had happened at Craigdon Enterprises, her temp agency had suggested she might need to seek representation elsewhere. When she asked who'd called them, they'd confirmed it was Nicholas. He'd made it clear to them her services wouldn't ever be required at his company again. There would be no reference.

Her lease on the studio was almost up. Though she hadn't heard from Christopher again, any day she expected him to come through with his threat to evict her. Apart from the youth club, there was nothing keeping her in Sydney. She needed a fresh start. Somewhere away from the memories of her childhood and most of all, of Nicholas. Somewhere no one knew her.

She'd start afresh and work her way up from the bottom, just like she'd done before. This time she wouldn't let dreams of revenge take over or make her lose sight of what really mattered. To love and be loved. To belong to a family. She had to believe she hadn't blown her only chance at that. It was the only thing that kept her going.

Nick frowned over the pile of papers scattered across his desk. Ever since his conversation with Sophia, he'd been determined to get to the bottom of things. He was glad he'd cleared the air between him and Logan, but he still wanted to see this through and that meant investigating this right through to the final conclusion.

Grace was sure Harper had known what it was like to be homeless. Then there was Harper's passion for helping the less fortunate. He only had to recall how much she loved working with the teenage girls and young women at the youth club, hoping to help them find a better path, increasing their chances of securing a job in the workplace.

At one time he might have scoffed at the importance of teaching young people about good grooming and hair and makeup, presenting one's best self in order to maximize opportunities, but after spending time with Harper at the youth club, he'd left with a different attitude.

She was so passionate about how the way someone felt about themselves and how they looked could make such a difference to their self-esteem and to their ultimate job prospects. Was it because she'd had personal experience with that? He knew her mother had died when Harper was seventeen. Had she been left to work that kind of thing out for herself? Could Sophia have been right? Could Harper and her mother have been caught up in his father's scheme?

So far, he'd found no mention of the name Wyburn and he'd been poring through papers for the better part of two weeks. He didn't know the name of Harper's mother, but Wyburn was an unusual name. He assumed if he found reference to it, there was a good chance it might be her.

He pulled out the last lease in the bottom of the current box and started to go through it. The owner of the building was listed on the lease as the landlord, along with his agent. Nick's gaze moved lower to where the tenant's details were.

Tammie Wyburn.

His heart skipped a beat. He kept reading as fast as he could. The usual conditions about no pets and no unapproved tenants were listed there, along with the name of the other person living in the apartment.

Harper Wyburn.

It was her. It had to be.

She was one of Dad's tenants… Tossed out on the street…

His heart beat faster. The lease was for a term of twelve months. It commenced on 29 April 2011. He did a quick calculation in his head. Harper had told him she was twenty-two. That meant she was thirteen when her mother entered into the lease. A year older when the lease came to an end. She'd been seventeen when her mother died.

What had happened in between?

He wished he knew. Somewhere along the way, the Wyburns' paths had crossed with Henry Craigdon who wanted their building for himself. In accordance with his Urban Renewal Program, once the lease had expired, he'd increased the rents to unaffordable levels. When the tenants defaulted, he booted them out. Over and over again, until he had the building all to himself and could do with it as he liked.

Nick felt sick all over again. The lengths his father went to for money… It was shameful. And Harper and her mother had been just a couple more of his victims. Innocent people caught up in his desire to create even more wealth.

Tammie Wyburn had died from malnutrition and pneumonia. No doubt her illnesses were directly related to being forced out of her home. It was no wonder Harper wanted to get back at the person she saw as responsible.

What Nick had more difficulty accepting was how Harper had decided to turn her need for revenge on him. She'd admitted she'd become aware of the news about Henry's death and had been momentarily taken aback. Then she'd re-grouped and had come for his son. Nick was now the one firmly in her sights and he'd been totally oblivious.

He remembered how she'd begged him to believe her

when she said it hadn't been like that. Or if it had been, things had changed for her somewhere along the way. She'd even said she loved him. He so desperately wanted to believe her, but how could he? She'd told him so many lies. Except she'd told the truth about what had happened to her and his father's involvement in it. What had she said?

"Your father ruined my life!"

He couldn't begin to imagine how tough life had gotten for her after her mother died. With no one to look out for her, support her, protect her… His heart went out to the young Harper and the last vestiges of his anger faded away. He still didn't like that she'd turned her need for revenge on him, but he could understand it. And the simple truth was, no matter what she'd done, he loved her.

And then he thought about Christopher. It was always possible Nick had it all wrong. Was it Christopher who had somehow discovered Harper's grief against Henry and seized an opportunity to cause trouble? Was Christopher the one who approached Harper with the idea to steal Craigdon secrets?

Not that it would get Harper off the hook. No one had forced her to do what she had, but it would make things slightly more palatable.

I need to find out. I need to know the truth…

With that in mind, he reached for his phone and dialed Christopher's number. His half-brother picked up right away.

"Nick! What a surprise!"

"This isn't a social call, Christopher," he said coldly. "Tell me everything you know about Harper Wyburn and you'd best cut the bullshit. I'm not in the mood."

"My, my, Nicholas. A little touchy, aren't we?"

"Start talking." His tone brooked no argument.

He heard a dramatic sigh on the other end of the phone. "Hey! She was the one who came to me."

"Why should I believe you, Christopher? You lie at the drop of a hat."

"Okay. I deserve that, but this time I'm telling the truth. I swear."

The revelation was a blow, but Nick was determined to see it through right to the end. "Keep going."

"Harper approached me about bringing Craigdon Enterprises down. Once she told me her reasons, I was happy to go along with her plan. Let's just say we were kindred spirits with a common goal."

"So it was all about the eviction," Nick stated flatly.

"Wasn't that enough? She watched her mother struggle through three winters, before the poor woman finally died."

"Shit," Nick cursed. He'd guessed something like that had happened.

"That's not all."

"There's more?"

"Yes. The real blow came when Harper confronted Dad about what he'd done."

Nick started in surprise. "She met Dad?"

"Yes. It was not long after her mother died. She tracked him down at the office. She accused him of killing her mother. He laughed in her face. Then he suggested they come to some arrangement that involved her sleeping with him. She refused."

Nick sat frozen with shock. Then anger reared its head, fast and white-hot.

Dad… You fucking prick… Harper was all of seventeen! How could you?

"Are you sure?" Nick asked when he finally found his voice.

"Well, I wasn't there, but do you think anyone would lie about something like that?"

Nick thought about it and agreed with Christopher. Though Harper had been deceitful about other things, she didn't seem the type to lie about something like that. Then there was what they all knew about Henry. He was a womanizer and a sleaze. He'd stopped at nothing to get what he wanted and it was clear he'd wanted Harper.

Nick was filled with a renewed sense of outrage. His father was no longer alive to pose a threat to him, but he sure as hell wouldn't have let him take another woman from him.

Harper is mine!

"Nick? Are you still there?"

Nick blinked. "Yes, Christopher. I'm still here."

"I'm sorry. You didn't deserve to be treated like that. I understand where Harper was coming from, but it was wrong for her to take her anger out on you."

"It's all right," Nick said. "I understand more than I did when I last spoke to her. I hate to admit it, but I wasn't really in the mood back then to listen to her explanation. I guess I'll give her a call and see if she's still willing to talk to me."

"You know she moved out of her apartment?"

Once again, Nick started in surprise. "No, I didn't. Where did she go?"

"I don't know, but one of her neighbors said something about her moving to Melbourne."

Nick's heart skipped a beat. "Melbourne? You mean, she's left Sydney?"

"That's what I heard. I'm not sure how reliable the source was."

Nick frowned as he was filled with a sudden surge of suspicion. "Why the hell were you talking to one of Harper's neighbors? How the hell do you even know where she lives?"

There was a long stretch of silence.

"Christopher." Nick's voice held a taut warning.

"Uh… I… Uh… I might have bought her apartment."

"What the hell are you talking about?"

Nick listened in growing anger as Christopher confessed about becoming Harper's new landlord.

Nick shook his head in confusion. "Why would you do that?"

Once again, there was a pause and once again Nick issued a barely contained threat. "Now is your time to come clean, Christopher. I won't ask you twice."

"Well, I… I… I might have threatened her with eviction."

"You *what*?" Nick shouted, aghast. "After knowing what she and her mother went through? You prick! How could you! You're as nasty and malicious as our father. I'm done with feeling sorry for you, Christopher. Don't show your face around me again."

"But, Nick! I—"

"No! No more! This conversation is over."

With that, Nick stabbed viciously at the phone and brought the call to an end. He stared down at his desk in disbelief. Christopher had cleared up some of the gray areas, but he'd also caused Nick even more grief. Harper had left Sydney. It was only a guess she'd headed for Melbourne. All of a sudden, it seemed imperative to talk to her. He scrolled through his contacts and found her number. He was met with a computerized voice.

"The number you're calling is disconnected. Please check the number and dial again."

"Shit." Nick thumped his desk in frustration.

How am I going to find her? How am I going to tell her how I feel?

He'd never felt more helpless. Then he had an idea. Picking up the phone once more, he dialed the number of her temp agency. After explaining the reason behind his call, he was put through to Harper's supervisor.

"Hello, Mr Craigdon. I understand you're asking about Harper Wyburn?" the wary voice on the other end said. "I hope she hasn't caused you any more trouble?"

Nick tried to stem his impatience. "No, nothing like that. I just need to contact her."

"I believe she's relocated to Melbourne. At least, that's where she told our HR department she was going."

"Do you know where in Melbourne?"

"Just a minute. I'll check her file."

The woman wasn't gone for long, but it felt like a lifetime. Then she was back again. "It looks like she's working with the Burke & Smith Agency."

Nick jotted down their details and then thanked the woman for her time. Next he dialed the Melbourne agency and confirmed Harper was indeed on their books. Unfortunately, they wouldn't provide him with her contact details, but they did tell him where she worked at that time.

Ending the call, Nick stared down at his notes. *Melbourne.* It would take him at least nine or ten hours to drive. Way too long, but what choice did he have? There was no way he was catching a flight. He hadn't been on a plane since that fateful flight with his father when he was sure he was going to die. He could still feel the absolute terror as the plane hurtled toward the ground.

But he needed to talk to Harper. What if she was about to do something really stupid, like run off overseas? He'd never track her down. She'd never know how he felt. The possibility was totally unacceptable. He had to find her.

Chapter Twenty Two

Harper did something she hadn't done since she was seventeen. She started chewing on her nails. During the time she'd spent living from hand to mouth with her mother, with no fixed place of abode, no certainty that she'd even eat that night, her nails had taken a battering. Often they were bitten down to the quick. After her mother passed away, Harper was so filled with helpless rage she was determined never to take it out on herself again. From that day on, she made a vow not to chew her nails and up until now, she'd kept it.

It pained her to know the reason behind her sudden lapse. It had been two long weeks since she'd left Craigdon Enterprises. Two long weeks since she'd seen Nicholas. Two long weeks to replay every sentence, every word, every *syllable* uttered that fateful afternoon. She'd always known being honest with Nick was risky, and even though she hadn't dared to admit it even to herself, secretly she'd hoped once he'd gotten over his initial shock, he'd find it in himself to forgive her.

But it hadn't worked out that way. She'd remained in Sydney a week after that terrible day, but he hadn't called. She'd attended her students' graduation at the youth club and though she'd been able to summon up a smile for her girls and spoke warmly about how proud she was of them, inside her heart was breaking. She'd looked around the gymnasium in a desperate hope that Nicholas might appear, but he hadn't. She'd left there that night knowing it was over.

Determined to put all of the pain and sadness behind her, she'd changed her phone number, packed up the few belongings in her studio and caught a bus headed south to Melbourne. She hadn't heard any more from Christopher, but neither was she going to wait for him to toss her out on the street. The memories *that* would have brought back would have set her back a long time and she wasn't prepared to take the risk.

She'd spent hours trying to decide where to go. She'd looked at Brisbane, but even the name reminded her of Nicholas. She looked at Perth. It was a long way away from everything familiar. She looked at Adelaide and thought the city was probably too small for her liking. Eventually, she'd decided on Melbourne.

It was far enough from Sydney that she'd never have to risk running into Nicholas, but a large enough city that it wouldn't be too hard to find employment. In fact, her previous agency had been kind enough to supply her with the name of another temp agency who they thought were looking for staff. She'd managed to secure a job the first day she arrived.

It was in a typing pool with fifteen other typists. The work was boring and monotonous, but it paid the bills. Though she had a nice little nest egg set aside thanks to Christopher, apart from splashing out on the dress she'd worn to the baptism, she hadn't been able to bring herself to spend any more of it. Knowing how she'd come by it, the very thought of that money now filled her with guilt.

She suddenly became aware her index finger was back in her mouth. She quickly pulled it out and surveyed the damage. She'd bitten down at least half of the nail tip. With a conscious effort, she put both hands back on the keyboard and moved over to the next section of the document she was in the process of completing.

Focus, Harper. Focus. Stop thinking about Nicholas. That boat has sailed. It's time to face reality. Nicholas Craigdon will never be part of your life…

"Harper, there's someone asking for you downstairs."

Harper looked up at her supervisor and blinked. "Excuse me?"

"I just had a call from the receptionist. There's someone downstairs who wants to see you."

Harper's pulse skipped a beat and then immediately went into overdrive.

Nicholas.

And then she had a reality check. She didn't know anybody in Melbourne and nobody knew she was there. Especially Nicholas.

Who could be asking to see me? It doesn't make sense.

"If you need a few minutes, you can take your break now," the supervisor added, waiting expectantly.

Harper shook her head in confusion, but pushed away from her desk. Slowly, she made her way to the lift. The whole time, her mind was in turmoil.

Who can it be?

Nick had never been more nervous. He thought climbing on board an aeroplane after vowing never to fly again had been difficult. It was nothing compared to waiting to see if Harper would leave her desk and come down to meet him.

From the information he'd gotten from her agency, he'd managed to find her workplace. It was a multi-story building made of glass and steel with contemporary pieces of artwork on the walls and minimalistic furniture. The greeting he'd received from the girl behind the front desk was friendly enough but had done nothing to ease his nerves.

He'd listened openly to the receptionist's end of the conversation with someone in Harper's department. From what was spoken, he was satisfied she was there. Now he had to wait and see if she responded to his request.

The *ding* of a lift snagged his attention. His gaze was immediately drawn in that direction. The silver doors slid open. *And there she was.*

His chest went tight. For a moment, he couldn't breathe. It had been fourteen days since he'd seen her. It felt like a lifetime.

She looked straight at him and he watched as the color left her cheeks. She stumbled slightly and then quickly regained her balance. For a few moments, she stopped where she was, as if unsure whether to continue.

His heart thumped. His hands clenched into fists. Sweat popped out on his forehead.

Come on, Harper. Keep walking. Please, keep walking…

Still she hesitated, and his gut twisted with nerves. He stood ramrod straight, his gaze unwavering, willing her forward. And then she moved. The tiniest step. And then there was another. A few more, each step a little more confident than the last. And finally she was there, standing right in front of him. Up close, he could see the apprehension in her eyes.

"Hello, Harper. It's good to see you."

"What are you doing here, Nick?"

Her voice gave nothing away.

"I came to see you." He glanced around them. "Is there somewhere we can talk?"

She didn't respond, merely walked past him and continued out through the front doors. He hurried after her. She stopped a short distance away, near a bench that had been built around a large oak tree. With her hands on her hips, she turned to face him.

Harper was trying as hard as she could to remain cool, calm and collected. From the moment she'd seen Nicholas standing there in the foyer of her building looking vulnerable and uncertain, she'd wanted to throw herself in his arms. But the memory of the last time they'd parted stopped her.

Was he here to tell her he was taking her to court? Or wanted her to pay back…? No. He'd have sent a lawyer for that. She desperately hoped his presence there meant he'd finally found it in his heart to forgive her, but she cautioned herself to take it slowly.

"Is this place good enough?" she asked.

He glanced around them impatiently, like he just wanted to have his say and get out of there. "This is fine."

She deliberately took a seat and took the time to cross her legs before looking up at him expectantly. He cursed beneath his breath and then spoke.

"I'm sorry about the way we left things. I said some terrible things."

She merely shrugged, but her pulse rate picked up its pace.

"Since you've been gone, I've had some time to think. I also did a little digging, and discovered the real reason you were so hell-bent on revenge."

She started in surprise. "You know about the eviction?"

"Yes. I also know why you blamed my father for your mother's death."

She opened her mouth to question him again, but he beat her to it.

"Christopher told me."

She blinked in surprise. "Oh." The last person she expected to come to her defense was Christopher.

"What my father did to you and your mother was unforgivable. He then compounded his unforgivable behavior by the way he treated you when you confronted him."

Once again, he'd taken her by surprise. Christopher had obviously been thorough when he'd brought Nicholas up to speed.

"Thank you," she murmured. It felt good to receive Nick's apology, even though she owed him one, too.

"I'm sorry about what I did," she said. "It wasn't right to take out my need for revenge on you. You were just as innocent in all this as I was."

His grin was hesitant, as if he still wasn't sure where he stood. "You apologized already, remember? More than once. I wasn't in the mood to listen."

She nodded. "I remember. Still, I mean it, Nick. I was way out of line." She looked at him. "What have you told Logan?"

"The truth. He's upset we lost those contracts, but he understands. I *made* him understand."

She sighed. "It would have been so much easier if you'd been as mean and nasty as your father. Then I wouldn't have found myself liking you."

"I'm nothing like my father," he said quietly.

She looked at him. "You're right. And I didn't expect that." She paused and then added, "At every turn you surprised me. I didn't want to like you, and I tried very hard not to, but you made it impossible. By the time you invited me to the baptism, I was already half in love with you."

"Only half?" he teased.

She smiled and some of her tension eased. Nicholas had also begun to look more relaxed.

"I accompanied you to that party because I wanted to, but I was also curious about Henry Craigdon's family. I wanted to meet them, see what kind of people could have loved and supported a man like that."

"And what did you decide?" Nick asked quietly.

Harper offered him a grudging smile. "I decided they were kind and sweet and funny, ordinary people with ordinary problems, hopes and dreams, just trying to get by, like the rest of us."

"You sound surprised."

"I was surprised," she admitted. "My dealings with your father had been less than savory. He was rude and arrogant and insufferable. I expected his family to be the same."

"But we weren't. Especially not me." Nick grinned. "Is that why you finally kissed me?"

She blushed. "I couldn't help myself. We were there, standing close. I was falling fast. You were everything I wanted in a man." She paused and then added, "It just happened."

His grin widened. "Hey, I'm not complaining. I'd like to kiss you again."

And just like that, the air around them became charged. Harper looked at him and saw the shadow of desire in his eyes that she was sure was reflected in her own. His lips parted on an indrawn breath. This time, she let him make the first move.

As if in slow motion, he sat down beside her. His head moved closer until there was nothing between them but air. And then his lips were on hers and she was lost. He kissed her softly, tenderly, as if reacquainting himself with her taste. Her arms crept up around his shoulders and she drew him even closer.

Just like that, the fire between them sparked to life. They kissed with frantic passion, over and over again. When his tongue pressed against her lips, seeking entrance, she opened her mouth and gladly let him in. When they finally pulled apart, they were both breathing hard.

"Wow," she said a little shakily.

Nick regarded her solemnly. "Yes. Wow."

She searched his face. "Does this mean you forgive me?"

"Love and forgiveness go hand in hand. You can't truly love someone without also being willing to forgive them. None of us are perfect. One day it might be me who makes a mess of things and needs your forgiveness. I'll never deliberately set out to hurt you, but I can't promise it won't happen someday. After all, we're going to be together for a very long time."

She laughed at his confidence. "Are we, now?"

"Of course."

He said it with so much certainty, she laughed again. "How much do you love me?"

"I love you with everything that I am. You're the woman I'm meant to have, my soul mate, my partner for life."

She cupped his beloved face in her hands and kissed him again. "I love you, too. More than I could ever have dreamed."

He pulled her close and sighed quietly against her hair. "I wish you didn't have to return to work."

"Me, too. But I get off at five. Only a few more hours to go. Where are you staying?"

"In the city." He gave her the name and address of his hotel. "Will you meet me there after work?"

She heard the faintest sound of uncertainty in his voice and kissed him hard on the lips in an effort to reassure him. "Wild horses couldn't keep me away."

He stared at her, his eyes filled with love. "I love you, Harper Wyburn."

She grinned, feeling impish. "Tell me again how much?"

He smiled. "You know how much I hate flying?"

She nodded. "Of course. You drove all the way to Brisbane just to avoid getting on a plane. Crazy."

His smile morphed into a grin. "Absolutely. So, despite the fact I own not only a Mercedes, but I recently acquired a Porsche, even those high performance cars weren't fast enough when it came to finding you."

She stared at him. Her eyes widened in sudden comprehension. "You *flew*?"

"Yep."

She shook her head in disbelief. "You got on a plane? For *me*?"

"Yep."

Tears mingled with her laughter. She felt overwhelmed by the strength of his love. He kissed her and then pressed his forehead to hers.

"Now you know how much I love you."

Chapter Twenty Three

Nick glanced at his watch nervously. It was only a few minutes past the last time he'd checked. Harper should have finished work by now. Any moment, he expected a call from downstairs, telling him she'd arrived. In all the wonder of rediscovering their love for each other, he'd forgotten to get her new number. Now he waited anxiously for her to turn up at his hotel.

Please let her come… I couldn't stand it if she changes her mind…

And then the phone beside the bed began to ring. Nick's heart leaped into his throat. He dived across the room and answered it.

"Mr Craigdon?"

"Yes."

"It's Jacob from reception. I have Harper Wyburn down here. She says she's a friend of yours."

Nick struggled to contain his relief. "Yes, that's right. Tell her I'm on my way down."

Hanging up the phone, Nick's body surged with excitement. She'd come, like she said she would. She hadn't let him down.

He left the room and hurried to the lift. Moments later, the doors opened and there she was. Standing only a few yards away, her face lit up when she saw him. Unable to help himself, he strode from the lift and took her straight into his arms.

Oblivious to any onlookers, he kissed her with everything he had. When he finally released her, she was breathless.

"Wow. I could get used to that kind of welcome." She grinned.

He grinned back, feeling impossibly happy. With their arms around each other, they walked back to the lift. They kissed and cuddled all the way up to the penthouse. The heavy petting continued down the corridor and into Nick's room. With almost frantic haste, they tore at each other's clothes, not pausing until they were both naked on the bed and pressed together, skin to skin.

Nick's sigh was one of pure contentment. "It feels so good to have you in my arms again. I've missed you so much."

Harper regarded him solemnly. "I've missed you, too."

Their kisses started out gentle, but as if a blowtorch had been applied, they suddenly erupted into a fireball of passion. Nick kissed every inch of her, from her lips and cheeks and eyelids, all the way across her collarbone and down her chest. He paused when he got to her nipples. Taking her breasts in his hand, he suckled one and then the other, flicking his tongue back and forth over the turgid peaks. Harper groaned and moved restlessly beneath him.

"Easy, honey. We have all night."

His words seemed to calm her. She relaxed back against the pillows and let him love her the way he wanted. Kissing his way across her ribcage, he moved lower down her flat belly and lower still. With his hands on her hips, he buried his face against her mound, breathing in her scent. And then he opened his mouth over her sensitive flesh and started stroking her silky folds with his tongue.

"Nick!" She gasped. Her fingers clutched at his head, burying themselves in his hair.

He continued his sensual onslaught, loving the sounds of her desire. Little whimpers of need, followed by gasps of delight… He loved that he could bring her so much pleasure… And he hadn't even started yet.

His tongue stroked long and slow, savoring her sweetness. The more attention he paid to her most sensitive flesh, the louder her cries of gratification. She'd released her hold on his hair and now clutched at the sheets. Her head moved from side to side with increasing speed. And then she was at the peak. She cried out in relief; her legs twitched, her chest rose and fell with the force of her rapid breathing. Eventually her breaths slowed. He eased himself from between her legs.

"That was amazing," she murmured with a smile, drawing him down beside her.

He grinned. "I'm glad you liked it. There's plenty more where that came from."

"I must be the luckiest girl in the world."

With that, she climbed on top of him, straddling him with her thighs. His eyes widened in surprise.

"You like being on top?" he teased.

She gave him a saucy look. "On top, on the bottom, maybe even from behind."

His gut clenched with white-hot desire. His cock was hard and throbbing. All afternoon he'd been nursing an erection, hoping the day might end with them in bed. Now she was here and he wanted to make it all about her, but he couldn't deny he was on fire. Just the thought of burying himself inside her silky warmth had his balls tightening with need. If it didn't happen soon, he might disgrace himself.

Harper's silky wetness was pressed against his cock. She rocked her hips back and forth over his groin, increasing the exquisite sensation. He reached up and took hold of her hips, encouraging her all the way. He didn't know how long he could last, but he wanted to enjoy every minute of it.

Leaning forward, Harper let her breasts fall across his face. He opened his mouth and snagged a nipple, suckling it. She groaned and he increased the pressure. She pressed down once again on his groin.

And then he couldn't stand it anymore. He had to be inside her. With one hand, he held her in position. With the other, he reached for a condom and handed it to her. Her eyes went wide with surprise.

"Are you sure? I've never done this before. What if I hurt you?"

"You won't hurt me," he rasped.

She tore open the packet and pulled out the condom. Tentatively, she took his cock in her hand and tried to slide on the condom. It took her a couple of attempts, but finally she had him sheathed.

She grinned at him in satisfaction. "What now?"

Desire surged through him. "Ride me."

Once again, her eyes flared wide with surprise and excitement. Positioning herself over his cock, she slowly impaled herself on his hardness. It was excruciating, but the pain of holding himself back from plunging inside her was so worthwhile when she finally seated herself to the hilt. They both gasped from the impact.

"Oh, God. You feel so good," he moaned.

"So do you."

She started moving slowly, rising and falling over his cock. With his hands back on either side of her hips, he guided her progress, increasing the pace as his desire burned ever hotter. And then he couldn't hold back anymore and with an almighty thrust he poured himself into her. His body was slick with sweat when he finally came back down to earth.

She looked down at him with eyes that were so filled with love it snatched away what little breath he still had.

"I'm sorry," he gasped. "You didn't come."

"Does that matter? I came before, remember?"

"Oh, it matters. Just give me a minute or two."

True to his word, in no time at all, he was ready and eager to go again. The way his body responded to her didn't surprise him. All he had to do was look at her and he wanted her.

This time he took it slowly when he positioned himself between her thighs. Sheathing himself with another condom, he inched into her wetness. She was slick from her earlier climax and he slid in easily and sighed. Moving his hips, he stroked in and out until she was once again flushed with desire.

Her eyes were open, holding his, silently encouraging him on. She reached up and pulled him down until they were lying chest to chest. As he picked up the pace of his rhythm, her fingers dug into his shoulders. She clung to him, her breath coming fast and then she reached her climax.

Crying out in triumph, she held him in a stranglehold. Gradually her breathing quieted and the tension in her body eased. He rolled onto his side and took her with him, looking at her with love. He pressed a soft kiss against her lips.

"Better?" he asked.

She smiled. "Better."

He kissed her again. "*That's* why it matters."

It was a long time later that Harper opened her eyes. She found Nicholas already awake beside her. He was smiling.

"You look happy," she said.

His smiled widened. "I *am* happy. More happy than I could ever have imagined."

She leaned up and gave him a soft kiss. "I'm glad."

She'd never felt so loved and cherished. Every moment with Nicholas felt right. She was so glad they'd overcome their differences. That he'd forgiven her for what she'd done. And then she remembered the one thing she hadn't told him.

"What is it?" he asked, noticing her frown.

She shrugged. "It's not really important, but… I don't want there to be any misunderstandings between us."

His expression sobered. "Should I be worried?"

She risked a smile. "I don't know. How badly do you need an EA?"

He frowned. "An EA? What are you talking about?"

She looked away. Heat crept across her cheeks. "I have a confession to make. It's about the job applications."

"For my EA?"

"Yes. Remember when I told you we hadn't received many?"

"Yes."

"The thing is, I fibbed. We received a lot. Hundreds."

"Hundreds? What did you do with them all?"

She kept her gaze fixed on the sheets. "I hid them in the bottom drawer of my desk."

His frown deepened. "What about when I told you to cull them and come up with a shortlist?"

"I ignored you," she said in a rush. She risked a glance in his direction.

His eyes widened in mock horror. "You *ignored* me? That was a direct order."

She nodded, trying not to squirm. "I know."

"What are you going to do about it?"

"What do you want me to do about it?"

"You disobeyed me. I think that deserves punishment."

Surprise and a little alarm surged through her. Her gaze flew to his. "You're going to punish me?"

A gleam of desire entered his eyes. He reached out and flicked her nipple with his finger. "Oh, yes. I have no choice."

Her belly somersaulted with need. Her hand slid across his bare chest, stroking his taut skin. "What did you have in mind?"

"I'm not sure, yet. I'll let you know."

She pouted in disappointment. "But I want to know now."

"All in good time. Serious decisions can't be rushed."

"Of course not." Her hand wandered lower until she circled his cock. It immediately came to life in her hand.

"Careful," he warned. "You're in dangerous territory now."

She smiled, her eyes wide with innocence. "Really?" She stroked her hand up and down his member. Within moments, he was erect. She bent over and took him in her mouth.

"Harper…"

She looked up at him, his cock still filling her mouth. "Yes?"

He made an unintelligible sound. Taking that for consent, she began sucking him in earnest, using her mouth, her tongue, her lips. His hips bucked against the mattress, but she didn't stop her assault.

Just when she thought he could take it no longer, he sat up and flipped her over. Before she knew it, he'd sheathed himself and had buried himself inside her. With her desire already fever pitch, it wasn't long before both of them cried out together.

Exhausted, she sank back into the mattress and gave him a triumphant grin. "I'll take that kind of punishment any day."

Nick chuckled and threaded his fingers in hers. After awhile, he spoke. "By the way, I was speaking to Zane McClintock. Christopher's been fired."

Harper sighed. "I know he's your brother, but good riddance, I say. He was way too easy to convince to become a part of my plan for revenge. I couldn't bear the thought that he was still in a position to hurt you or your company."

"Half-brother," Nick corrected. "And you're right. I'm glad he's gone. By the way, do you think you can come back to Craigdon Enterprises because thanks to you, I still don't have a permanent EA."

She poked out her tongue and tossed a pillow at his head. His raucous laughter filled the room. The joyous sound of it made her smile.

Note to Readers

I do hope you have enjoyed reading Nicholas and Harper's story. If you've enjoyed this book, I would really appreciate it if you could leave a review at Goodreads and your favorite digital retailer. Every review increases visibility and helps other readers to find books they enjoy.

Receive a free book when you sign up for my newsletter if you like to receive news on upcoming stories, release dates, book launches and other snippets. I love to receive feedback from my readers. Please feel free to contact me at chris@christaylorauthor.com.au.

Sophia is the next book in the Craigdon Family Dynasty series. Keep reading for a sneak peek:

Excerpt from

Sophia

The Craigdon Family Dynasty

Book Five

CHRIS TAYLOR

Chapter One

Sophia Craigdon snatched another glass of champagne from a tray carried by a passing waiter and emptied half of it in one swallow. She was already onto her fourth glass and she'd barely been there an hour. It wasn't that she didn't enjoy attending a glitzy family function, but they were celebrating her brother, Joel and his fiancée, Sheridan's engagement party. Everyone was so goddamn *happy*. Smiles and laughter were everywhere. It was sickening.

Of course, she was happy for her brother. For years, Joel had seemed content to play the field. Though he'd had one long-term girlfriend, he'd given her the flick right after he inherited ten million dollars. He'd gone on a trip to Europe and from all accounts, he'd had a great time. Not the least with several exotic-looking women, if his Instagram feed was anything to go by.

But now he'd met Sheridan McClintock. She was the daughter of Sophia's late father's biggest competitor. It proved for some uncomfortable moments early on, but it was obvious the two lovebirds had worked things out. They'd been kissing and cuddling all evening, barely taking time out to greet their guests.

Restless, Sophia circumnavigated the formal dining room

where most of the guests were gathered. The party was supposed to have been held outdoors in the lush gardens of Craigdon Manor, but a thunderstorm had rolled in a few hours earlier and plans had been quickly changed. The three-piece band had been moved inside and were now set up in her mother's music room, after moving the grand piano to one side. Most of the guests wandered in and out between the two rooms, leaving Sophia no escape. Unless she wanted to hide in the kitchen with the caterers or slink off to her old room upstairs, there was nowhere to go.

She reached for a canapé and popped it into her mouth. She wasn't in the least bit hungry, but she had to admit, the caviar was good. Not that she expected anything but the best for a high society do such as this. Though Joel was a detective in the city and not really into the whole extravagant party scene, it seemed Sheridan had wanted to make a splash and had invited all of her family's friends and quite a number of her work colleagues.

It was a who's who of the social pages. She recognized several prominent businessmen, along with the Lord Mayor of Sydney. Sheridan's brother, Zane Forrest was there, along with a famous model hanging off his arm. There were also a number of politicians, bankers and lawyers, all vying for attention. No wonder she wanted to escape.

She took another gulp of champagne, this time emptying the glass. She wasn't in the mood for the lovey-dovey atmosphere. The truth was, she'd been out of sorts for most of the year. Ever since her father had died unexpectedly from a heart attack and had left her almost nothing in his will.

Most of her brothers had inherited ten million dollars. Her sister, Isabella had received double that. Then there had been a fifteen-million dollar gift to some weird charity. And yet Sophia had received a paltry one-hundred grand. It was barely enough to pay off her student loans. An insult, that's what it was. It was more than eight months since the reading of the will and she was still hopping mad.

Catching sight of another waiter, she pressed forward through the crush of people and set her empty glass down on the tray. She immediately swiped another one.

"Thank you," she muttered to the waiter and turned away.

Once again, she swallowed half the contents before coming up for air. It was lucky she was a seasoned drinker. No one spent four years at university without learning how to hold their liquor. It was a right of passage and one she'd exuberantly embraced. At the memory of her university days, a reluctant smile tugged at her lips.

"Ah, there it is. I was beginning to think we wouldn't see your smile ever again."

The teasing comment came from her brother, Callum. He followed it with a peck on her cheek and then stepped back and drew his fiancée, Grace close. Grace looked up at him and smiled at him so tenderly it nearly made Sophia sick. Just another loved-up couple. They were everywhere.

"There's no need to look so happy," she replied in a churlish tone.

Callum gave her a serene smile. "Happiness is good for the soul, little sis. You ought to try it sometime."

Sophia gave a non-committal grunt and took another gulp from her champagne. Callum continued to regard her calmly, but now a slight frown creased his forehead.

"You might want to take it easy, Soph. You're looking a bit flushed."

"Last time I checked, I was past the age of consent, Callum. Keep your advice to yourself."

"Whoa!" he replied and held his hands up in a sign of surrender. "I didn't mean any offense." He paused and then added more quietly, "I'm worried about you, Soph. You haven't been the same since Dad died."

Swift anger ignited inside her. She glared at her brother. "Surely you don't have to ask why?"

He compressed his lips and nodded. "Of course not. And I understand. But you've got to let the anger go. It's eating you up inside."

She curled her lip up in disgust, even as tears pricked her eyes. "Easy for you to say. You weren't done over like I was. You got everything you could have dreamed. A release from Dad's stupid promise that you give your life to the church, along with a tidy sum of ten million dollars. You did all right."

"I'm not disputing that," Callum continued in a gentle tone. "Just like I agree you were dealt a shabby hand. It wasn't right and it wasn't fair, but don't let it destroy you. You're better than that."

Bitterness flooded her veins. She blinked back tears of pain. "Am I? Apparently our father didn't think so."

Callum's eyes filled with love and concern. Stepping forward, he put his arm around her shoulders and drew her close.

"I hate seeing you like this, Soph. It's like you've let him win. Dad did something unforgivable to you, but you can't let it ruin your life. You have so much going for you. You're young and beautiful and smart. You've just finished your university studies. The world is yours for the taking. You can do anything you want."

She looked at him and was filled with gratitude for this big brother she loved so much. "Thanks, Callum. I appreciate that."

He gave her another peck on the cheek. "It's true. All of it. You need to believe it, too."

She sniffed and nodded. "You're right. I'm a good and decent person, no matter what Dad did. He's the asshole, not me."

Callum smiled. "Thatta girl."

Sophia managed to smile back and then she looked at Grace. "Sorry about that. It must be the champagne. I was feeling sorry for myself. All the love in this room, it's a bit hard to take." Her gaze encompassed Callum. "But I want you to know, I'm so pleased for you guys. In fact, I'm thrilled you've found each other and fallen in love. It's a beautiful love story and I'm so proud to be part of it."

"Thank you, Sophia," Grace replied, giving her a soft smile.

"Well," Sophia said in a brighter tone, "not long now until the wedding. Are you getting nervous?"

Grace laughed. "Not nervous about getting married, but there's still so much to do. We only have six weeks left. I'm not sure how we're going to get everything ready in time."

"You'll be right," Sophia assured her. "You have my mother on board. She can organize a wedding with her eyes closed, even one as elaborate as yours."

Grace worried at her bottom lip. "I'm not sure it was a good idea setting the date right before Christmas. It's been so hard to secure caterers and decorators, enough chairs and tables for the guests, champagne buckets… The list goes on."

"I'm sure everything will work out just fine," Sophia assured her once again. "It will be the best wedding ever."

Grace shot her a grateful smile. "Thank you, Sophia. You always seem to know what to say to make me feel better."

Sophia shot her a tight smile. "I'm glad I have the ability to make someone feel better."

"Now, now Soph," Callum quietly admonished. "We're not doing this again. Come on. We're at a party."

Sophia forced a brilliant smile. "You're right. Let's have another glass of champagne. I want to toast the happy couple! Or should I say, *couples.* You seem to be multiplying."

She gazed around the room and spied Joel and Sheridan sharing another kiss. Her brother, Nicholas, and his new girlfriend, Harper Wyburn, were also getting down hot and heavy in one corner. It was Nick's first serious relationship. He looked besotted. Sophia was happy for him, even if he'd ignored her many pleas for a job at Craigdon Enterprises.

In the end, things had worked out and Sophia had managed to secure a temporary position at Mosman Primary School. It had been a lucky break. Not many schools took on new staff in the last term of the year. Besides, Sophia really liked Harper. Even better, Harper seemed to really like Nick. Sophia hoped the relationship would last the distance.

Sophia sighed. No matter where she looked, happiness abounded. She needed to find somewhere else to hang out. With a muttered excuse in Callum and Grace's direction, she made her escape.

Weaving through the press of people, she couldn't help but grin at Grace's children as they stole handfuls of handmade chocolates off a platter. Seth was ten and Alyssa was eight. They'd become a regular fixture at Craigdon Manor. Sophia's mother, Elizabeth was pleased to have the rooms once again filled with the noise and laughter of children and had welcomed them with open arms. Once Grace finished rehab, she'd be living at Craigdon Manor fulltime until the wedding. Sophia was sure her mother was looking forward to having female company again, especially now that Isabella was moving out.

Ever since Sophia's sister, Isabella had met her boyfriend, Raine Fairfax it was inevitable the two would end up together. Though their path to true love hadn't been easy, anyone could see they were made for each other.

After attending university and then working in the rural city of Armidale, Isabella had returned to Sydney right before the unexpected death of their father in February. Though she'd moved back home and was still living there, it was only a matter of time before she left for good. Raine lived in Brisbane and had a successful business there. As a doctor,

Isabella was more mobile. It made sense for her to be the one to relocate.

Sophia had only spoken to her sister about her plans the day before and Isabella had told her she expected to make the move after Christmas. With Callum and Grace's upcoming wedding and the usual Christmas fanfare that went on in the Craigdon family, she'd decided to wait until then.

Sophia had mixed feelings about her older sister moving interstate. She'd always looked up to Isabella and admired her for her grit and determination and her seemingly effortless way of always looking sensational, no matter what the occasion. And of course, she loved her fiercely and would miss having her around. Sophia had also gone to university in Armidale and even though the two sisters hadn't shared an apartment, they'd socialized often enough.

But there were many times during their childhood that Sophia had felt inferior and jealous of her sister. It had been no secret that their father had favored Isabella over Sophia. He hadn't even tried to hide it.

Even in death, Henry Craigdon had gone out of his way to rub salt into the wound. He'd left Isabella the hefty sum of twenty million dollars. To Sophia, he'd left a mere pittance. It had been yet another hurtful blow in a long series of painful experiences she'd had with her father and now he was gone forever. There was no one to rail against, no one to blame. All that was left was for her to overcome the hurt and pain and bitterness that sometimes overtook her and get on with her life. It was easier said than done.

Sophia made a beeline for a sideboard where rows of champagne-filled glasses stood. She picked one up and took a gulp. The tart alcohol slid down her throat, cool and crisp. Most people would be well on their way to being sozzled with all the alcohol she'd drunk, but for Sophia, it had barely taken the edge off.

Intent on escaping the room, she turned and headed toward the exit. On her way, she spied her half-brother, Christopher Barrington. Though he was family, she never could work out why her mother kept inviting him to family functions. He didn't even try to fit in or pretend he was happy to be there. He was a serial pest who went out of his way to make trouble for her family. It seemed all he wanted to do was criticize and complain about the family who had only ever tried to accept, love and support him.

She ducked away to avoid him. She wasn't in the mood for his acerbic tongue, or to get caught up listening to another round of his complaints. The way she saw it, Christopher brought the misfortune on himself.

Finally breaking clear of the crowd, she left the dining room and wandered across the hall into her father's study. She hadn't been in there since the reading of the will, more than eight months earlier. The room was dim, with most of the curtains drawn. She assumed her mother kept it that way on purpose. It was a room that had always been dominated by Henry. Even though he was gone, it didn't seem right to intrude on his space. But right now, she had to escape the party and her father's office seemed like a good place to go. It was the one place no one would come looking for her.

Flopping down on one of the comfortable leather couches, she took another mouthful of champagne and sighed.

"Sounds heavy."

She jumped. The sudden movement caused her to slosh champagne all over her dress. She blinked in surprise as her cousin, Flynn moved from out of the shadows. He'd been standing near one of the floor-to-ceiling bookshelves that lined the room. A thoughtful expression creased his face.

"Flynn! What are you doing here? You startled me."

"Sorry about that," he replied. He moved closer and then sat beside her on the couch.

A quick grin turned up the corners of his mouth. Tall and broad-shouldered with thick blond hair, brown eyes and a killer smile, unlike her brother, Nicholas, Flynn had always been popular with the ladies. Sophia didn't have to wonder why. On top of the exceptional good looks, Flynn was a lawyer and an all-round decent guy.

"That sigh sounded like you had the weight of the world on your shoulders, Soph. You're at a party and an engagement party at that! You should be on top of the world. Your brother's found the love of his life."

She grimaced. Flynn was family. There was no need to pretend with him. "I've had better days. Hell, I've had better years. Don't get me wrong, I'm thrilled for Joel and Sheridan. And Callum and Grace. And Isabella and Raine. And even Nick. Did you meet Harper? Did you see the way he looks at her? He's besotted. Good on him. He deserves to find a woman who loves him."

Flynn shot her a curious look. "Then what's with the frown?"

Sophia sighed again. "I'm sure you already know the answer to that."

"Are you talking about your father's will?"

"Of course. What else do you think's been consuming my time all these months? It's so darn unfair!"

To her horror, tears filled her eyes. She angrily swiped at them with the back of her hand. She refused to waste more tears on her goddamned excuse of a father.

Flynn put his arm around her shoulders and drew her close. With another sigh, she rested her head on his chest. Though they were cousins, they were as close as if he were another one of her brothers. She'd always found it easy to talk to him.

"Talk to me, Soph. Shout, cry, scream. Let it all out, honey."

His gentle words were her undoing. With a gasp, she poured out her anger and hurt. He sat and listened, a strong, silent presence, offering comfort without words. When at last she finished, he tightened his arm briefly around her shoulders.

"Feel better now?"

She gave him a shaky smile. "Yes, I do. And I'm not one bit sorry for the things I just said."

"You have no need to be sorry. Uncle Henry treated you appallingly." He paused and then added, "You have options, you know. Legal remedies. You could always sue the estate for a bigger share."

She grimaced in distaste. "Like Christopher? No, I don't think so."

"Hey," Flynn said gently. "Don't be too hard on Christopher. He was treated even more shabbily than you. Cut him some slack."

She compressed her lips and remained silent. What Flynn said about Christopher was true, but her half-brother wouldn't get any sympathy from her. She had enough to deal with on her own and no matter how hurt she was about the way her father had treated her under his will, she wouldn't be suing anyone.

"Logan told me you were looking for a job at Craigdon Enterprises," Flynn said, changing the subject.

Sophia nodded. "Yes. I was. Given that Daddy left the company to your brother, I approached Logan first. I graduated from university back in February and I still didn't have a job. On top of everything else, it was getting me down. Logan told me to speak with Nick. After all, he was the managing director in charge of the day-to-day running of the business."

"So did Nick find you something?"

Sophia shook her head. "You'd think as the managing director's little sister he'd have shown me some favoritism, but no. Nick played it by the book. He told me I didn't have the skills required for anything senior. The best he could offer me was a junior admin position." She pulled a face. "I'm university educated! As if I'd be willing to take on a minimum wage role like that."

Flynn grinned and she could tell what he was thinking, but wisely, he chose to remain silent. "So," he said instead, "what are you doing with yourself?"

She gave him the first genuine smile she'd managed all night. "It seems Nick did me a favor, after all. I was lucky enough to get a job teaching at Mosman Primary School. A maternity leave position."

"That's great news! How's that working out?"

Chapter Two

At the thought of the twenty-three kindergarteners currently under her supervision, Sophia reluctantly smiled. "It's working out okay. I didn't expect to enjoy it so much."

Flynn frowned. "But didn't you just spend four years at university to become a teacher?"

"Yes, and I really enjoyed my studies, but in the back of my mind, I always thought I'd come and work with Daddy in the family company."

Flynn shot her a wry look. "Like teaching and the cutthroat world of property development have so much in common."

Sophia blushed. "You're right. But I spent so much of my life thinking that's how things would go. And now it's all gone pear-shaped."

"But you enjoy teaching. You just said so."

She sighed again. "You're right. I should forget about my dream of working in Craigdon Enterprises. After all, with Daddy gone, it's never going to be the same."

"From what Logan tells me, your brother's doing an excellent job as managing director."

"Of course he is! Nick was born to take over the reins from Daddy. I still don't understand why Daddy didn't see it that way, too." She flushed, suddenly becoming aware of what she'd just said. "I don't mean to offend Logan. He's a great guy. It's just that…" She shrugged, feeling helpless.

"I know what you mean. We were all shocked when that came out. Even Logan. He had no idea."

Sophia shook her head, bewildered. "Why would Daddy be so cruel to Nick? I mean, nothing against Logan, but Nick's his flesh and blood. It's like the stunt he pulled on me. A lousy one-hundred thousand dollars. Barely enough to cover my student loans."

"I thought there was more for you in the will."

She made a sound of disgust. "Only if you count that stupid condition about me having to get married."

Flynn regarded her solemnly. "Perhaps it's something you should give serious consideration."

Sophia almost choked on her champagne. "What? Getting married to some random just so I can inherit?"

"Hey, we're talking about five million dollars. That's no small change. In exchange for only a year of marriage, I don't think it's a bad trade."

Laughter bubbled up inside her. "Oh, that's rich, coming from the perennially single Flynn Craigdon! What would you know about marriage? You go through women like a university student goes through a keg. Can you even remember the name of that girl you dragged to Annalise's baptism?"

Flynn merely laughed. "Of course. Casey. Boy, was she a firecracker."

Sophia looked at him with one eyebrow raised. "Was? Do I take it the fiery Miss Casey has been replaced already?"

Flynn shrugged. An embarrassed flush stained his cheeks. "Yeah, things didn't work out. She was a bit too clingy. Started hinting that we should move in together. Hell, we'd barely known each other a month."

Sophia shot him a dry look. "Why aren't I surprised? She's only one in a long line of women you've refused to allow yourself to get close to. Admit it, Flynn. You're a commitment-phobe. You can see why I'm not falling over myself to take marital advice from the likes of you."

Flynn grinned, completely unrepentant. "That might be true Soph, but I'm not the one looking to lose five million dollars. Suit yourself. I know what I'd do."

With that, he leaned over and pecked her on the cheek and then stood. "I'm going to re-join the party. I'm sure there's a pretty woman or two who might be willing to spend some time with me." He winked.

Sophia reached for a cushion and tossed it toward his head. Flynn deflected it easily and laughed.

"What were you doing in here, anyway?" she asked, curious. She looked around the dim study and fought off a barrage of memories. "No one comes in here anymore."

Flynn's expression sobered. "I wanted to get away from the noise and frivolity for a while. I found my way in here without really thinking about where I was going." He paused and his voice lowered. "I still can't believe he's gone."

Sophia was immediately beset by emotions. She hated that the primary emotion she felt whenever she thought of her father was pain. Even now, more than eight months after his passing, she still hadn't been able to let go of it. Still, no matter how much hurt and pain her father had caused, he was still her father and despite everything, she'd always loved him. It was the reason she'd craved his love and attention. If he hadn't mattered to her, if his opinion hadn't counted, she never would have bothered setting herself up for disappointment time and time again.

"Don't go there, Soph." Flynn's voice was soft and soothing.

She forced a sad smile. "You're right. There's no point. He's gone. It's time to put all of that aside and get on with my life, living it on my terms the best I can. Right?"

He smiled. "Right."

With that, he held out his hand and helped her up. She gave him a hug. "Thanks, Flynn."

He looked at her in surprise. "For what?"

"For everything. I don't know what I'd do without you."

He shrugged, a little embarrassed. "Of course you do. You have four brothers of your own. Not to mention two more male cousins. I'm sure you would have found someone to listen to your woes."

She poked her tongue out at him and grinned.

"Brat." He chuckled. "Come on, let's go and have some fun."

Sophia left Flynn chatting up an attractive brunette wearing a skin-tight leather dress that left little to the imagination. She accepted another glass of champagne from a passing waiter and wandered outside. The rain had cleared away and a makeshift dance floor had been set up on the paved area surrounding the pool. The band was now playing loud music. A handful of people were moving on the dance floor, including her cousin, Noah and her sister, Isabella, who'd managed to tear herself away from Raine.

Noah was Flynn's younger brother. Whereas Flynn had bucket loads of confidence, Noah was the complete opposite. He was every bit as good looking as his older brother, but was too shy for his own good, especially around women. One place he did shine was the dance floor and right now he was carving it up with Isabella.

Sophia took a sip from her glass and smiled ruefully. It was typical of Noah. There were at least a dozen eligible women at the party who would have jumped at the chance to partner him, but instead he was helping his cousin through the intricate steps of a salsa. No wonder he was still single.

Still, there was no rush to get to the altar. She ought to

know. She'd grown up knowing her parents only stayed together for convenience and no doubt financial reasons. A costly divorce wouldn't have benefitted either party. The only ones to win would be the lawyers. Her parents weren't stupid.

But the lack of love between them had left Sophia with a sour taste in her mouth when it came to the state of marriage. She'd long declared she'd remain single for the rest of her life. And her father had known that. No doubt that was the reason he'd punished her with the ridiculous clause in his will. Only another reason to despair at the apparent enjoyment he took from causing her hurt.

She glanced at her watch. She'd barely been at the party a couple of hours.

I wonder how long before I can sneak out?

As if privy to her thoughts, her mother materialized beside her.

"Sophia, darling. I hope you're not leaving? You've only just arrived." Her mother pecked her on the cheek. "You look beautiful, as usual. I love what you've done with your hair."

Sophia touched her brown locks a little self-consciously. Out of deference to the occasion and her frightfully expensive dress, she'd gone to the hairdresser earlier that day and had instructed the woman to jazz up her boring color. It wasn't fair that Isabella had been born with the most gorgeous white-blond hair and even her brothers had shades of dark blond like their father or black, like their mother and Sophia had been stuck with plain brown.

To her relief, her hairdresser had worked magic and the blond highlights she'd added brought out the richness of Sophia's brown hair. She'd left it out and it fell in long waves across her shoulders.

"Thanks, Mom. Given the occasion, I thought I should make an extra effort."

Her mother smiled gently and then slowly her smile disappeared. She looked at Sophia with concern.

"What's the matter, darling? Why do you look so glum?"

And just like that, the hurt and pain Sophia had nursed for more than eight long months ignited into anger. "Wouldn't you? Daddy left me next to nothing! I don't understand! I tried so hard for him to love me. Why didn't he love me, Mom?"

To her horror, her voice cracked on a shard of emotion and tears burned behind her eyes. Her mother's expression softened. She leaned over and tenderly brushed Sophia's long hair out of her eyes.

"Of course he did," she said quietly, but she didn't meet Sophia's eyes.

"No, Mom. He didn't. We both know it. There's no point in denying it. And his last malicious act reinforces that. What kind of father holds out the promise of five million dollars to a penniless student but only if they agree to tie themselves up in matrimony? I mean. What is this? The nineteenth century? He knew how I felt about marriage. And what about Isabella? Why didn't *she* have to get married in order to inherit? Daddy knew she felt the same way I did. He'd never force something like that on his precious Isabella." Sophia shook her head. "I still can't believe she's had such a total change of heart."

Her mother looked over toward Isabella who was still enjoying herself on the dance floor with Noah and then sighed. "I guess she wasn't planning on being swept away by her Prince Charming. None of us can predict the future. You shouldn't look at this as such a weight around your neck, darling. Forget about the money. The trust fund I set up for you when you turned eighteen was very generous and I'm more than happy to top up your account. You're hardly penniless. We both know you don't need the money from your father."

Sophia's shoulders slumped. Her anger of just a few

moments ago had eased. She looked at her mother. "I know, Mom and I'm extremely grateful for everything you've done for me. But it still hurts. It's not so much about the money, but that Daddy set things up that way. And he only did it to *me*. Almost like he wanted to punish me."

"Don't be silly. Besides, you weren't the only one he dealt with so harshly."

Sophia stared at her. "You mean, Nick?"

"Yes. He was devastated when your father overlooked him as the CEO of Craigdon Enterprises. He's worked there for years. Every afternoon he was there, learning the ropes, even while he was still attending school. If it weren't for Logan's generosity, I don't know what Nick would have done."

Almost on cue, the double glass sliding doors that led from the main house to the pool area opened and Nick and Harper spilled out. They were holding hands and laughing. They both looked so happy. So removed from the brother of eight months ago who'd been shocked and devastated when he'd realized the company he'd given his everything to had been gifted to someone else.

Sophia sighed. "I'm so glad he's found Harper and that things are working out for him at Craigdon Enterprises, but I still can't help wondering what the hell Daddy was thinking."

Her mother didn't reply. Instead, she busied herself accepting a glass of champagne from a passing waiter. Sophia tossed the rest of her wine back and replaced it with a fresh glass.

"Let's not think about your father right now. It's your brother's engagement party. A time for celebration. Okay?" She clinked her glass with Sophia's.

Sophia offered her a reluctant smile. "Okay."

"That's my girl." Her mother leaned over and kissed her on the cheek. "I love you, Sophia."

"I love you too, Mom."

Chapter Three

The bright, mid-afternoon sun bounced off the lake in shards of diamonds and had Sophia reaching for her sunglasses from her perch on one of the wooden park benches not far from the water. After all the alcohol she'd consumed the night before, it was a wonder she didn't have a hangover, but she'd always been lucky that way. There were some advantages to being a seasoned drinker.

She'd come down to the man-made lake at Penrith to enjoy some peace and quiet away from her family. As much as she loved them, she'd had about all she could take. Most of them had spent the night at Craigdon Manor and had stumbled downstairs for a late breakfast in groups of twos and threes. Callum and Grace and her children had still been there when Sophia had left to get some fresh air. No doubt they'd be gone before she got back. Grace still had another week of rehab. Though she'd been given a leave pass to attend the engagement party and then spend the night, she was expected to return before the weekend was over.

A couple of sailboats with brightly colored sails drifted past, disturbing a handful of wood ducks. A group of white ibis stood on the water's edge, stately on their spindle-like legs, watching with curious eyes. The grassed area was filled with families picnicking, children laughing and playing games. It was a happy scene, a peaceful scene and one she enjoyed.

She'd always loved kids. It was the main reason she'd gravitated toward a career in primary school teaching. She loved the honesty of children, their unfiltered, undiluted reactions. So different to the adult world. So different to her father's world.

For years, she'd wanted to follow in Henry's footsteps and carve out a name for herself in the world of property development. She hadn't wanted to strike out on her own. She would have been content to work under her father. But it seemed no matter how hard she worked or what she did to get her father's attention, he'd dismissed her at every turn. Eventually she faced the reality he was never going to see her as a potential business partner, or even a senior executive. He couldn't have cared less about her interest in Craigdon Enterprises.

So, she'd looked elsewhere to make her mark and had ended up in Armidale completing a four-year university degree. Her time there made her realize the reason she'd liked working at Craigdon Enterprises was because it was a way to get her father's attention and hopefully, his approval. She didn't actually *like* the cutthroat world of business.

What she really enjoyed was being around young children and interacting with them. She liked the feeling of being important to them and making a difference in their lives. She'd come to realize that even more since starting work at Mosman Primary. She'd only been there a couple of weeks, but already she looked forward to going to work each day.

It was the kids who made all the difference. The kids gave her a sense of fulfilment. They made her smile. Nick had been right to turn her down for a job at Craigdon Enterprises. He was the one who'd told her to put her degree to good use. After all, she'd just used her entire inheritance to pay off her student loans.

She'd finished her degree with honors and was so proud of the effort she'd put in. She'd graduated only weeks before her father's death. He'd barely acknowledged her achievement. She'd still been smarting over that when he died.

The gurgling sound of young laughter snagged her attention. She looked to where a small boy was playing with a soccer ball, kicking it toward a good-looking guy, who kicked it back to him. As she watched, the young child swung hard with his foot and completely missed the ball, instead falling over onto his butt. Though the lush grass softened the impact, Sophia braced herself for tears. But instead the same unrestrained laughter rang out. She couldn't help but grin.

Though she wasn't keen on the idea of marriage, that didn't mean she wasn't keen on kids. She definitely wanted kids one day. As far as she was concerned, the two weren't mutually exclusive. She couldn't believe her father left her five million dollars only on the condition that she marry. Just like it did every time she thought about it, her blood started to boil, ruining her good mood. Her father's actions were ridiculous. Barbaric, even.

But then she remembered what Flynn had said. Five million dollars was a lot of money. It could set her up for life. Yes, she had the money in her trust fund and she was very grateful for that, but it fell far short of the inheritance she'd been entitled to from her father.

Maybe I could put up with someone for a year in order to get it?

A year wasn't all that long, after all. She'd spent four years at university and that time had flown by. She was going on twenty-two. Not old by anyone's reckoning. Even after a year of marriage, she'd still be in her twenties. With five million dollars in her pocket, she'd be free to do as she chose. She couldn't imagine wanting to give up her work as a teacher, but she'd have a lot of options in front of her, that's for sure.

There was one big problem she was avoiding. Even if she got to the point where she decided she could marry someone for money, what kind of man would go for that? And how would she find him? They had to do more than just marry. They had to convince her mother and Callum they were the real deal. Not an easy thing to pull off with a stranger.

"Look out!"

Jolted out of her reverie, Sophia looked up just in time to avoid a flying ball. She ducked and the ball sailed over her head. The good-looking guy scooped his son into his arms and came jogging toward her. He gave her an apologetic smile.

"I'm so sorry," he said, his eyes crinkling at the corners. "That nearly took your head off."

She shrugged and tried not to notice that he was even more good looking up close. His caramel-colored skin, wide nose, and thick dark hair were evidence of an Aboriginal heritage. On top of that, he had the most incredible green eyes. Despite herself, her heart skipped a beat.

She wasn't easily impressed by anyone. Growing up in an ultra-wealthy, well-known family meant there were plenty of people throwing themselves at her, wanting to impress her, both men and women. It had been that way all her life. She'd learned to be very choosy about the people she spent time with. Everyone wanted to be her friend, but not all of them had her best interests at heart.

But here was a guy who set her pulse racing and all he'd done was smile. It was ridiculous. He was obviously here with his son, no doubt happily married to some equally gorgeous woman. That's the way it usually went.

Coming to her feet, she moved around the bench and picked up the ball. He set down the child and Sophia crouched down and handed it to him. The boy grinned.

"What do you say, Beckett?" the man said.

"Thank you."

Sophia smiled. "You're welcome."

She stood and was once again on eye level with the boy's father. "Cute kid," she said. "He looks like you."

The man grinned. "Yeah, much to my brother's disgust."

She frowned in bemusement. "Why would your brother care?"

"Probably because Beckett's his son."

"Oh." Her face flamed. Unable to help herself, her gaze slid to his ring finger. It was bare. Still that didn't necessarily mean anything. Lots of married guys didn't wear wedding rings, especially if they were involved in manual labor, like a tradesman.

"I'm Jarrod Sampson."

Belatedly, she noticed his outstretched hand. She shook it briefly. "Sophia Craigdon."

"Of Craigdon Enterprises?"

She cursed under her breath. She should have given him a fake name. It was too late now.

"Yes."

"I heard about your father's death. I'm sorry."

She blinked in surprise. He sounded so sincere. "Thank you. It's been a difficult adjustment. He was larger than life. He left a big hole to fill."

"I know what you mean. I lost my father a couple of years ago. Car accident. One minute he was here and the next he was gone. He was a big part of my life. My hero. I still miss him," he added quietly.

Sophia thought about her father. He was a long way from being her hero. Still he was the only father she'd had and she'd loved him. She still couldn't believe he was dead.

"I'm sorry," she said and realized she meant it. She'd only just met this guy and already she cared that he was grieving.

"Thanks." He sat down on the bench and she sat down beside him. She noticed he kept a close eye on Beckett, who was now kicking at dry leaves, laughing with glee as they fluttered around him.

She smiled. "How old is he?"

"Three-and-a-half."

"A good age."

"Yes. Do you have kids?"

She quickly shook her head. "No, no. But I've spent the past four years studying kids. I'm a teacher."

The admiration in his eyes filled her with warmth. "Good on you. That's one job I could never do."

"But you're here with Beckett and having a great time. I was watching you. You're a natural."

He quirked an eyebrow, somehow managing to look even more sexy. He followed it with a grin. "You were watching me? Should I be worried?"

She blushed again and was immediately annoyed with herself. No one made her blush. Ever. She was usually so totally in control of every situation.

"Not like that," she hurried to explain.

He laughed. "Hey, don't sweat it. I'm joking."

She managed a smile, but was still embarrassed. In an effort to distract him, she changed the subject.

"So, are you a property developer? Is that how you knew of my father's death?"

He laughed again. "No. I'm a cop."

"Oh."

"Disappointed?"

"No, of course not," she said truthfully. "In fact, two of my brothers are cops. And a cousin. I have a lot of admiration for people who are prepared to put their life on the line to keep us safe."

"You make me sound like superman." He followed the comment with another sexy smile. His white teeth were in stark contrast to his tanned skin. A three-day growth covered his cheeks, adding to his attractiveness. His thick, wavy hair ruffled in the slight breeze. She itched to run her fingers through it.

Crazy!

"So, what brings you to the park this lovely Sunday afternoon?"

His question jolted her from her reverie. She opened her mouth to give him some glib answer and found herself confiding in him instead.

"I came looking for some peace and quiet."

He shot her a knowing smile. "Big night, huh?"

She smiled. "Yes, a family celebration. My brother's engagement party."

"Ah. You overindulged."

She grinned. "Maybe. But I'm one of those lucky people who don't suffer from hangovers."

He looked at her in mock envy. "Oh, please no! You're not one of *those* people, are you? Don't take this the wrong way, but I hate you." He softened the words with a teasing smile.

She laughed. "Oh, don't worry, so do my brothers and sister. I seem to be the only one out of the six of us who inherited the trait. I'm not complaining. It comes in handy."

"I'll bet. So, you're one of six. That's a pretty big family."

She saw the friendly curiosity in his eyes. "You knew about my father. I assume you also know something about my family."

He shrugged. "Only from what I read in the social pages."

She smiled, but it came off more like a grimace. "Then you'll be completely up to date with all the lurid details."

"Why don't you tell me yourself?"

She looked at him. There was something about him that inspired trust. Maybe it was the fact he was a police officer.

"It isn't all nice," she finally said.

"What family doesn't have a few skeletons in the closet?"

She smiled briefly. "Don't say I didn't warn you." She drew in a deep breath and eased it out on a sigh. It felt like she'd been angry and tense for months. Eight months, in fact. Ever since her father died and his lawyer had disclosed the contents of Henry's will: the good, the bad and the downright ugly.

"I'm the youngest. I have four brothers and a sister. My father's estate was considerable, but for reasons known only to him, he didn't divide it evenly. Some of us were treated very favorably and others, not so much. He left the family company to one of my cousins." She was helpless against the bitterness that lined her voice.

Jarrod regarded her somberly. "I take it you were in the latter category."

She compressed her lips and nodded grimly. "Oh, yeah. I'm not sure what I did to deserve it, but I was left a paltry sum compared to most of my siblings."

"I don't understand what kind of father could do that to his kids," Jarrod mused.

Sophia' lips twisted in a grimace. "Don't worry, it gets worse. He added a further clause just for me. I can inherit a larger sum of money if I marry."

Jarrod shook his head in surprise. "Wow, that's the weirdest thing I've ever heard. Who does that? Your father really must have wanted to see you married. I take it you're against the institution?"

She shrugged. "My parents weren't exactly good proponents for marriage. Both of them had affairs. Besides, I'm twenty-one. Who wants to get married at my age?"

"So why did your father insist on such a ridiculous condition?"

"I don't know. To punish me?"

"Why would he want to do that?"

"I don't know that either, but the truth is, though I tried so hard to please him, I never felt like he loved me."

"That's too bad," Jarrod said softly.

The compassion in his green eyes nearly undid her. She bit down hard on a surge of emotion. She refused to feel sorry for herself, or waste another minute on asking pointless questions. Her father was dead. She'd never get an answer.

A short silence fell between them. Jarrod was the first one to break it. "So what are you going to do?"

"I don't know. My cousin, Flynn thinks I should find a willing groom and take him to the nearest registry office."

Jarrod laughed. "Let me guess. Flynn's happily single, right?"

"Right."

They laughed together. Sophia couldn't believe how comfortable she felt. *Weird.* They'd only just met.

"So, are you married?"

He shook his head and smiled. "No."

"Happily single, right?"

"Right."

She flicked a glance at him. "What are *your* thoughts on marriage?" Her face flamed with embarrassment, unable to believe she'd dared to ask him, but he merely shrugged.

"I'm not against marriage. My parents were together for nearly thirty years."

"It's a long time."

"Yeah. You get less for murder." He winked.

They laughed again and it felt good. It seemed like years since she'd been so relaxed and carefree and she owed it all to the man seated beside her.

"Do you come here often?" she asked and then hoped he wouldn't think her too forward. To her relief, once again he seemed to take her question in his stride.

"Yeah. Most Sunday afternoons. I take Beckett to the park to give my brother and his wife some alone time."

She looked at him with admiration. "That's really nice of you."

He shrugged and looked a little uncomfortable at the compliment. "They recently lost a baby. Thirty-five weeks. It was still born. Taking Beckett away for a few hours means they get time to grieve properly."

"Oh, no! That's so sad."

Jarrod shrugged. "It happens."

Another silence fell between them. Sophia was the first to break it. "Is Penrith home for you?"

"No. I live in Surry Hills. My brother, Jacob and his wife, Natalie live out here. Beckett likes to come to this park. It's easier for me to spend time with him outdoors. My bachelor pad isn't set up for kids."

"Uncle Jarrod! Uncle Jarrod! I want the ball!"

Beckett ran toward them. Jarrod laughed and kicked the ball toward his nephew. The boy took an almighty swing at it and missed. Once again, he toppled over onto the grass and once again, instead of tears, he rolled on the ground with laughter.

Sophia chuckled. The kid was too cute. And so resilient. A testament to his upbringing.

Jarrod got up and went to him. Crouching low, he tickled the child until he was screaming with laughter and begging his uncle to stop. Jarrod cajoled Beckett into standing and having another go.

Beckett got to his feet and lined up the ball.

"C'mon, little mate. You've got this. Keep your eye on the ball. Take your time."

Listening his uncle's encouragement, Beckett took another big swing. This time his foot connected. The ball went high. Both Jarrod and Sophia cheered. Jarrod turned and winked at her, grinning wide. Her stomach flip-flopped.

God, he's gorgeous.

Belatedly, she realized she was staring. Looking down at her feet, she busied herself collecting her Gucci handbag from where she'd stowed it beside the bench. She needed to leave before she completely lost her dignity. With that thought in mind, she stood and smoothed down her dress.

Jarrod returned to her side. "Well, it's been nice talking to you, Sophia Craigdon. I hope you enjoy the rest of your Sunday afternoon."

Flustered by his nearness, she could barely bring herself to look at him. "You too, Jarrod Sampson."

"Maybe I'll see you around sometime?"

She shrugged dismissively. "Maybe."

"Good luck with the husband hunting."

She looked up and caught his teasing grin. Once again, her heart somersaulted. "Thanks." With that, she turned and made her escape.

SOPHIA is available for preorder at all of the digital retailers. It will be released on 31 January, 2021.

About the Author

Chris Taylor grew up on a farm in north-west New South Wales, Australia. She always had a thirst for stories and recalls writing her first book at the ripe old age of eight. Always a lover of romance and happily-ever-afters, a career in criminal law sparked her interest in intrigue and suspense. For Chris to be able to combine romance with suspense in her books is a dream come true.

Chris is married to Linden and is the mother of five children. If not behind her computer, you can find her doing the school run, taxiing children to swimming lessons, football, ballet and cricket. In her spare time, Chris loves to read her favorite authors who include Richard North Patterson, Sandra Brown, Kathleen E Woodiwiss and Jude Devereaux.

You can find out more about Chris and sign up for her newsletter at her website:

http://www.christaylorauthor.com.au

www.ingramcontent.com/pod-product-compliance
Lightning Source LLC
Chambersburg PA
CBHW060759190726
48285CB00002B/492